Other Books in the
Velvet Glove Series:

THE WILDFIRE TRACE *by Cathy Gillen Thacker*
THE KNOTTED SKEIN *by Carla Neggers*
LIKE A LOVER *by Lynn Michaels*
THE HUNTED HEART *by Barbara Doyle*
FORBIDDEN DREAMS *by Jolene Prewit-Parker*
TENDER BETRAYAL *by Virginia Smiley*
FIRES AT MIDNIGHT *by Marie Flasschoen*
STRANGERS IN EDEN *by Peggy Mercer*
THE UNEVEN SCORE *by Carla Neggers*
TAINTED GOLD *by Lynn Michaels*
A TOUCH OF SCANDAL *by Leslie Davis*
AN UNCERTAIN CHIME *by Lizabeth Loghry*
MASKED REFLECTIONS *by Dee Stuart*
THE SPLINTERED MOON *by Leslie Davis*
A LOVER'S GIFT *by Lynn Michaels*
JAMAICAN MIDNIGHT *by Sherryl Woods*

Look for upcoming titles in the
Velvet Glove Series:

TANGLED MESH *by Lee Karr*
EDGE OF RECKONING *by Marianne Joyce*

Rachel Scott

Stalk A Stranger

AVON
PUBLISHERS OF BARD, CAMELOT, DISCUS AND FLARE BOOKS

STALK A STRANGER is an original publication of Avon Books. This work has never before appeared in book form. This work is a novel. Any similarity to actual persons or events is purely coincidental.

AVON BOOKS
A division of
The Hearst Corporation
1790 Broadway
New York, New York 10019

First Avon Printing, October 1985

AVON TRADEMARK REG. U. S. PAT. OFF. AND IN
OTHER COUNTRIES, MARCA REGISTRADA, HECHO EN
U. S. A.

Printed in the U. S. A.

WFH 10 9 8 7 6 5 4 3 2 1

STALK A STRANGER

Chapter One

Unexpectedly, the dark and winding road twisted sharply to the left. Bianca quickly hit the brake, grabbed the stick shift, and forced the wheel to the left down the steep incline.

Instantly she felt the first jolt pierce the white knuckles of her hands, shoot up her rigid arms, and then shimmy down her spine as the tires of her '83 Celica bounced out of one deep rut and immediately smashed into another, kicking up high clouds of dust in its wake.

Then the unfamiliar sounds of a muffled explosion went off beneath the chassis and collided in her head. She took a deep breath of chilled air and held it, blinking rapidly before her blue-gray eyes froze open with terror. For one horrible, paralyzing moment, she was certain that the car's frantic bucking had ripped apart the engine, or that something just as bad would set off an even worse explosion.

Catapulted out of what she hoped was the last chug hole in the county road, once again she slammed her high-heeled sandal down hard on the brakes, hit the horn by mistake, and shivered at the possibility of being blown to kingdom come at the worst, and stranded in the middle of nowhere at the least. Old Boerne Stage Road was deserted at this hour of the night. Where in God's name would she find help if she needed it?

Slowly she eased her black satin shoe off the brake pedal, careful lest she go careening down the hill. Perhaps she should have followed Arthur and Marianne's advice. It would probably have been wiser— fine time to realize it—undoubtedly safer, to spend the night at their place instead of trying to leave their anniversary celebration at two in the morning to drive more than thirty miles home . . . alone.

She stared straight ahead into the single line of darkness dispersed by the beam of the headlights. Alone. She had lived with that word a long time now. And it still had the power to trap her with grief and self-pity, to frighten her, to beat down her rationality. Widowed and alone. On a night like tonight she was certain that the ghosts of her dead dreams hid from the stars behind the shadows of a clouded moon. Protected by the dim light, ghosts could throw out the long arms of the past and seduce her from the present. It was easy, really. On nights like tonight she sometimes forgot to put up a fight until it was too late. Too often she had let those ghostly arms drag her down into memory.

Determined to be rational and sensible, she fought off the impulse to clench her eyes shut and block out the shadowed gloom that lurked outside the car and inside her heart. So the road rolling down from the dark hill was deserted, so what? The car hadn't stalled, had it? As for the explosion, she was so keyed up she must have imagined it, spurred on no doubt by the heavy chords of the Wagner tape she now regretted having chosen for the ride home. She hadn't heard a second explosion. She didn't need to worry about getting help out here in the middle of nowhere because she wasn't going to be in any trouble.

"That settles that!" she exclaimed aloud.

Immediately she felt better. Her hands encased in black lambskin relaxed their hold on the wheel, her rigid spine eased itself back into the driver's seat. She downshifted into second gear and turned the wheel to take the curve to the right. She wasn't going to let an overstimulated imagination ruin what had turned out to be an enjoyable evening. It had been, in fact, the first party she had honestly enjoyed in the last four years. By God, she wasn't going to ruin it now. She had even found herself mildly interested in a man, one of her brother's colleagues, who had shown considerable interest in her. A smile passed briefly across her face as she remembered his witty repartee that had made her laugh.

Laugh—it had been a long time. Too long, her brother, Arthur, had told her repeatedly in the last two years, an opinion strongly shared and voiced by Marianne, his "Amen" section, as Bianca had privately dubbed her. Well, she was in for it now. Neither her brother nor his wife could have missed the fact that she had chosen to spend most of her evening in the company of the intelligent, urbane cardiologist they had introduced to her. Brother or sister-in-law, or both, would no doubt call her on Monday morning, if she were lucky, to find out her reactions; on Sunday morning, if she weren't so lucky, to insist that she date the man "for her own good."

She approached the last intersection before she reached the well-lit smooth asphalt of Interstate 10. "I might as well go out with him a couple of times," she said aloud, and extended a hand to raise the heater's temperature. "What can it hurt? At thirty, what have I got to lose?"

The second smile which might have lit up her face became instead a frown which furrowed her nicely arched brows. There was a vehicle at the intersection's stop sign. Although minutes before she had been lamenting the isolation of the road, she was now uneasy at the sight of the dark red automobile that came into view. She shook her head, fingering with one hand the strand of pearls across her breast, as she tried to dismiss the eerie feeling eating away at her mind's hold on the rational and the sensible.

Cautiously she braked to a stop a good fifteen feet behind the car that announced PORSCHE in large silver letters beneath its sloping rear window, with 928S below that. The silk ribbons of her white shawl swished on her arm as she shifted into neutral to wait her turn. There wasn't any traffic. If her experience of the last ten minutes was any indication, there wasn't going to be any. Yet the car didn't move. The line between her brows deepened. How long was the driver going to sit at the stop sign, for heaven's sake? She had always been under the impression that any Porsche 928S painted in brilliant metallic red took off at the slightest provocation. She felt her chest muscles tighten, her breathing become labored again. She didn't want to sit on the horn, but she didn't know what else she could do.

She flattened the heel of her hand on the wheel's central disk. The brief blast made no impression. She leaned forward, peering into the tinted glass of the sloped window ahead. She couldn't be absolutely sure, but she thought the head of the driver wasn't where it should have been. Maybe he was busy reaching into the glove compartment or searching for something on the passenger's seat. Then why didn't he respond to the horn blast? She shook her head. No, the head of the driver was definitely tilted to the right at a disturbingly odd angle.

Bianca felt a sudden chill begin in her extremities and move into her tightened chest. She tried to tell herself that her body was merely reacting to the record low temperatures predicted for south Texas, which had moved in earlier than expected, but she knew better. Her heart began an erratic beat to warn her that something here was very wrong indeed. She'd be a fool not to obey the instinct that told her danger was in front of her and that she ought to flee right now for dear life.

With a quick precautionary glance at her left side-view mirror and an unsteady hand on her stick shift, she threw the transmission into reverse. A woman alone at two o'clock in the morning didn't have any business investigating suspicious-looking situations.

It wasn't until she pulled her white Celica alongside the Porsche to pass on the left that the question that had plagued her for the last four years struck her with numbing sharpness: *If someone had gotten to the scene of Richard's automobile accident in time, had called EMS in time, would he be alive today?*

Even considering the injuries he had sustained, the EMS paramedics and doctors had said that fifteen minutes, perhaps as little as five, might have made a difference. Moisture began to collect in her wide eyes, and her hand on the wheel went limp. *If only I had immediately followed Richard in the second car the way we had originally planned, I might have been able to save him, or I might have even been able to warn him about the oncoming truck that was . . .*

There they were again, those grisly, ghostly arms that could rip her out of the present and drag her down into aching memory. She wouldn't let it happen tonight. She pulled her mind away from the self-recriminations which had never brought her anything except endless suffering and trained it instead on what she had to deal with now.

This isn't the scene of an accident, she admonished herself severely, *but the driver could be hurt, could have had a heart attack? I know CPR. Arthur's made sure of that. If I let fear prevent me from helping this driver, won't that be the same thing as abandoning Richard?*

She put an end to circuitous deliberation. Flinging open the door of her Celica, she stepped out into the night, instantly aware of how vulnerable she was. The predicted cold front had finally blown in, earlier than expected, and with a vengeance. It slapped her unprotected face, cutting through the open weave of her white shawl, and whipped the thin silk of her turquoise dress around her slender legs. Whisking the long strands of silver-blond hair out of her eyes and pushing them back into the full coil at the top of her head, she fervently prayed that her instinct to help another human being was correct. As she made her way against the gusting wind toward the other driver's door, she wasn't at all sure that it was.

Even before she actually reached it, she could see that, in spite of the cold, the window on the driver's side was lowered more than halfway, the stereo's mellow rock carrying out into the wailing wind. As she crossed the last three feet of the distance, she bent her head down and immediately made out the figure of a man. His limp upper body covered in a thick sweater was slumped to the right over the steering wheel, half of its weight apparently supported by the console and the stick shift, the other half by the wheel and the dashboard.

Without a moment's hesitation, her hands stopped trying to hold onto both her shawl and her coiffure and grabbed the door handle instead. It wouldn't give. She thrust her hand into the window opening and fumbled with a series of invisible knobs until she finally heard the click of a lock. Pulling out her arm, she swung the door wide open. The dark red interior was instantly bathed in a soft overhead light, allowing her to see a head of honey-colored hair and a broad back covered in a pale wheat sweater with a high horizontal band of blue below the wide shoulders.

She leaned into the car. "Are you hurt? Can I help you?" she asked breathlessly, on the outside chance that the man was conscious. Dear God! The size of him made her wonder how she'd ever be able to move him if she had to. How in the world would she manage if he needed CPR? She put a tentative hand on his shoulder. Perhaps if she . . .

She heard no more than a faint moan escape lips she couldn't even see, but it was enough to encourage her. She watched as the head of dark honey hair turned ever so slightly in her direction. He was conscious! "Thank God!" she exclaimed aloud as she felt the door behind her whip back with the wind and bite into her calves. She gasped at the unexpected impact.

"I'm . . . here to help you," she managed to blurt out, hoping the words might reassure him. "Don't try to move just yet."

A guttural noise that sounded as though it had come up from a cracked throat responded, but she didn't take the time to decode the message. She lifted the heel of her left shoe and forced the door back against the wind, this time making sure it clicked into place, then fumbled at the steering column and the instrumentation panel until she was able to locate the keys and turn off the ignition. Suddenly silence. No engine hum. No mellow rock. Afraid that he would only slip further and hurt himself even more, she positioned her left knee against his trousered leg on the leather bucket seat, and leaned in to support his head with her left hand and his shoulder with her right while she pulled him back into an upright position. Fortunately, the driver's seat was pushed back far enough that she could just wedge herself between his body and the wheel.

But the advantage she gained by the new position wasn't enough. She pulled, but it wasn't the gliding of his body and her arm along the leather seat that she heard. It was the distinct sound of silk ripping at her sleeve and her waist. She kept pulling. In spite of the wind and the cold, perspiration beaded on her upper lip and in her palms. He was a big, broad-shouldered man, and she simply didn't have the necessary strength. A second time she threw her weight forward, her body bent at the knee and waist, and tried to bring him up with her. Still she couldn't budge him. And she had to. Out here help was unlikely to ride by. She straightened up again.

Lifting her left knee, she delicately repositioned it between his legs for better leverage and swiveled so that her body directly faced his, her back flat against the steering wheel. This time she leaned over to her left as far as she dared, leaving the support of the wheel. Precariously balanced, she was parallel to his sprawled form, her leg and back muscles screaming at the performance she was ripping out of them.

Enunciating each syllable in a loud voice, she commanded him, "Try flattening your hand on the seat and move your upper body to your left." He didn't make a move. "I can't do this without you. You've got to give me some help."

Resting her chin on top of that honey hair and pressing his head onto the rise of her breasts, she gripped the driver's headrest with her right hand for leverage and wrapped her left arm more securely around his shoulder, lifting her own shoulder to cradle his head. Slowly she began to pull him with her toward the driver's side, all the while hoping to God that one of them didn't fall on top of the other in the process and make matters worse. Just when she thought she would fail a third time and be crushed by his weight, she heard another faint moan, felt him turn his face at her breast, and realized—thank God!— that he was helping her help him.

Anticipating the low ceiling, she ducked her head in time as they both came up, her face sliding down until it lay flat against his clean-shaven cheek, his left hand firmly grasping her right leg for support. Her breasts were shoved up against his hard chest muscles, which rose and fell with labored breathing, and the weight of him embedded the beads of her pearl necklace like hot stones into her flesh. She felt the gasps of his breath warm against her neck, his lips icy cold against her earlobe. The deep fragrance of a masculine cologne mingled with the scent of pipe tobacco and the natural musk of his body. She was dizzy with sensations.

Within seconds she was aware that both of her hands and much of her lower right arm felt damp, cold and damp. Silk dress and ribboned shawl stuck to her skin. Dreading what she would discover, she slowly moved her face away from his and pulled away one hand. With a convulsive start, she realized that the sticky, gooey substance that had matted his hair and was soaking through her silk dress and leather fingers of her gloved hand was undoubtedly blood.

Blood!

The alarm resonated in her head. She sucked in air and held it. Suddenly, she was viciously catapulted back into time long past. She was staring down at the face of a stranger, but she didn't see it. Instead she saw herself, wild and hysterical, desperate and despairing, trying to break through restraining arms to the side of the fair-haired man whose slim, mangled body ambulance personnel were trying to lift from his wrecked car.

She heard another muffled sound of pain, saw the curl of fogged breath rise from a bruised mouth she could now see. She flung the back of her hand against her mouth and in anguish she cried out, "Richard!"

Sobbing convulsed her body, caught in her throat, strangled her heartbeat. It was her husband! Dear God! This man whose frame was broken by steel, whose flesh was ripped apart by sharp metal was her beloved husband. She wanted to throw her arms around him and with the strength of her love erase the ghastly image, bring him back to what he had been.

Then all of a sudden, with a sick feeling in the pit of her stomach, her muscles froze before she could follow her impulse. She knew where she was, and though her vision was blurred by unbidden tears, she saw only a few inches away from her own the face of the man whose head was thrown back against the red leather seat.

It was this stranger who had called out to her in pain, not her dead husband. Bianca saw the strong planes of a memorable face carved by the dim light of the car and the eerie shadows of the moon. She swallowed down hard the agony that tried to consume her and watched closely as the stranger moistened his dry lips with a slow, deliberate tongue.

Without warning, he laid a limp and bloody hand flat against her startled face. She flinched at the touch of ice-cold flesh. His heavy lids fluttered open. The sight of yellow, wide, unseeing eyes burning brightly into her own made her cringe. Hypnotized by their intensity, she couldn't escape.

"Why?" he hoarsely whispered above his labored breathing as though he were begging her to give him understanding. The hand on her right leg tightened. "Why?" His voice was fading.

She bent slightly forward, trying to study the strong features tangled in pain as if they might be able to dispel his confusion and her own. His hand slipped down her face, ripping off the pearl in her pierced earlobe and marking a trail of blood down her smooth right cheek and naked throat before it came to rest on the rise of her breast. She was certain he could feel her wildly beating heart beneath his hand.

Filled with the certain knowledge of her betrayal, his eyes and voice angrily demanded, "Why did you do this to me?"

Chapter Two

BIANCA forced down her fright and her memories. This was not Richard Cavender. This was a stranger whose difficulty she could not confuse with her own past, or she would be of no use to him at all. A stranger whose peculiar eyes had the metallic gleam of madness.

Immediately she dismissed any attempt to deny the accusation of a man close to delirium. "Look, I've got to go get help," she told him, pulling her wits together and her eyes away from his accusing glare.

Fighting against the emotional turmoil aroused by the weight of his hand familiarly placed on her breast, she strained the muscles of her upper arm to free her hand from its prison between his unyielding shoulders and the driver's seat. She had to get to a phone. She had to call EMS and her brother. The hospital had to be alerted. She wasn't any medical authority, but she was relatively certain that this man needed immediate assistance or he might go into shock.

"Don't worry—I'll be back as soon as I can." She spoke each syllable distinctly in low, soothing tones. "I promise."

She threw her weight back against the wheel to steady herself at the same time she tried to swivel on her knee to get out of the car, but his hand wouldn't release her, nor would his wild, unseeing eyes. Abruptly the hand at her breast grabbed the shawl collar of her neckline, frantically bunching up the turquoise silk in a determined fist while his other hand rode up the length of her leg, lifting the silk as it went, touching her hip briefly, then mercilessly grabbing her behind the neck.

Jerked forward with a start, she managed to keep herself from slamming into him only by swiftly flattening her palms beside his head on the leather seat, but she wasn't able to keep her hips from sliding down onto his leg, or his leg from slipping warmly between her thighs. She heard the syncopated gasps that passed for breathing between them and felt the rise and fall of his chest beating madly into hers. She was so close to him that she could see his nostrils flare as his heavy breathing became even less regular; so close that she could count the scores of curly lashes on the unflickering eyelids, see the cut that marred the left side of his swollen lower lip.

His stealthy fingers began to creep up the nape of her neck, then dug into her hair. She shivered uncontrollably and closed her eyes in pain. For a brief, unsettling moment she had a vision of herself and this man with wild yellow eyes caught like lovers in an attitude of horror, locked forever in this bizarre embrace.

"Let me go," she breathed, trying to keep the fright and pleading out of her voice.

Unmoved, he pulled her closer until her knee pressed intimately into the juncture of his legs. His face was so close to hers that when her lips tried to form words again, they rubbed against his lips. Without realizing the consequences, she put out a tentative tongue to ease the dryness of her mouth and licked not just her own lips, but his as well.

Oh, dear God, help me! she prayed, her mind and heart pounding with awareness of this hideous distortion of lovemaking. "If you don't let me go, I can't help you," she tried to reason with him, and straightened out her right arm to put some space between them. But her confusion over the unnameable current passing between them only deepened; with the distance gained, she found herself staring once again into his glazed, fever-bright eyes, hypnotized by the possibilities she saw there.

He turned his head slowly from side to side just once in silent negation. She could hardly believe it. He wasn't going to cooperate. He tightened the hold his fingers had on her hair and once again pulled her toward him, pressing her cheek against his, pressing her ear to his mouth. She was so close to him she felt the Adam's apple in his neck ripple against her throat as he swallowed.

In a hoarse voice nearly strangling on its own stunned pain he whispered brokenly, "Shot . . . phone . . . use it." He took another ragged breath. "Need . . . hospital." His hand released her collar. From the corner of her eye she could see that he was gesturing at a box between the instrumentation panel and the console.

Shot? She wrestled down her own pain and tried to think clearly. Her head was pounding, her chest ached, her body shivered with cold. The explosion she had heard must have been the blast of a gun.

"How can I drive your car?" she tried for a gentle tone of reason, knowing she couldn't move a man of his size out of that bucket seat, never mind not knowing the first thing about using a car telephone.

"I'll help you . . . help me," he interrupted her with a variation of the words she had spoken to him. He robbed the air for the oxygen his lungs needed, seeming to gain strength with each labored syllable. "You drive this car—hospital two miles away." The fingers he had entwined in her hair splayed out to cover the crown of her head. The heel of his hand he buried in the nape of her neck. He anchored the weight of his right hand onto her shoulder. He wasn't going to let her go.

Bianca tried not to think too hard about the fanatic

quality in his voice and in his physical hold on her.
She tried not to think about his leg that moved between her own legs each time a spasm of pain coursed
through him. She tried not to identify the spasm that
coursed through her own loins each time he warmed
her.

Did he still believe that she had shot him, and was
he trying to detain her to harm her in reprisal? Or,
realizing that he had made a mistake about her identity, did he now suspect that in her absence the criminal who had shot him might return to finish him off?
Was that why he wouldn't let her leave him? She
studied the face she didn't think she would ever forget. What had he done to become someone's victim?
What was she getting herself into by helping him?
Were homicidal maniacs lurking around the dark
corners of the surrounding hills? And were they going
to come gunning for her?

She didn't have forever to make a decision. She had
to put an end to the questions swirling in her brain.
He might be right: Possibly she could save time by
driving him to the hospital herself, that is, if she could
somehow dislodge him from his position behind the
wheel of the Porsche.

"All right," she finally yielded, "we'll try it your
way." Immediately his hand slid out of her hair and
down her back until it dangled alongside her extended leg.

"Good," he mouthed the word as his head began to
roll forward onto his chest.

Bianca supposed he was trying to nod. Afraid that
he couldn't support himself, she caught his chin in her
hand and gently eased his head back into place. She
ducked her head, inadvertently touching his cheek
briefly with her own, and raised herself on her left
knee, trying her best not to press suggestively between his legs again. She threw the weight of her body
toward the open door to disentangle her limbs from
their cramped position in his lap. As she slipped away,

his dangling hand negligently rode up the inner length of her right leg, the unintentional intimacy shooting a powerful sensation between her thighs. On unsteady legs she left the car, the imprint of his cold hand still on her flesh, the memory of the sensation impossible to erase.

In a flurry of activity, she parked her Celica on the side of the road, turned off the heat and the ignition, and switched on the emergency lights. When she returned to the Porsche, she was astounded to find that he had somehow contrived to situate himself on the passenger's side. Had she misjudged the extent of his weakness and his injury? Only his left leg dangled on the driver's side of the console now, his head shoved into the corner of the right-hand window. She could hear his ragged breathing and see his sweatered chest expanding and contracting dramatically with the effort he must have exerted just moving. For the first time she noticed where the sweater's pattern was obliterated by the dark stain that covered his upper left arm and the side of his chest.

Instantly she got into the driver's seat, hardly noticing the blood that had dampened and darkened the leather, and, bending down, put one firm hand on his ankles above the dark loafer and another in the bend of his knee.

Though he emitted a deep, anguished moan at the disturbance and glared at her as though she were evil incarnate, he whispered hoarsely, "Help you . . . help me," and, albeit clumsily, moved his leg when she moved it. Unexpectedly, he lifted his arm and ran his fingers lightly over a strand of platinum hair that had fallen across her cheek. "Silk hair," he said, his voice a gasp of pain and surprise. "Silk face." Then, as though he had said and done as much as he could, the curly lashes fluttered shut over those preposterously bright eyes and he slumped against the door, his long body crumpled up in the passenger's seat.

Eliminating at the outset any fumbling attempts

to use a car telephone that would only delay her, she turned on the ignition, switched off the stereo, and, throwing the stick shift into first gear, fishtailed around the corner, determined to reach the emergency room before the man beside her died from shock or loss of blood. Methodist Hospital, where Arthur was chief of staff, was at least ten miles to the south and west, contrary to this stranger's misguided perception that he was within two miles of it, but she was determined to reach it within minutes. She certainly had the machine to do it in.

Exactly seven minutes later, she sailed onto Medical Drive doing an even eighty-five. She knew now was the time to sit on the horn, just as Arthur had explained years before. She whipped into the lane leading to the emergency entrance and hit the brake and the power window button at the same time. The instant she saw the door attendant dart out of the building like a white flash, she leaned her head out the window and yelled, "This man's been shot!"

"We'll get a stretcher!" the attendant yelled in return and whirled back into the building.

"Have someone get Dr. Arthur Lamont here immediately," she called out just in time to his retreating form. "His sister needs him."

Concentrating on maneuvering the powerful car up the ramp, she almost didn't catch the guttural whisper of the man next to her. "Allergy . . . penicillin, sulfa drugs," he breathed.

"Don't worry, I'll tell them," she promised, jerking to a stop in the space reserved for an ambulance.

"Please . . . I can't . . ." came out on a wisp of breath.

She pulled the keys out of the ignition and turned to face him, throwing a protective arm across his chest. "You'll be all right now. My brother will see you get the best possible attention." His eyes opened again for only a second. "You'll be . . ." She stopped on the last breath of reassurance for she could see, from the way his head slumped forward, that he had just lost consciousness.

Her long, lovely legs, marred by the wide runs in her hosiery, were crossed one over the other, her hands resting on her kneecap. Bent forward at the waist, she stared down at the tip of one satin sandal damaged beyond repair and the ripped bodice and bloodied sleeve of her favorite dress. Even her rose enameled nails had the dark brown stain of blood beneath them, even though she'd been wearing gloves. That night four years ago she had come away from Richard's side in much the same state. Her appearance had mattered as little then as it did now. She remembered having wondered then if she would ever care what she looked like again.

She turned her wrist. It was four-thirty A.M. With typical grace, she rose from the chair and walked toward the hospital bed. She ran her hand along the cool white sheets. Richard had never made it to surgery or to a hospital bed. When she had broken free from the people trying to constrain her and had reached for his hand as he lay mangled on the stretcher, his clear blue eyes had already been glazed over with the sightlessness of the dead. She fell on him then, her tears a river in which he could not be reborn. When she was pulled away, her face was streaked with blood.

She closed her eyes against the pain, feeling the burning moisture collect in the corners of her eyelids. She took several deep breaths to steady herself against the effects of a long sleepless night and the trauma of memory. But when she opened them, she didn't see the dawn ease out the moon on the other side of the window. Her mind kept showing her, instead, the image of a broad-shouldered, muscular body, sweatered chest, and corduroy-covered legs pulled from the Porsche and laid on a stretcher. Under the bright lights she had been able to see just how much damage the bullet had done to his arm. But she couldn't be sure if the blood that splattered his face and neck were an indication that he had been hit elsewhere besides.

She hadn't been able to help herself. Though Bianca knew the orderlies had to move swiftly in the best interests of the patient, she had cringed with pain when she saw how roughly he was being handled. She felt the tightening of an unwelcome, and inexplicable, bond between this man and herself and an overwhelming urge to inform the orderlies he was not alone. She had insisted on walking beside the stretcher, holding his limp hand in hers all the way into the building and past the swinging doors toward the operating rooms until, in spite of her protests, she was adamantly barred from going any further.

"He's got an allergy to penicillin, sulfa drugs," she reminded the orderlies for the third time, only retreating to her solitary vigil outside when they told her they could best care for her husband without her assistance.

An hour or so later, Arthur's assistant had come out of the operating room to tell her that he would live. She took comfort in the message. She could accept a great deal of responsibility for it, too. And she would wait for him here in Room 407 as she had been instructed until he was wheeled in from recovery.

"For God's sake, Bianca! You look like hell!"

She whirled around at Arthur's unusual greeting, nearly losing her balance on a loosened heel. When he'd arrived at the hospital, he had gone straight to the operating room; following surgery he had sent down a message that he would be staying with the patient until all vital signs were normal, and she in turn had sent up a brief explanation of her involvement. Consequently, he hadn't seen her since she had left the party.

"Are you sure you're not the one who should be recovering?" he demanded as he walked briskly toward

her, shoving his arms into the sleeves of his jacket,
his black head of hair lowered like a charging bull's.
"Are you bleeding from his wounds or your own?
What in the hell is wrong with your ear? My God, do
you mean to tell me that goddamn son-of-a-bitch
whose life I just saved did this to you? Why didn't
someone tell me you needed attention? What in the
hell is going on here?"

She clamped her hands on either side of her ringing
head. "Arthur!" Her voice was a quiet shout. He was
silent. "I'm all right, just bruised." When she was relatively certain he was listening, she dropped her
hands and her volume. "It's his blood, not mine."

"Not on your ear it's not!" The brother who stood
no more than two inches above her head stared into
her wide open eyes. "You're missing one pearl earring. Where is it? Did he rip it out of your ear, for
God's sake?"

She should have taken precautions against her
older brother's bullying protectiveness, which had
gone underground only for as long as she had been
married. She could stand up to him. She almost always had to. But it was such a strain. "He didn't know
what he was doing. I really don't think he meant to
hurt me."

"Don't *think?*" Arthur leaped on her admitted confusion. With a firm hand he turned her head so that
he could study the damage to her earlobe. "Don't
move—I'll be right back," he announced and abruptly
left the room, still muttering obscenities to himself.

When he returned seconds later, cotton swabs and
alcohol in hand, he proceeded to minister to her ear—
of all things! And she submitted to the absurdity only
because she knew it was his way of working off tension and because she was weak from relief. News from
the recovery room had to be very good or Arthur
would have told her the moment he had entered the
room. When he dabbed antiseptic on her damaged
earlobe, it hurt a hell of a lot more than it had when

the wounded man had ripped her earring out. She told
him so. He grunted in disbelief.

When he stepped back to inspect his handiwork, she
looked at the brother who was the living image of
their Italian grandmother; she herself had retained
only a first name from that familial strain and a
deeper skin tone than one would expect to find in a
woman with platinum-blond hair.

"Are you going to tell me how he is?" she asked,
folding her hands primly in her lap.

Arthur didn't answer her question right away.
Giving her his back, he disposed of the cotton swabs
and scrubbed his surgeon's hands at the basin. "What
in the hell were you doing with a man like that?"

She could hear the controlled tension in his voice.
"A man like what?"

"A man who could be shot at!"

Since it had also occurred to her to distrust a man
who had been someone's target practice, she didn't
point out the flaw in his reasoning. "I didn't plan my
evening, Arthur. I just happened to come upon an incident I couldn't in good conscience leave."

He dried his hands on a towel and turned around.
"I wish your conscience wasn't so damn demanding."
She didn't remind him that if Richard had been discovered by someone of equally refined conscience, he
might be alive today. He hadn't forgotten. "When
they called me at home I thought it was *you* who had
been in the accident."

Belatedly she recalled how her shouted instructions to the emergency room attendant might have
misled him. The minutes between his house and the
hospital must have been dreadful for him. "I'm
sorry," she said softly.

"I had hoped I would never see you looking like this
again." His voice was weary with emotional and
physical exhaustion.

She'd thought she had done a good job of combing
her hair back in place and washing the blood off her

face and hands. "Like what exactly?" she asked, needing specifics somehow, though she knew exactly what he was talking about.

"Like all the life had gone out of you . . . a second time."

She closed her eyes. When she opened them, a rather sad smile curved her lips. "I can't order my fate, Arthur, and neither can you. And besides"—she tried to put a little bouyancy into her voice—"this man's alive, isn't he?" When he didn't answer, she pressed him for affirmation in a tight voice, "Isn't he?"

"Yes." He replaced the towel on the rod and conceded, "But he wouldn't be if it hadn't been for you. He must have sustained that gunshot wound only minutes before you found him." She waited patiently for him to continue. Now that he could talk about medical facts, the emotional fervor of the moment before, she knew, would dissipate. "From the damage we discovered, he must have been shot at close range. But, fortunately, he was shot with the bullet of a low-velocity twenty-two-caliber revolver."

"Ah," she said in understanding. "The famous 'Saturday Night Special'. How appropriate." She paused for a second, then made herself ask, "Did he suffer any permanent injury?"

He shook his head. "All that will remain are two scars. One near the shoulder where the flesh of the upper arm was ripped away at the entry point, and another at the rib cage where I had to go in to explore the wound and retrieve the bullet." He frowned at her worry. "He's damn lucky. The projectile had already lost much of its force before it slammed into him, probably because it hit another target first."

"Like what?"

He shrugged his shoulders. "My guess is the car, but who knows? And when it did hit him, it entered the muscle of the upper arm, took a splinter of bone off the humerus, which in turn deflected the bullet to the chest wall, where it lodged next to the rib cage. It didn't pass into the chest cavity. No punctured lung, no damaged organ. As I said, Bianca, he's goddamn lucky."

"Then I hope you've saved the bullet." She made a flippant attempt to dissolve his gloom. "Maybe he'll want to make a lucky charm out of it."

She was saved his response because at that moment the door swung open. Two green-garbed attendants wheeled a stretcher into the room. A man with a shock of dark honey hair and ashen skin lay on it. My God! She was momentarily stunned at the sight of him. How much closer to death he looked now that they had saved his life.

Arthur must have correctly interpreted the jerking motion she made when she got to her feet. "All surgery patients look like this, Bianca. Believe me, considering the trauma his body's sustained, he looks damn good. He must have been in prime physical condition before the shooting."

She nodded her head and tried to believe him. "We don't even know who he is." Her voice was a bit shaky as she turned her head away when the attendants began to lift him from the stretcher to the bed. When she looked back, they were arranging the covers over his long legs, tanned and sprinkled with curling golden hair.

"No. He didn't have any identification on him. The police will probably be able to track him down through the license plates on his car, assuming it *was* his car."

She refused to encourage his skepticism about the victim's reputation. "He'll be needing someone with him for the next five hours or so, won't he, Arthur? At least to see that he doesn't pull those IVs out of his hand?"

"It would help," Arthur answered without thinking, then stopped when he saw the intent in her blue-gray eyes. "You don't need to be reliving tragedy, Bianca, by staying here."

"I won't be." She didn't know if that was an outright lie. Wasn't that what she had been doing before Arthur walked in?

"Bianca, I mean it. This isn't Richard."

"I know that."

"Do you?" Arthur's brows collided in a scowl. "Get this straight, Bianca. He is *not* your responsibility."

She looked over at the man lying on the hospital bed who had no one but herself to care about him right now. A muscle spasm in his lower jaw worked madly. His face was a stone tablet of pain. She looked at her brother again. "Isn't he?" she inquired softly.

Bianca lifted her head at the sound of movement on the bed. Carefully she put down the cup of hot tea she had agreed to drink in return for Arthur's agreeing to leave her in peace with his patient. The other half of the prescription, hot chicken soup, she had managed to swallow two hours ago. She got to her feet just in time to prevent the patient from yanking out the IV he was fumbling with as he turned on his side.

Looking down on the good bone structure over which his skin was beginning to look a little less like ash and more like pale nutmeg, she spoke gently. "My name is Bianca Cavender. You've been through surgery to remove a twenty-two-caliber bullet from your chest wall, but your doctor says you're going to be all right, that is, as long as you leave all the essential tubes in place."

His curling lashes fluttered on the dark circles above his cheekbones before his eyelids opened. The color of his skin might have been severely changed by surgery, but she was elated to see that the bright gold color exploding around the irises of his eyes had not. The lids shut down, then opened again, the second time a little less laboriously as he surfaced from the anesthesia.

In slow motion, painful to watch, he raised a hand to rub his index finger across his bruised and swollen lips.

"Here, I have something to make that feel better," she offered, reaching for the jar on the table to her immediate right. With a caressing finger she began to apply a thin film of colorless gel to that part of his mouth not covered by a butterfly bandage.

"Thank you," he mouthed, his tongue darting out on the first syllable to touch the tip of her finger.

In alarm she withdrew her hand, amazed at the strength of her response to the unintentional familiarity. "Of course," she mumbled, trying to slow down her quickened pulse, but the enigmatic smile that had begun to turn up one corner of his mouth defied her attempts. Surely he wasn't sufficiently conscious to have intended the familiarity or noticed her reaction to it.

"Must have hit mouth on—"

"—the wheel of your car, or the stick shift," she volunteered when his voice trailed off, eager to end her confusion through conversation.

He blinked once, twice. She thought he must have slowly come into focus, for his eyes fastened first on her hair, then on her dress. Distrust visibly narrowed his eyes into sparkling chips of glass. A new tension perceptibly dropped the corners of his bruised mouth.

"I won't hurt you," she rushed to assure him. She scrutinized every plane of his face to see if he believed her, but she couldn't tell. "I don't know your name," she said hopefully.

His lips began to move slowly as his eyes widened, almost as though he recognized her. "Ja . . .," he tried, but abandoned the effort. Closing his eyes, he slid one lip over the other.

"Jason?" she tried to help him out, putting one hand beside his white pillow.

Slowly he turned his head from one side to another. He opened his eyes again. "Jared," he breathed at last, and then added, with strength gradually infusing his voice, "Beren . . . son."

"Jared Berenson," she repeated. As interesting a name as the man who laid claim to it. Wouldn't the hospital staff be elated to hear it? Though the police had probably discovered his name by now, they hadn't, to her knowledge, called it in. "Well, Mr. Berenson, you owe me a new silk dress." She casually posed, and heard a ghost of a laugh rumble in his bandaged chest.

Somewhere he had learned that the first thing one should do after awakening from anesthesia was to move, for he seemed to be forcing himself to come to life beneath her eyes. She watched as he completed three knee bends on each leg. Then he attempted a couple of shoulder rolls with his right side, but he bared his teeth in a grimace of pain when he tried the left.

Recovering, he raised one brow only. "Do I owe you one silk dress?" he inquired with a faint smile once again on his lips as though the idea amused him. "I thought I owed you my life."

"At the scene of the crime, you accused me of having tried to deprive you of it," she teased him in return as she bent her head toward his to hear him better.

Suddenly she felt the cool pressure of his right hand on her cheek and the nape of her neck, and she shivered at the memory the contact called up of the night before when his hand had marked her face in blood. She put down the memory. All he wanted now was for her to bend down further still, probably because his voice, strong enough for a riposte or two, was fading fast. She lowered the steel bar on the bed. His hand never left her face or her neck.

"Silk hair," he said, staring into her eyes. "Silk face."

"You do remember," she breathed, her heart racing at the seductive sound in his voice.

"Never forget." She saw the knot in his throat move as he swallowed hard. "Come closer . . . to me."

With the weight of his hand to guide her, she lowered her blond head down to his. But his lips were not at her ear as she had anticipated. They were no more than an inch from her own. Quite suddenly, he pulled her toward him to eliminate even that inconsequential distance and faintly pressed her lips to his. The gel on his lips made it easy for hers to glide into place. She parted her lips. He parted his. Tongues flicked quickly against each other once, twice, then disappeared into each other's mouths for a second, no more, and then instantly retreated.

Startled and more than a little ashamed of her initiative, she pulled herself up, trying very hard not to let him see how deeply the kiss had disturbed her.

"Momentary delirium," he acknowledged casually, his hand still a weighted caress on her face.

Her heart was in her throat. "Your sudden gesture of thanks," she made herself ask, "or your false accusation against me last night?"

His hand slipped from her face to the bed, searching for her hand as it went down. He entwined his fingers through hers. "You want to know too much," he whispered. "Better not to know."

She straightened her back. Something in the wary way he watched her with glimmering eyes made her believe that he intended the ambiguity in his words because he wasn't absolutely sure she deserved to be absolved of the crime.

She opened her mouth, newly kissed, to assert her innocence, but his curly lashes fluttered down again and he drifted into sleep, holding fast to her hand for the lifeline he very likely didn't trust.

Chapter Three

"ALL right, Mr. Berenson, so far what we've got is that on returning home from a cocktail party at the home of the comptroller you employ, Charles Roper, you stopped your car at the intersection of Trail's End and Old Boerne Stage Road at one fifty-two A.M. on Sunday. Handy things, those digital clocks tucked into the dashboards. A car, whose make you didn't note, was stopped at the four-way sign to your left."

Harry Denman of the Bexar County Sheriff's Department was speaking to Jared Berenson in a hard voice that verged on sarcasm, though Bianca couldn't fathom why he should take an aversion to the man who was the victim of the gunshot wound, not the perpetrator. From her position on the chair at the foot of the hospital bed, she studied the balding man in the rumpled olive-drab trench coat who was standing between the patient and the window. Maybe the protective streak she had built up over the last thirty-two hours for the victim made her susceptible to imagining animosity that wasn't there.

"It was when you shifted into neutral that the driver's door of the other car swung open," Denman continued with a glance at the deputy who had accompanied him, apparently as a mute note-taker.

Jared Berenson was sitting up in his hospital bed, sufficiently recovered from the trauma of his wound and his surgery of the previous day, Arthur decreed, to tolerate police questioning. His color was decidedly improved, Bianca noted, though he still hadn't adjusted to the extra weight of the elaborate dressing across his chest and a splint that frustrated every attempt he made to move his left arm.

If he was aware of Denman's peculiar attitude, Berenson didn't indicate it by so much as a flicker of an eyelash. And the hoarse, ragged voice she had first heard from him was now replaced by a strong, rich baritone that rang with the confidence of a man who had nothing to hide.

"Correct," he told Denman. "Before I realized anyone was coming toward my car, I heard a loud banging against the window. When I turned at the sound, I saw a fist flattened against the glass and a woman whose features were distorted by crying and fear."

"What did she look like?" Denman demanded.

Berenson stared at the investigator, but he must not have heard him. "Of course, because it was such an isolated spot, I was immediately . . ." He paused in mid-sentence to reach for the glass of water on the bedside table. Belatedly he realized the limitations his disability imposed. "Damn!" he exclaimed through clenched teeth as his shoulders fell back on the pillows, no water glass in hand.

"You were immediately suspicious?" prompted Denman, not the least interested in Berenson's disability or discomfort, while Bianca had to restrain her impulse to jump up and help the patient.

"Wary," Berenson overrode the investigator's eager interpretation after catching his breath. "I could see only part of her twisted face because the wind whipped her yellow hair across it and she kept jerking her head over her shoulder to her right as if she expected someone to accost her."

Denman glanced keenly at Bianca's blond head. She stared him down.

The patient looked from one to the other, no visible emotion on his face. "I remembered thinking that she must be cold because she kept clutching to her neck a white fur jacket that she was wearing over a dress— turquoise, I think, maybe dark blue." He shook his head. "I can't be sure."

"What did you do?"

"I did what any man raised by a good mother would do," he answered with a smile for the irony. "I lowered the window to help the lady in distress."

"You and Ms. Cavender must have been raised by the same good mother," barked Denman in a voice devoid of approval.

"Good people are everywhere," Bianca said in a firm voice, immensely glad she hadn't confided to him what had really driven her to help the victim.

Denman didn't respond. "And then what happened?"

Berenson drew his brows together in concentration. "I heard noise behind me, maybe running feet, although how I could have heard that over the stereo I'm not sure."

"The stereo wasn't turned at a very high volume when I found you," Bianca offered.

"Maybe I turned it down before I lowered the window." He spoke thoughtfully as he looked at her. "In any case, when I heard the noise, I suddenly knew something was wrong."

"Did you now?" Denman looked skeptical. "Was that because you were expecting something wrong?"

Berenson rubbed a hand across his stubbled chin as though he were trying hard not to rise to the bait. "The silver barrel of a gun suddenly appeared out of nowhere. Out of reflex, I tried to push it away." He looked down on the bandages covering the fingers of his left hand. "My fist slammed into the barrel of the gun at the same time I heard a deafening blast."

"Who shot you, Mr. Berenson? The woman in the white fur and turquoise dress?"

"I don't know. There could have been someone else

who rushed me from behind once she had waylaid me."

"If so, wouldn't you have seen that person?"

"Once I saw that silver barrel, my eyes were riveted to it. I never saw anything else."

"Do you mean that you can't corroborate Ms. Cavender's story?"

Uncrossing her legs, Bianca sat up straight in her chair. "Mr. Berenson and I haven't had much time to talk. He doesn't know what my story is." Denman was looking at her as though *she* had waylaid Berenson. But if he believed that, why did he think she would have brought the victim to the hospital?

Berenson interceded. "I can tell you only that I remember nothing after the blast except burning pain until I heard Ms. Cavender's voice and felt her hands on my face."

Bianca waited for him next to tell the police that he had accused her of shooting him, but he said nothing more. Nor did she.

"Mr. Berenson, you're a man who's a rather muscular six feet two, right?"

"Correct."

"And Ms. Cavender, you're a rather slim-bodied five feet—hmmm—"

"—seven," she offered. What was he getting at?

He scratched his chin with the fingertips of a broad, hairy hand and transferred his gaze from her to the victim. "Don't you find it incredible, Mr. Berenson, that a woman of some hundred fifteen pounds could move you from the driver's seat to the passenger's?"

"But I told you," Bianca interrupted, "that I didn't do it alone." Her reward for that assertion was a scathing glance.

"I must have helped her," offered Berenson.

"In your stunned condition?"

"Well, anything's possible—you know, like a man who can suddenly lift a car with his bare hands to save his child caught under the wheels."

"And yet you have no recollection of doing that?"

"None at all. But I don't think it's unusual, considering the trauma I must have gone through."

Bianca had had enough. "Of course it isn't!" She was on her feet in an instant. "It's no medical secret that the human body can do incredible things, even surpass its own physical strength, when it's really concentrating all its energy on one particular task alone. And a lot of studies have shown that the person rarely remembers what happened because he didn't accomplish the task consciously."

Denman's voice was as cold as his face was hard. "Thank you, Ms. Cavender, for enlightening me." He turned his attention to the victim. "Look, Mr. Berenson, whoever shot and robbed you went through a helluva lot of trouble to make the crime resemble the M.O. of a much publicized wanted gunman who's ambushed five other men in this area."

"Two of the men died," his assistant offered an addendum, the first time he had opened his mouth.

"You're telling me that I wasn't shot for my wallet and my gold watch?" inquired Berenson mildly in a voice totally devoid of the shock that Bianca felt. "What made you draw that conclusion if my assailant did such a helluva job in disguising the intent?"

"Easy." Denman reached into his olive-drab coat and pulled out a cigar. Bianca shot him an look of reproach before she walked to the table to pour herself and Berenson a glass of water. Chagrin crossed Denman's face and he stuffed the cigar back where it belonged. "The county sheriff and the city police chief have purposefully kept back one important detail of the gunman's style from the news media."

Putting one glass in the patient's right hand and lifting the other to her lips, she asked, "I guess you wouldn't care to share that information with me and Mr. Berenson, would you?"

"No, Ms. Cavender, I wouldn't."

No, nor anything else, from the looks of you.

"Mr. Berenson, why do you think someone would go through the trouble of an ambush?"

"I don't know why anyone would want to kill me."

Denman's brows went up. "I didn't say kill you."

Berenson took a long swallow of water, then with a wry twist of his mouth asked, "Can't judge intent by the failure to accomplish it, is that it?"

"Exactly." The investigator looked decidedly unhappy. "How about giving us a list of the people you think would want to harm you. The usual—vengeful wife, forsaken lover, betrayed business associate—for starters."

The usual? Bianca put down her glass and walked back to her chair. What did Denman know of Berenson's private life that would make him assume he lived by these standards?

"I still can't help you out." A hard edge had crept into the patient's voice. "I am without a vengeful wife since I have never been married. My most recent *affaire de coeur* is happily married to another man, at last. And, to my knowledge, I have never betrayed a business associate."

"Sometimes, Mr. Berenson"—Denman matched each of the hard-edged syllables with his own—"we find that an ambush like this one results from the victim's having been involved in illegal activity. His partners in crime find a way to punish him for having double-crossed them."

"Are you accusing me of a crime, Investigator Denman?"

"No."

"Good."

The atmosphere in the room crackled with static electricity. Even the deputy looked up from his copious note-taking. Bianca certainly hadn't imagined the animosity barely concealed beneath the surface before. It was very real now, and she sensed that there was more to come, even though Denman tried to shed his abrasive manner.

"You maintain close ties with Mexican business-men, don't you, Mr. Berenson?"

"Certainly," he answered without hesitation. "In my work, it's necessary."

"Two particular ties are with the Elizondo and the Albañez families, who have interests in the north-eastern state of Tamaulipas, isn't that correct?"

"Yes. My father established those ties. I've contin-ued them because they mutually benefit all three family businesses."

"Are you aware that both of those families are al-leged to be involved in Mexican underworld opera-tions? Operations whose U.S. contacts are under FBI investigation?"

"No, I am not." Each syllable punctured the air with angry emphasis. "And, furthermore, I do not be-lieve that Pedro Elizondo or José Albañez, the two family representatives I have closest contact with, have ever been involved in underworld activity."

Denman lowered his puffy lids in a scowl. "Your immediate defense, I suppose, could be commend-able."

"I believe justified loyalty to good friends is always commendable, investigator."

"Ah, 'justified,' " crooned Denman, "that's the key word, isn't it?" Berenson gave him no answer. "What do you suppose led the FBI to identify these families as the link to underworld activity between the two borders?"

"I can't imagine."

Suddenly Bianca noticed how strained Berenson's face had become. With exhaustion? Or with trying to keep his own secrets?

"Can you tell me anything about their banking and hotelier interests which could be, shall we say, sus-picious?"

"No."

Denman's face tightened at the unequivocal neg-ative. It was a moment or two before he tried again.

"Has either man ever approached you about acting as an agent for any transaction, apparently legal, to be consummated in the States?"

"Never."

Denman put his hand on the foot of the bed and leaned forward, if not in menace, then definitely in impatience over the victim's lack of cooperation. "Then in what way have you dealt with either man?"

"José Albañez was good enough to notify me five years ago when a large ranch in the state of Tamaulipas went up for sale. Pedro Elizondo made it possible for two other Mexicans to joint-venture with me to buy the property and its livestock since Mexico won't allow any foreigner to own more than forty-nine percent of a Mexican enterprise."

"What did you and your father do in return for the favor?"

"For the *favor*"—Jared Berenson drew out each word to let the man know just what he thought of the implication—"we employed two hundred previously unemployed Mexican farm workers and made what had been a derelict piece of property financially solvent, *even* tremendously profitable."

"How did that 'mutually benefit' Elizondo and Albañez?"

"Elizondo made his money on the bank loans, which were repaid with interest, and in my case, with U.S. dollars, and Albañez made money on the increase in value of his adjacent property." A muscle in Berenson's jaw was working madly. "Nothing illegal there, investigator. Straightforward entrepreneurship, American-style."

Denman narrowed his cynical eyes. "What else do Elizondo and Albañez dabble in besides banking and hotels and land values?"

"You will have to ask them for yourself. What my friends do for a living is their business—it's not my style to check out their bankbooks first."

She had to hand it to him. Clever and neat—and

evasive. What was Jared Berenson trying to hide? she wondered.

The rest of the investigation dragged on until, convinced that the patient would surrender no more information on highly placed Mexican families, Denman left, defiantly pulling his coveted cigar out of his olive-drab pocket as he went.

Bianca crossed the room to close the door that he and his deputy had failed to shut. Returning to the foot of the bed, she studied the patient's face, framed by hair the color of clover honey burnished with red and gold threads. The curly lashes of the closed lids were spikes of shadow on the blue circles beneath the eyes. The nostrils of the well-formed nose flared with each deep inhalation of breath. Was he trying to steady his heartbeat, calm his anger? Was his lower lip thrust out with belligerence, or with concentration?

Suddenly the lids flew up and he fixed her with a bright stare that unnerved her. What had she done to deserve it?

"I woke up to your voice and your hands on my face, Ms. Cavender." It was a slow and formal repetition of what he had told the investigator. "Your appearance was—as Denman suggests—fortuitous, wasn't it?"

She was tired. She wasn't in the mood to be held in suspicion for attempted homicide, if indeed that was what Berenson was doing to her now. "Well, yes, I'd say you were damn lucky that I came along when I did—actually." Her voice sounded strong, thank God.

His eyes assessed her, falling from a study of her very blond head of hair to her body defined and revealed by a dress the color of ripe purple grapes. "Why would a beautiful woman like you take a chance on rescuing someone in a stalled car at two in the morning? Weren't you afraid?"

"Yes."

"Then why did you do it?" His voice was softer now. She closed her eyes and swallowed hard. Would it be a thankless rescue after all? Was this new note of persuasive gentleness in his voice merely trying to coerce a confession out of her? She felt the pressure of tears building in her eyes, the telltale sign of the strain she'd been under.

She opened her eyes, giving him a direct blue-gray stare. "Because I thought you needed someone and I was the only someone around."

"Doesn't it strike you as oddly coincidental, Ms. Cavender, that you happened on the scene so soon after the shooting?"

She looked down for a moment, feeling the tension in the room begin to rise again. She wasn't up to a resurrection of this theme, especially when it couldn't be put down to momentary delirium. Wrapping her hands around the lowered rail on her right, she looked up and caught his hard glare again. "What are you driving at, Mr. Berenson? If it's what the investigator was trying to suggest, you're going to have to be more direct than that. I didn't understand what he was trying to imply either."

"Investigator Denman suspects that you were in on the plot to ambush me."

That was certainly direct. More direct would have been to tell her exactly what Jared Berenson suspected of her. "How do you think he can explain then the fact that I brought you to the emergency room and alerted my brother to get a surgical team together to save your life?"

"Perhaps he is hypothesizing that once you saw I was more seriously hurt than planned, you took matters into your own hands to see that I didn't become a fatality."

". . . So I wouldn't become an accomplice to a murder?"

"Precisely."

"Then you've been holding out on the sheriff's deputies, Mr. Berenson." His brows went up and a question widened his eyes. "To believe I'm an accomplice in crime means that you must also believe you were ambushed. If you believe in the investigator's ambush theory, you must know that someone does have a reason to harm you, even to kill you."

Silence seeped into the room and into the spaces of her beating heart. What was this man guilty of that he was so quick to suspect her of guilt? What had she done by becoming emotionally involved in his pain, his life? And she was involved. Oh, he wasn't Richard. Arthur didn't need to fear that she would ever confuse the two men. They weren't anything alike, not physically, and not temperamentally. Though it was true that in having assumed responsibility for his physical survival, in having taken steps to ensure it, she felt an undeniable bond growing between them, even alongside the suspicion. She was caught in an emotional tug-of-war—how could she win?

He raised his good right hand, palm upward, extending it toward her. "Bianca," he called her first name softly, "come here." She didn't move. "Please."

He was playing with her heart. She knew it. She just couldn't resist it. Slowly her hands released their tight hold on the metal rail and she walked the few feet that took her to his side. Their eyes met, golden lights searching for soft blue-gray depths. She wished she didn't find the face, with its dark heavy brows and its well-defined mouth, so appealing, so compelling.

He let his hand travel with a lover's familiarity along her arm. God help her, she didn't stop him. "Forgive me, Bianca. I'm sorry for my thoughtless accusations because it couldn't be true and because it distressed you. Please, if you can, forgive me."

The man had power all right. With his physical strength the strength of his personality had apparently returned. Should she guard against it? She felt the brick wall of her defenses disintegrate into dust, and a flood of feeling could have bowled her over if she hadn't been so accustomed in the last four years to controlling strong emotions.

"Forgiven," she quietly pronounced with a smile pulling at one corner of her mouth as she looked down on him. She resisted the impulse to place a hand over his. "Forgotten as well."

"Thank you." Though he had gained the exoneration he had asked for, he didn't drop his hand from her arm. He kept the golden glints in his eyes trained on hers and let his hand find its way to the nape of her neck, where he rubbed a few platinum strands of hair between his fingers. "This wonderful color doesn't come out of a bottle, does it?"

In spite of herself, she laughed. She hadn't been expecting a light comment after so tense a moment and so familiar a touch. "Even my hairdresser would sign a testimonial," she vowed, with a hand raised in Girl Scout fashion.

Capturing her upraised hand, he smiled broadly in return, then lightly moaned when the cut on his lip reminded him of his condition. "Do you ever wear it down?" he asked before she could sympathize.

"Only when I don't want to act my professional age."

He laughed, this time remembering not to accompany the laugh with a broad smile. "Will you invite me to the next performance?"

"You'll be the first on my dance card, Mr. Berenson."

"If you're toying with my affections," he warned her, lowering his chin onto his chest and lifting his eyes until his lashes nearly touched his brows, "you'll be *very* sorry."

"Why, Mr. Berenson," she started to protest saucily, but the words never surfaced, for his determined hand eased her face down to his, and before she could say anything else he was gently moving his head from side to side, letting his lips slide against hers.

"I can't open my mouth very well." He whispered the husky apology against her lips and instantly followed it with the gentle command, "Open yours."

And like an obedient idiot she did—before she could question her behavior and the tortuous road he was leading her down.

Immediately he rewarded her obedience with a cool, moist tongue that shot into her mouth, teasing her warm interior with firm, pleasurable strokes. And she, instead of realizing the danger in his persuasion, carefully maneuvered one arm above his head and the other between his splint and his chest, instantly stimulated by the touch of him against her breasts as she gently eased herself onto his chest. Tentatively she began to twirl her tongue around his tongue, trying not to let him see how she craved the taste of him in her mouth even as she felt herself melting into his unresisting lips. With one leg anchored to the floor and the other bent at the knee under her, she wasn't aware she was ever so slowly easing her hips onto the bed until her leg touched his. Then a powerful, marvelous inner pressure seemed to shoot itself between her thighs; a delicious, aching need that made her dizzy. She heard his deep breathing mingling with her own as his hand went down her back and fell to her hips.

It wasn't until she heard the deep agonized moan of pleasure well up in his throat and felt the lifted knee of his left leg rest against her waist that she began to have a vague sense of what was happening between them. She withdrew her tongue from his mouth, the stain of embarrassment hot on her cheeks, the shine of mystified passion in her eyes. What must she have been thinking of? This man was a post-op patient, for God's sake!

"Did I hurt you?" she whispered against his lips, thoroughly humiliated by her behavior, her body frozen in suspension above his.

"You bet you did," he growled without a second's hesitation while his hand roamed eagerly up and down her back, then forward beneath her arm, almost touching her breast. "Plenty. But it's not where you think, baby. The pain from these gunshot wounds are going to take time to heal. The pain you inflict, however, could easily be alleviated now by . . ."

"I'm sorry. I . . . I don't know what came over me." She searched her mind for a graceful exit line but drew a blank.

"It's okay," he soothed in a crooning sound, his delight with her eagerness clearly shining in his eyes and in the hand that moved deliberately onto her breast. "We've got time. My wounds aren't going to hinder me forever. In the meantime, you wouldn't like to climb between the sheets with me, would you? Even with my disability, I could give one helluva try at being one helluva great seducer."

"God forbid!" she cried, shaking her head as she pushed herself up into a rigid sitting position, his hand following her retreat.

He had lightened with humor what could have become a very embarrassing situation, but now suddenly the smile on his face was gone. "You're such a lady, Bianca. But you must be one hell of a woman to have had the guts to stop for me on Old Boerne Stage Road."

"Am I going to be sorry that I did?" she queried him earnestly.

He rubbed his hand along the curving line from breast to waist. "I can't answer that, can I?"

And he didn't answer it. Nor, she realized much later after leaving the hospital, did he ever deny that someone might have had a good reason to gun him down.

In the following days, Jared Berenson received at least forty visitors, making Bianca laugh at her earlier perception of him as a victim without family or friends who required her devoted attention. Two sisters, a half-dozen nieces and nephews, first cousins galore, and two elderly parents who were made to believe their only son had been injured in a hunting accident—all came carrying chocolates and flowers to the patient who basked in the attention. In actuality, Jared Berenson was a successful, influential, and reputable businessman whose produce brokerage firm was the largest of its kind not only in San Antonio, but in all of south Texas as well.

Nevertheless, in spite of Arthur's renewed objections, she had continued to visit him once each day, though there had been no recurrence of their physical intimacy. Just as well with her. She needed time to unravel the web of her feelings in the vacuum of chastity.

It was getting close to eight o'clock on Wednesday night, four days after the shooting, when she walked down the corridor to Room 407, wishing that she had had the time to change into something more appealing than the stark white blouse and corporate suit of charcoal gray she had worn to her late business appointment.

Her knock was answered by the patient himself, a mild reprimand on his tongue and a pout on his lips. "I had almost given up on you," the rich baritone informed her quietly.

She arched her brows at the complaint, her gaze quickly taking in the full length of the man robed in a chocolate dressing gown piped in ivory. "I didn't realize you were counting so much on seeing me."

"Lying so early in our relationship, Bianca?" he inquired in a low, seductive voice and shook his head in mock disappointment. "You ought to be ashamed."

"Of being such a poor liar that you found me out so easily?" she rallied, and then realized that two pinstripe-suited gentlemen were in the room. She looked back to the patient for assistance.

"You're just in time to meet Martin Goerner," he said as he gestured to the taller and younger of the two men, "director of trucking operations at Harvest Enterprises. And Charles Roper," he added, directing her attention to the man whose pale eyes studied her behind rimless spectacles, "comptroller of everything Harvest Enterprises owns."

"Jared tells us you're a CPA, Ms. Cavender." It was Roper who was speaking as he extended a pale hand.

"Yes, that's right," she answered, accepting his hand that felt like dry parchment and then Goerner's firm grasp before taking the chair to which Jared directed her.

"Private practice?"

"Why, yes. For the last four years anyway. Before that I worked with a large firm—to get experience and contacts." Something in Roper's manner made her think of the unpleasant Investigator Denman. Jared was standing behind her. She felt his hand slide from the back of the chair and rest casually on her shoulder.

"I keep up with the aspiring careers of local CPAs, Ms. Cavender. Never know where I might find an especially bright mind for the company." She couldn't imagine what he was leading up to so she placed her clutch purse on the bedside table and waited quietly for him to tell her. "Are you the Bianca Cavender who six months ago uncovered an accounting fraud in the national headquarters of a restaurant chain?"

Roper wasn't kidding. He *did* keep up with his homework on rising careers. "One and the same, Mr. Roper," she acknowledged with a slight inclination of her head.

"Clever detective work." It was Goerner's turn to give her the once-over.

She looked at the speaker, whose broad face and high cheekbones revealed anything but praise. "Actually, I really hadn't been able to unearth much evidence, Mr. Goerner." She crossed one shapely leg over another, resigned to settling in for the inquisition. "I merely followed a hunch that checking accounts had been created for nonexistent employees so that payroll checks could be deposited in them and the embezzler could withdraw money from the accounts as he needed it."

"Quite a hunch," Jared mused aloud. "Quite a scheme."

"Yes," she agreed, "but in the final analysis the books will always lead you to a criminal. It's all a matter of reading clues into the books and following your hunches." She turned to the man whose scrutiny of her had never wavered. "You know that, Mr. Roper."

"Indeed, I do," he answered in a peculiar voice, but the look in his eyes was lost in the glare from the bedside lamp, which bounced off his rimless glasses.

"Apparently, from what Jared tells us, you had another hunch that paid off as well," offered Goerner, pulling back his coat to put his hands in his pockets. "Like the hunch that something was wrong at the stop sign."

For that hunch you ought to look a damn sight more grateful. "No doubt about it, Mr. Goerner. Instinct is a marvelous thing."

He looked at her archly. "Isn't it strange that there was such a striking resemblance between yourself and the woman who first accosted Jared? How can one explain such a coincidence?"

She heard Jared clear his throat and threw herself into the answer before he could defend her. "Frankly, I, for one, make no attempt to explain coincidence, nor do I feel I should have to." She was growing increasingly resentful of the implied accusations which seemed to be coming at her from every source lately. "As for your first statement, none of us can be sure that the woman looked like me at all. A turquoise—maybe blue—dress, a white fur jacket, and yellow hair that partially concealed her face do not exactly add up to my twin, Mr. Goerner."

He had the grace to look ashamed. He dropped his eyes briefly and then glanced up again. "Maybe my concern for Jared has made me too suspicious."

She noticed he hadn't bothered to apologize. "Obviously it has."

Taking out his car keys from his pants pocket, Goerner said abruptly, "I guess it's time Charles and I said good night." He looked a little uncomfortable, jingling the keys in his hand, then continued, "Jared, we've arranged for the conference meeting to begin at three tomorrow afternoon so that you'll have plenty of time to take care of checking out of here before you're due at the office."

"That should even give me a few hours of rest at home," Jared responded, seeing them both to the door like a proper host.

Clasping her black leather purse securely beneath her arm, Bianca rose to take her departure as well. The pleasure with which she had anticipated her visit had dissipated. In its place was the bitter aftertaste of resentment.

"Don't go."

She turned around at the command spoken in a very different tone from the one moments before. He must be in greater pain than he had let on. "Why? Do you need me? Do you need a nurse?"

"I have a favor to ask of you." She tensed at the deadly earnestness in his voice. "I convinced your brother to discharge me from the hospital today with arrangements for me to stay in this room until nine tonight." She looked skeptical. "Right now I need to get to my office to study the fine print on the merger contract before that conference meeting tomorrow."

Was he telling her the truth? Surely someone could have brought the papers to him in the hospital. "Why did you let those two men think that you were spending the night here?"

He shrugged his shoulders but he didn't answer her directly. Walking over to her, he put a hand on her arm. "Please do this last thing for me. If I could drive myself, I would, but you know as well as I do that I couldn't manage the shift and the wheel at the same time. Not yet."

Half of her wanted to protest about his motives for lying indirectly to his friends. Why did he need to sneak out of the hospital? What did he need to conceal?

The other half felt the pull of an undeniable bond. It was that half that said, "All right. If you're sure it can't wait, I'll drive you to your office."

The late night was damp and windy and starless as Bianca and Jared drove into the large parking lot of the produce distributorship that comprised the major part of the holding company called Harvest Enterprises, Inc. She slipped her white Celica easily into the parking slot reserved for him, noting that the moisture was coalescing into long thin needles of ice that splintered when they hit the windshield. Getting home tonight was not going to be easy.

She switched off the engine and the lights before turning to him. "Now what?"

"First off," he answered, his hand promptly on the door, "we discover, if we can, what accounts for the absence of the security guard who should have shot out of that side building like a resolute arrow when you parked an unfamiliar automobile in my slot."

That didn't sound very promising. In fact, in view of the circumstances that surrounded everything about the man sitting next to her, his left sleeve limp at his side, it sounded ominous. Bianca began to suspect that whatever happened tonight would only justify—if not increase—the vague uneasiness she'd felt from the moment she entered his hospital room two hours ago.

"Do you want me to wait for you here in the car?" she asked.

"Good God, no! At this hour? I want you where I can keep an eye on you."

Why? Is someone keeping an eye on us? The fear immediately leaped to mind. *Is someone out there stalking him while the moon is conveniently shadowed by clouds? Will I through association become part of the quarry?*

Even after he had gotten out of the car, she still sat there, an uncertain fear preventing her from following suit. She knew she didn't want to enter the multi-storied Gothic building in front of her any more than she wanted to wait for him alone in the car. Was she safer with him or away from him? Suddenly the evening wasn't just dark, it was black as pitch; not just starless, but friendless as well. Even the facade ahead was less architecturally interesting than inimical. The bulbous eyes of its hideous gargoyles jutting out of the lacy stonework watched every movement of every human who entered there. When Jared opened her door to give her a hand, she took it, but she couldn't help wondering if she would be sorry.

Reluctantly she walked up the steps toward the pointed arch of the double doors, trying to remind herself that the gargoyles were inanimate, albeit grisly, creatures and that the parking lot behind them was what it appeared to be—deserted. She took a quick look to her left. Long beige trucks identifiable by the logo of harvest baskets and cornucopias over-flowing with fruits and vegetables were lined up in neat, even rows. Some were parked in utter darkness unpenetrated by even the dimmest light. Others were situated near the high pole lamps within whose strong shafts of light she could see the ice needles drizzling down, just as she could feel them pierce her cheeks. Shivering, she lowered her chin and tried not to think that one of those trucks might be sheltering the same assailant who had waited to ambush his victim on an isolated country road.

Jared ushered her into an office building whose vaulted foyer supported by massive columns made her think of a mausoleum. "This is more than odd," he said, his brow creased in chagrin as he closed one of the huge doors behind them. After pocketing the keys, his hand went immediately to her elbow.

She went absolutely still, her feet immobile on the plush carpet. She didn't move anything except her lips. "What's odd?" Her voice sounded distinctly hollow even to her own ears.

"Benjamin!" he called loudly, then quietly listened to his own unanswered syllables reverberate off the cold walls of the emtpy foyer and down the corridors that shot off from its sides.

He looked down on her frozen face. Unexpectedly he flicked a remaining ice crystal from her brow with a light stroke of his finger. Looking as though he had surprised himself with the gesture as much as he had surprised her, he kept his finger against her face, letting it slowly travel into the hollows of her cheek before resting it on her lower lip. She resisted the natural impulse to moisten her mouth with her tongue, her eyes growing wider the longer he prolonged the contact. She saw the Adam's apple in his throat move up and down as he swallowed hard. Breathlessly she waited for him to say something, too confused by unwelcome desire and genuine fear to break the peculiar mood herself.

He shook his head slightly as if to clear it. When his finger left her mouth, his voice resumed a matter-of-factness that let her heart resume its regular beat. "Benjamin is the security guard who's usually stationed near the entrance. I've never known him to miss his night shift."

"Any theories?" she asked in nearly as casual a tone.

"None. If there had been any trouble, he could have set off the alarm with the electronic panic button he carries in his pocket." In spite of the assurance, worry lines creased his brow. He slipped his good right hand across her back and up to her shoulder. "Come on. We can take the elevator down the hall to the fourteenth floor. Then, unfortunately, we'll have to walk up a couple of flights to get to my office since the private elevator leading to the executive floor is temporarily out of commission."

As soon as the doors of the stairwell swung shut behind them, she heard him mutter under his breath, "What in the hell is going on here?"

"You know, Mr. Berenson"—she chanced a touch of levity as she peered apprehensively into the drafty blackness and forced her feet in the direction of the risers' shadowy outline—"the City Public Service Board requires that you pay your bill for the privilege of electricity, or they take the privilege away from you."

He laughed mirthlessly, an eerie sound that spiraled up the stairwell. "I'll have Charles speak to our accountant about the delinquency first thing tomorrow morning." His hand pressed more firmly into her shoulder bone as they made the ascent.

They entered what Bianca assumed was a two-story penthouse on the top floor. What light there was came through the long, narrow arched windows at each end of the elegantly appointed reception room. She looked up to study Jared's expression. She couldn't read it. She saw only a tightly clenched jaw and a pursed mouth. When he cast his eyes down on hers she could see that they were alight with a determination to discover why things were not as he had expected to find them. He dropped his hand from her shoulder to flip the light switch. Darkness prevailed, dispersed only in two milky shafts of moonlight.

One would think that a man who had been ambushed and left to die would have been hesitant to proceed in view of so many inauspicious signs. Why wasn't this one? she wondered. For that matter, why wasn't she?

"My office is right beyond the next room," he explained as he put the key in the lock and ushered her into a room whose utter darkness was unrelieved by any natural light pouring in from a window.

Both of them instantly noticed the warm glow of light leaking out between the floor and the doorframe of Jared's office. Bianca heard his deep inhalation of breath at the same time she heard her own. From a stairwell which should have been brightly lit but wasn't, they had come to an office which should not have been lit, but was. Suddenly it seemed terribly important to find out why.

On cat's feet they crept to the door. Jared whipped out a key and shoved it into the lock. She put a hand on the knob to help him instead of having the good sense to get out of harm's way. Immediately they saw the light behind the locked door go out. They heard drawers slam shut and muffled footsteps race across the room. Without warning her, as soon as the lock clicked open, Jared kicked the door flat against the inner wall, yanking it out of her grasp. In the same instant an unidentifiable figure hurtled like a speeding bullet between the two of them, knocking her off her feet as he shot away into the darkness.

"Goddamn!" Jared shouted as he was thrown up against the doorjamb, his injured shoulder and arm taking the entire brunt of the fall.

Pitched forward into the room, she remembered inhaling the scent of wet wool and feeling rough fabric scratch into her cheek as the figure made its swift escape. Too disoriented to cushion her fall with outstretched hands, she hit the floor with a thud, the reverberations of Jared's curse ringing inside the injured recesses of her skull.

Chapter Four

Her eyes were tightly shut against the pain reverberating in her head and shooting like a rocket from the base of her neck down to her toes and straight back up again. Cautiously she tried moving her head which had been slammed into the dubious cradle of her outflung arm, every nerve ending in her cheek and neck burning like fire. Slowly she pushed her lids open; her eyes were glazed.

At first she saw only vague purple outlines partially revealed by a flood of moonlight from the numerous windows along the outside wall of the room. One of those blurred outlines moved. Somehow she had the presence of mind to realize that it was Jared struggling to a kneeling position from which he could spring to his feet. Without a second's hesitation, she threw her body to the right and flung out her hand, reaching for that part of the purple shadow where she thought his feet might be. She grabbed his ankle, mercilessly embedding her fingernails into the flesh above it.

"For God's sake, stay put!" she screamed even as she simultaneously tried to hold air in her collapsing lungs. "Don't be an idiot! You'll never catch him now." Her fingers sensed the relaxation of his calf muscle as he hesitated. She dug her nails deeper into the flesh. Her chest hurt when she took in breath again. "If your incision hasn't already opened, running after him now will undoubtedly do the trick! Is that what you want?" He rocked back on his heels and steadied his weight with the palm of his good hand flattened on the floor. "Just be grateful he only knocked us down. He didn't *shoot* us down."

"No doubt it's better to be stabbed by your nails and slowly bleed to death!" he spat at her.

"Yes, it is!" she lashed out in return, anything to keep him immobile. Only when she was sure he wasn't going anywhere did she gradually relax the hold she had on him and then drop her hand altogether. His anger didn't affect her. She knew it sprang from frustration over his physical helplessness, which she had had the very bad grace to remind him of. "Sorry," she murmured, catching her breath, "I wasn't trying to hurt you."

For a moment or two a chilling silence settled on the room. Then, in the heavy shadows she saw him get to his feet in one fluid motion and extend his good hand to help her as well. She pretended not to see it—how could she lean on his support four days after his surgery?—and scrambled to her feet on her own efforts.

Without a backward glance, without a break in his long, smooth stride, he quickly flipped the switch of a cordless lamp by the door, casting a soft glow over the central section of the room, walked behind a large mahogany desk, and with a rigid index finger jabbed a variety of buttons on the instrumentation panel that dominated the desk.

"Damn!" he muttered under his breath and immediately jabbed out another series. The thin curl of his lips told her that the motion hadn't produced the results he had expected.

He glanced up to see her standing beside the leather chair directly to the left of his desk. She had one slightly trembling hand on the chair's arm and the other hand at her heart as she tried her best to catch her breath. "Are you all in one piece?" he asked while he picked up the phone and punched in five numbers.

"Slightly battered, but one piece," she managed, pushing a runaway strand of blond hair back into the lost cause of her coiffure at the same time he barked into the receiver.

"J. Berenson here. Wherever the hell you are, Benjamin, sound the alarm, call the police, and get the hell over here to my office." He slammed down the phone and winced with the pain when the action jarred his physique. "I wasn't expected back until Friday morning," he said tonelessly.

She stared at him, wondering if he would tell her if he had seriously reinjured his wounds. She took a deep shuddering breath. "And you think that someone made a move before he, or she, thought you would return?"

"It's possible."

"Why would someone want to go to all the trouble?" But he didn't answer her. Denman's ambush theory wasn't so farfetched after all. She waited for the shuddering in her chest to subside, then asked, "Why an ambush and then a break-in? Why wouldn't your enemy have broken in on the night he shot you when he could be sure you wouldn't be here?"

Still he didn't answer her. Instead he began to search the large, two-story room with his eyes as if he were trying to discover purpose in the mad disarray of papers on his desk and others scattered on the Oriental carpet beneath it as well as the wall safe whose lock was marred by smoke burns.

She felt a throbbing at the base of her skull push its way up and around the curve of her head like a vise. She didn't want to think about his silence or the more unsavory ramifications of the evening's escapade. Instead she slid down into the leather chair before her knees went out from under her and tried to care about her appearance. One more pair of Hanes's best marred by runs from toe to thigh and a sturdy suit that had held up far better than the turquoise silk had weren't, unfortunately, enough of a distraction. When she looked up to ask him what, if anything, he had discovered missing from the safe, the room began to fill with bodies and noise.

First came a horrified Benjamin, whose behavior took Bianca by surprise. He acted far more like a faithful family retainer than a security guard, clucking over "Mr. Jared" like a grandmother hen and explaining that he had been investigating a sudden power loss in this part of the building; otherwise, he would have been on the spot to protect "Mr. Jared" and "his lady." The arrival of the police close upon the heels of Benjamin finally silenced the dear old gentleman's worry, but it didn't dismiss him. He felt it his duty to stay close to Mr. Jared, "just in case." Had there been an instance before, Bianca wondered, when his employer had needed his protection?

"Well, Ms. Cavender," Investigator Denman said as he came into the room with a loose-limbed man who identified himself as Lieutenant Barber of the city police, "it seems you are destined to be at Mr. Berenson's side when trouble catches up with him." He grinned.

"And who can fight Fate, investigator?" Bianca parried, not in the least amused by his attempt to make some quick associations at her expense.

He wasn't much amused by her attitude either. The grin disappeared. "Are you quite sure the two of you met only four nights ago?"

"Quite sure, investigator," she answered crisply.

But he wasn't going to let go of his juicy bone. "Must have been instant attraction, then."

It was Jared who answered without bothering to hide his disgust. "You're dead right. It was love at first bloody sight."

What was Denman doing here anyway? Unlike Old Boerne Stage Road, this area was in San Antonio's city limits, not under Bexar County jurisdiction. Bianca looked straight at Barber. "Why is the sheriff's department here tonight?"

Denman didn't like the slight. Before Barber had a chance to answer, Denamn pushed his lips into a tight expression and then released them with a smack. "Because," he said, "the city knows the sheriff's interested in this case."

"What 'case' is that?" demanded Jared, who was now sitting on the chair behind his desk. "When did the two incidents involving Ms. Cavender and me become a 'case'? *Before* or *after* they occurred?"

Bianca sensed that Jared was trying to trick Denman into telling him directly that he was a suspect in a preexisting case. Denman, merely shrugging his olive-drab shoulders, didn't fall for it. Was the investigator avoiding a direct accusation because his department was still searching for the evidence to make the accusation stick?

She felt very tired suddenly, the effects of fear, the surprise apprehension of the intruder, and the fall finally beginning to take a toll on her stamina. Jared didn't look fazed, but as the investigation-interrogation continued and both of them were called upon to give blow-by-blow accounts of the evening from the moment they left the hospital until the police arrived on the scene, she could hear the strength of his voice fast declining. His back was ramrod straight in his chair, as though he knew that if he relaxed even one muscle, the rest would crumble, and from time to time she noticed that he ran a hand across his upper arm and side as though to massage away the pain.

Lieutenant Barber, a pleasant enough looking man in his early forties, asked, "Has anything else, any seemingly insignificant detail, come to you which you think we should know?"

"Not a thing." Jared may have been exhausted but his response was brisk. "Nor can I think of a reason for anyone to want to shoot me, kill me, rob me, or burgle this office. I'm not even convinced that the person who broke into that safe tonight was after money any more than you are."

"What makes you think that?" asked the police lieutenant, who didn't sound as though he would believe the answer he'd get.

"The person who was in this office tonight had to have been highly familiar with the building or he never would have executed such a smooth break-in or made such a clean getaway. Apparently he knew how to cut off the power to this specific area, which is a rather tricky thing to do. And I wonder if he didn't use the acetylene torch on the safe because he didn't want to be identified as someone who knew the combination."

"Did you have any information in it which specifically deals with international transactions?" Barber asked with a glance at the safe, which one of his men was dusting for fingerprints.

Jared cast a here-we-go-again look in Denman's direction. "Are you referring to business transactions with Mexico?"

"Any and all international affairs, Mr. Berenson," came the deadpan reply.

Jared's voice was equally devoid of recognizable emotion. "All that was in that safe is pretty much what is still in that safe—titles to Harvest Enterprises properties and nonnegotiable securities. If anything is missing besides the thousand dollars in cash, I don't know what it is."

"Conspiracies have a way of twisting and turning until their beginnings and endings aren't always distinguishable from each other."

"What precisely is that supposed to mean, lieutenant?" Jared asked, his rigid back coming away from the chair. "You'll have to tell me, since I don't know the first thing about conspiracies."

But Bianca was afraid that she knew exactly what the lieutenant had meant. And if the city police as well as the county sheriff were interested in the possibility of an international conspiracy masterminded by, or supported by, Jared Berenson, they must have gotten their information through federal agencies that had a case under investigation. Miserably she stared at the man whose burnished head of hair was set at a proud angle on his strong neck and broad shoulders, this man who had a claim on her heart. What had he done, what was he involved in that had led the FBI to him? And if the FBI could really point to him, why were these local police fumbling around with their innuendos? Why didn't the FBI simply charge in with a formal indictment?

They were questions she was not going to find an answer for tonight. When Benjamin closed the door behind him, Barber and Denman in tow, she was standing at the edge of the desk, left alone with a man who was generating a great deal of criminal activity around himself, and her as well, by association.

She was grateful that the noise and blustering confidence of the detectives were finally gone, but in their place was an uneasy silence weighted down with newly awakened anxieties. Without warning, behind her she felt the soft pressure of a hand at the nape of her neck, then the soothing cool massage of gentle fingers that slipped inside the collar of her blouse. She shivered.

"Bianca . . ." She could feel the warm breath of his words on her neck. "I'm sorry. I was so angry and frustrated about that prowler in my office that I never even thought I might be jeopardizing your safety by trying to catch him in the act."

"I had plenty of time to back out of our little search party. I didn't." Lifting her shoulder and tilting her head to the side, she rubbed her cheek on his hand before she realized she shouldn't have.

"You could have been seriously hurt."

"I wasn't. You could have been hurt. But you weren't."

He rested his chin on the top of her head without

ceasing the cool massage of his fingers inside the white cloth. "Nonetheless, I'm sorry. I should never have asked . . ."

"Forgiven." As soon as the word was out, she felt his body slip between her and the desk. She could feel the warmth of his thighs move against the curve of her hips. Her pulse quickened.

Against every highly developed instinct for self-preservation she possessed, when she heard his silent request to turn around, she obeyed it, brushing against the muscular strength of his legs when she did, and comforted by it. He kept his hand at her neck, his arm resting behind her shoulder. When he raised his splint, she slipped her hand beneath his injured arm and alongside his rib cage. As she moved her other arm behind his back she stepped a few inches to her left, making it possible for him to hold her without hurting himself.

"Are you wondering what you got yourself into by coming to my rescue four nights ago?" he asked softly, his breath light on her face.

She looked up into his strong features and the glittering lights of his golden eyes. "Among other things," she acknowledged against his lips the instant before they touched hers. She closed her eyes and let her heart swell with feeling. His kiss was sweet, tingling like tomorrow's promise on her lips. She gasped a little when he eased his leg ever so slightly between hers.

"Like what?" he asked as he kissed her brow, then the fallen lids of her eyes.

He pulled her closer, persuading her to press herself against him. She felt a delicious sensation rise in her loins, which frightened her and simultaneously made her unaccountably sad.

"Like how do I deal with the way you're stealing my heart," she answered in a soft and husky breath, shaking her head at the impossibility of her dilemma. The biological rhythm he was orchestrating with the deft movement of his upper leg between her thighs was indisputable proof of the futility in her effort.

He threw back his head, a light laugh at her problem rippling in his throat. He fixed his bright gaze on her wide, unblinking eyes. "You can't, Bianca. The ancient philosophers tell us that if you save a man's life, you are thereafter responsible for it." His leg moved suggestively between hers again. His good hand fell from her shoulder and down her back, down the narrow mound of her hips, and pulled her even closer. "And you know it."

Her false denial was whispered into the mouth that instantly closed over hers, hushed against the tongue that took advantage of her startled, parted lips. She was lost in the taste of his flesh inside her own.

She began to kiss him, his full lips, his sweet tongue, his hard face, his strong throat, hesitantly at first and then, to her shame, a little frantically. It had been so long, so very long, and she was heady with the excitement of wanting him and of his wanting her in return. He was fire and she had for so long been encased in ice. Surely she could be allowed this one indiscretion, she argued with herself while he stepped back and rested his hip on the edge of the desk at the same time he pulled her between his legs. She was so eager for touching, and exploring, and discovering. He had come into her life at the right time. How could he be the wrong man?

But he could be and probably was, she forced herself to admit. And she resisted the temptation to run her hand along his leg as she was yearning to do, for what he was inciting was a perilous attraction. It defied reason, and common sense told her to run as fast as she could from the danger in his arms.

But it wasn't until she heard a deep sound, part pleasure, part something else, well up from his throat, that she summoned the will to pull her face away from his. "I'm sorry," she whispered, her voice quivering with a fervor that deeply embarrassed her. "You must

be in terrible pain." She tried to withdraw her arms
from around his back, and her hips from his enclosing
warmth, but even though he was handicapped by a
useless arm, she was no match for his strength. "You
slammed into the door before we fell," she persisted
in spite of his refusal to let her go. "That must have
been dreadful. We shouldn't be . . ."

The face she looked at now was rock hard, his nostrils flared from deep breathing, lips still slightly
bruised but parted with passion. "It's the pain you inflict, Bianca, the pain the doctors can't treat, that I
feel right now." His leg wrapped around hers and his
hand pulled her thighs into his so that she couldn't
escape and couldn't misinterpret his reference. Suddenly she was frightened but just as suddenly her
fright dissolved as his lips began to curve in a wry
smile of ironic amusement at himself. "Tell me the
words to say that will convince you to ease that pain?"

She shook her head, confused by the way he balanced intensity with humor. "I would have thought
the first pain would have diminished the desire of the
second."

He laughed, but it was a deep growling sound, all
animal, all male. "Not for me, sweetheart. Not when
I'm with you. Aren't we damn lucky?"

"Are we?" She glanced meaningfully at the arm he
carried in a sling, a little angry at the obstacle it
presented, and a little relieved. "We couldn't possibly . . ."

He stilled the protest of her lips with a light kiss.
"Of course we could. Biological drive coupled with
emotional attraction," he assured her with easy confidence, "is the mother of sexual invention. Isn't it?"

He spoke lightly, but she could still feel the heavy
rhythm of his heart expanding and contracting his
chest. Distance. She needed distance, or God only
knew what this man would have her agreeing to. "I
wouldn't know, Mr. Berenson."

"No time like the present to learn." His voice was

like supple velvet. "I think I could manage to perform any activity you would like to encourage."

In his eyes was a direct challenge. She was weakening in their light. And she mustn't. What did she know of this man? And really, what did she know of herself, except that a four-year fidelity to the memory of one man might be a very good reason to suspect the integrity of her wildfire response to the sexual advances of another. She looked away and searched her mind for something to bolster her resolve.

It wasn't hard to find. He hadn't said one word about the police suspicions, never offered her an explanation about his dealings with the two Mexican families the authorities were so interested in. Shouldn't he have leaped to reassure her with hard and fast evidence that he was innocent of their implied accusations? Surely he couldn't be so full of confidence that he took her trust for granted, just as he apparently took her attraction for him. He had distracted her, she decided, purposefully so, away from the interrogation with a quick game of masterful seduction—and one she'd been all too eager to participate in.

He was apparently adept at reading her mind. "You're looking at me as though you believe I'm a criminal."

She flattened her hand against his chest and took a step back. "A practiced seducer, a skilled deceiver," she spelled it out for him.

She would have liked to believe in the momentary confusion that pulled at his brows, the hurt surprise in his eyes, but she wouldn't let herself. She could feel the heavy beat of his heart against her palm when she managed the words, "It's been a long evening."

For a moment he didn't say a word. He bit down on the corner of his lower lip and inched his bandaged hand across his chest until it smothered hers. "Why don't you tell me lies instead, Bianca. Tell me that you trust me and I'll do my best to turn what has been a long and tedious evening into a beautiful and memorable night."

A brief spasm convulsed her body. He must have felt it, too. "I can't lie." *I wish I could.* "Besides, you don't know me."

"Oh, but I do."

She shook her head. How could he? "There hasn't been enough time."

"But there has been enough experience."

"Has there?"

"When people wrestle with fear and danger together like we have, they let their social masks slip. We haven't had time for artifice, you and I. No time for games. I saw you as you are four nights ago. I liked what I saw. I like what I see. I want to see more."

She swallowed hard. So he had felt and understood the uncommon bond that tied them to each other. She would be a fool, though, to admit that she believed in it as well. *"I* don't know *you."*

"No. You probably don't." His voice was sad. "Or you don't like what you know, don't like what you see."

She felt cheated by his response. She had been expecting to hear an explanation of his Mexican connections, a declaration of innocence. She stared into the hooded bright eyes and lamented her fate. Her heart, so long buried in the memory of one man's violent death, was now shadowed by the fear of another's culpability in crime. Where did that leave her?

Alone.

His hand moved up from her hips to her waist. His head came down to nuzzle warmly in her neck. She felt the breath of his whisper, "Another time, Bianca." Moments passed in unbroken silence. When he lifted his head to look down on her again, he said, "You're probably right. I'm guilty"—she held her breath,—"of wishful thinking. I couldn't handle anything more strenuous right now than one last kiss.

The first time we make love together shouldn't be a disappointment for either one of us."

He paused with a raised brow to give her ample opportunity to deny his assumption of what their future would be like. But she said nothing.

"Until then, good night." His final kiss, when he bent to give it to her, was sweet on her lips, though his final words were a torture of anticipation. Something to dream on.

When she finally closed the door on the dark, windy evening and her last client, she slipped the deadbolt lock and safety chain into place. Turning around, she leaned her back against the door for a moment. Her half-smile slowly disappeared with the exhaustion that hung heavy on her shoulders and weighted down her limbs. It had been an exceptionally long day, one of those twelve-hour workdays in a week that had seen too many. Last week had been a nightmare from which she had not yet awakened. Even now she wondered how much of it she had lived, how much she had dreamed.

Because she had insisted last Wednesday night, after that last good-night kiss, that his wounds be reexamined, she had driven Jared Berenson back to the hospital emergency room where capable hands redressed them. When she offered to drive him home, he turned her down. If she stayed with him at his place until morning, he said, her tempting presence might further jeopardize the healing process of his injury, and if she left, she would be driving home alone over deserted streets at one in the morning.

"Can't take the chance on your rescuing any other bachelor in distress," he had teased her with an engaging grin. "I'm having a hard enough time seducing you now. I don't think I could handle the extra competition."

It had been days now, six to be precise, since his taxi had followed her to her doorstep and then taken him

home. And she considered that a very long time not
to hear from a man who had declared that their lives
were joined because she had saved his, a man who believed that fear and danger had made them intimate.
She had heard absolutely nothing from the man who
had made her imagine what making love with him
might mean in her life.

Pulling herself away from the door, she walked the
length of her small foyer past the japanned credenza
that held the day's mail. Tomorrow she would see to
it, every bit of it, she promised herself. When she
reached the foot of the staircase that led to the private
residence on the second floor of her office-townhouse,
she sighed and bent at the waist to slip off her high-
heeled pumps.

She ought to be grateful Jared Berenson hadn't
called. All that was rational told her how grateful she
ought to be. At least not hearing that rich baritone
voice, not seeing those eyes flecked with gold, not
feeling the warmth in his body's embrace saved her
from fighting that endless battle between wanting to
believe he was innocent and suspecting that he had
indeed done something to attract an FBI investigation.

"Then why don't I feel grateful instead of disap-
pointed, even angry?" she demanded of the empty
foyer.

Shoes in hand, she climbed the stairs toward a hot
cup of coffee. It was then that the doorbell rang. She
stopped in her tracks and creased her brow. What appointment had she forgotten in her weariness? She
couldn't think. Oh, well, she sighed a second time,
balancing her hip against the banister as she slipped
her shoes back on. She couldn't be expected to put in
a normal schedule this week when she had had such
an abnormal one the last week, could she?

Down the carpeted risers she went, past the un-
characteristic bundle of unattended mail, toward the
safety chain and the deadbolt lock, and the second

peal of chimes. When she finally opened the door to her caller, her heart leaped into her throat.

The very reason for her disrupted schedule and disturbing dreams stood there looking down on her, those bright, intelligent eyes emanating all at once a fatal virility and an irresistible, refined charm. A wicked and disarming combination. How did he manage it?

Her mouth opened slightly. *Hello—Good evening— Won't you come in?* She could have said any of those things to him, standing there in a brown leather jacket with the left sleeve lying flat against his arm, but she closed her mouth without uttering even the suggestion of a sound. Just when she had about decided that she might never see him again, just when she had convinced herself that not seeing him was for the best, here he was—the physical height and breadth of him that overwhelmed her, the something special in his eyes that held her captive—making her feel foolishly determined never to be grateful again.

"Not even a 'Gee, but it's good to see you again'?" asked Jared Berenson, his burnished head cocked to one side. "I'm here to tell you, sweetheart," he confided sotto voce, "you're hell on my ego. It's a fragile structure, after all." His protests to the contrary, he stepped confidently across the threshold, taking his welcome for granted.

Recovering at last, she replied dampeningly, "The last thing you need is ego fortification. I would have voted for humbling if someone had given me the choice." The pout on his lips made her wonder what had really kept him away. "Have you been all right?"

He raised a brow at her concern. "I had a few bad days. High fever, chills, the works." One shoulder lifted to shrug off the inconvenience of a relapse. "It's over now."

"Arthur should have told me." She put a hand to the empty sleeve, the soft brown leather smooth beneath her fingertips. "He wouldn't have betrayed any professional scruples by telling me. I might have been able to . . ." She stopped herself before she admitted too much. As it was, she heard an anxiety in her voice she'd do well to bring under control.

He shook his head. "Arthur wasn't terribly sympathetic. Said I had brought it all on myself with macho heroics." A smile touched the corners of his mouth. "Besides, I didn't want you to know. You've already spent too much time worrying about me." He put a gentle silencing finger to her lips. "I've brought something for you."

Until then she hadn't even noticed that half-concealed between the hindrance of his sling was a large package wrapped in silver foil and white satin ribbon. He lifted his splint to release the package into his good hand.

"For me?" she asked, inordinately pleased and embarrassed by his gesture.

"Yes. For you."

Suddenly she was aware that her light wool dress was floating against her legs in the breeze of December's damp night air and quickly moved to close the door behind them. Still strangely hesitant to take the package he extended toward her, she said, "Please come in," as she led the way toward the staircase.

Puzzled, he looked up at the staircase ahead, then smiled wickedly. "Aren't you going to open it first? Don't you want to know what it is?"

"Of course, I do," she answered, realizing from the look on his face what he must be thinking of her eagerness to ascend those stairs. "These are my offices down here. I actually live on the second floor, where I thought I'd open the gift." She bit her lower lip. "I didn't think you had come to see me on business."

"Oh." A note of real disappointment entered his voice, mixed with laughter at his erroneous deductions. "And I thought you must be dying to get me up to your boudoir." His cordovan loafer touched the lowest riser at the same time her high-heeled pump did. Their eyes met for a second.

She took the package then and laughed at him and at herself. "Mr. Berenson, must I remind you of your disabilities? You must learn to control your eagerness."

"You just may have to do that for me, Ms. Cavender." He scratched his temple with his index finger as they ascended the staircase side by side. "I'm too single-minded to win at self-control, and I can be a very difficult and demanding patient."

"Then I'll just have to be a very difficult and demanding nurse."

"Is that your threat or your promise?" he asked as they stepped up to the second floor gallery.

"Most definitely my promise," she answered, leading the way to the open doorway of her living room, which occupied the central space on the floor.

"Be careful, now, Ms. Cavender," he suggested, his mock severity suddenly replaced with the real thing. "I'm a man who expects a woman to keep her promises."

"You're in luck, Mr. Berenson." She moved her hand in the direction of the light switch as they entered the room, and wondered if she had imagined that a meaning more intense lay beneath his repartee. "I've never broken one."

His voice was pitched seductively deep. "I'll remind you of your perfect record if you ever try."

Her pounding heart caught in her throat and she couldn't for the life of her think of a clever riposte that would conceal all that she was really feeling.

She touched the switch, and her living room, decorated with a fine though eclectic eye for period furniture, sprang to life. Country French chests flanking a marble fireplace boasted art nouveau lamps while Victorian velvet sofas the color of rich claret lounged on either side of a Middle Eastern brass coffee table. In the center of the table, a cobalt blue porcelain vase sprouted a lush arrangement of purple hyacinths and red roses, baby's breath, and yellow daffodils.

Bianca wondered if he had noticed the photograph of the fair-haired young man on the mantel or the photograph of the bridal couple leaving the arched doors of a church, which hung on the east wall.

"The room looks just like you," said Jared, smiling as he walked toward a claret sofa, oblivious to the chaos his last words had caused.

She walked around the table so that she could sit on his uninjured right side. "Will I be sorry if I ask how so?"

"Modern and old-fashioned." She relaxed. "A strong woman who won't let me forget she's a lady. All the pieces in your puzzle fit together nicely."

"I wish that were really true," she said aloud without meaning to, and then avoided his raised brow that encouraged more confidences. The name of San Antonio's most exclusive women's store was embossed in an oval label in the lower right-hand corner of the box she held in her hands.

"You've done a damn good job of convincing me the pieces fit. Now open the gift."

She instantly sat down on his right side, package in her lap, their knees almost touching. She was nervous. If she discounted her brother, and she did, she hadn't received a gift from a man in four years. Removing first the ribbon, she deftly slipped her rose-enameled nails between the foil wrapping and the tape that secured it on all sides. She pulled back the white tissue, her hands suddenly arrested when she saw what was nestled in the box. The soft folds of turquoise silk highlighted with intricate beadwork were fashioned in a designer dress far more expensive than the one she had discarded little more than a week ago. A smile of pleasure lifted her generous mouth, her long hands gracefully poised above the gift.

Jared spoke in soft reminiscence. "I distinctly remember that the first words I heard after surgery were, 'You owe me a new silk dress.' "

Unthinkingly she put her hand on his arm. "I never meant for you to take that seriously."

He was quick to put his hand over hers, infusing her with his warmth. "Oh, but I take my obligations very seriously, Bianca. In fact, I went through a lot of trouble on your account. When I finally found what I wanted, I had to find the right size. Fortunately, I had the memory of having seen you and having held you." He shrugged his broad shoulders and then grimaced at having forgotten the incapacity of the left one. "I described a tall, willowy, full-breasted figure to the salesperson and she said a seven would do." When he looked at her directly, she suspected that he intended for the words to excite her. "I hope the color is right. I never really saw it that clearly."

"It's perfect," she said quietly, flushed with unwilling excitement at his familiarity, both in choosing the dress and in telling her how he had determined the size. She fingered the flanged shoulders piped with glittering beads. "Thank you very much."

"It was the least I could do in return for all that you did for me. Of course, there are other ways in which I'd much rather express my gratitude—as well you know." His voice went a notch deeper. "I'm just waiting until you're ready to receive my full attention. The truth is, I'm only patient because these confounded wounds inhibit the full expression of what I have in mind."

She couldn't imagine that anyone had ever accused him of being anything less than unconscionably bold. What was needed here was a politely evasive reply now that he was situating his arm along the sofa ledge behind her, for all the world looking perfectly at home. But she needn't have worried. He released her hand and beat her to an abrupt change in topic.

"I must confess at this point that I'm here under false pretenses."

"Oh?" Immediately she went on the qui vive. "Was the gift a bribe?"

A flame of reproach flashed in his eyes, then died down. "No, not at all. But it's only half the reason I've come."

"I see." Rustling the tissue back over the silk, she replaced the white box lid and slid the package onto the coffee table. She swiveled on her hips to face him, the fingers of her hands entwined in her lap. "What's the other half?"

"Business."

She stared at him, struck by the good, strong bones of a face accustomed to success. A man with his extensive business interests didn't come calling on a one-woman CPA firm.

He thrust out his lower lip and arched a brow at her cynical response. "I'm glad I waited to tell you or you might not have invited me upstairs at all. And I would have hated to miss seeing where you live, how you live."

Did she imagine that he had moved an inch or so closer in the time it took her to blink? "And how do I live?" was out before she could weigh the consequences of getting off on personal tangents again.

"As expected. With elegant simplicity." His voice went gentle. "And with memories."

So he had seen the photograph of Richard on the mantel, and their wedding photograph as well. "Memories are the gifts time gives us," she said very slowly, steadily. She felt sad, wanting to say more, and tense, wishing she had said less.

"Undoubtedly," he answered, still in that deep voice filled with gentleness. "And in time, time continues to give us more."

She understood. There was a future for everyone, whatever the past had offered. But he knew nothing of her past.

"When you were married, did you and Richard live here together?"

So he did know. Who had told him—Arthur? "No. We had just bought the place the month before he died. We were moving the last trunkload of boxes here when his car was hit." She prepared herself with tightly laced fingers for questions about the accident, but they didn't come.

"Arthur said that you started your own practice shortly after the accident. You're a courageous woman."

"Am I? I don't suppose I've ever thought about it in those terms. Private practice is what we had planned to do together. That's why we bought this particular townhouse with its floor division in the first place." Unconsciously, she slowly kneaded the heel of one hand in the palm of the other, rumpling the slate-blue wool of her dress. "When I was left to do it alone, I simply did it."

He shook his head at her emotionless rendition of the last four years of her life. "That couldn't have been easy."

Harder than anyone would probably ever know. "It's true I didn't have the security of a guaranteed salary, but, on the other hand, being self-employed gave me little time for self-pity. I had to get to work and earn an income. I had to pursue my contacts while they still remembered me."

"Your hard work has paid off, hasn't it?"

She stilled the motion of her hands, relaxed her spine a degree or two now that he had steered the conversation back to business. "In most months I have as much work as I can comfortably handle."

"No desire to expand?"

"I'm not in the race for megabucks, if that's what you mean." She wondered if he guessed that some of the joy of working to make a professional name for herself had died when she lost the one person she was to have shared it with. "Peace is a more precious commodity. I can't buy that."

His pupils were surrounded by shooting sparks of gold when he looked at her, a nice complement to the yellow oxford shirt he wore beneath his leather jacket. "Would you make room for one additional client?"

"Yes, of course I would. Neither my schedule nor my bank account is so full that I could afford to turn down a good client." She looked at him thoughtfully as she got to her feet. She supposed he would tell her what was on his mind in good time. "Could I get you a hot cup of coffee, tea? Something stronger?"

"I'm still on too much medication to risk the 'something stronger.' You'll have to be enough in that department." Getting to his feet, he flashed her that same disarming smile she had seen when she had opened the front door. "But hot coffee, strong and black, sounds great."

How easily he made her forget that she might have something to fear in him. He followed her into her kitchen to the right of the living room and, coming up beside her, immediately reached into the kitchen cabinet she opened to pull out two earthenware cups and saucers. Too close to him for comfort, she decided, stepping quickly to the side and busying herself with filling the creamer and the sugar bowl. From the corner of her eye, she saw the irrepressible smile on his face that let her know he knew he confused her, and that he enjoyed her confusion.

With her finger she pointed to the corner nearest the oven to distract him. "There's a canister of chocolate chip cookies over there."

"Homemade?" he asked hopefully, moving with unselfconscious eagerness in its direction.

"Naturally. They're my weakness."

"I'd like to be another," he said, and took canister, creamer, and sugar with him to the living room, picking up paper napkins as he went.

Such a throwaway remark, but it had thrilled her—undeniably. Such a simple thing, his coming to help with the coffee, but its very simplicity and naturalness pulled at a heartstring that had fallen into disuse and, therefore, made her dilemma so much more difficult, made her, for a moment, imagine as he came back into her kitchen that they were . . .

"We were discussing business, weren't we?" she asked, this time to distract herself.

He leaned one hip against her countertop and swiveled his head on his shoulders to adjust his sling, giving no sign of having heard the abruptness in her voice. "I've had a little time to think over the events of the last week and a half, and I've been trying to find an explanation that fits the facts."

Different from Denman's, she surmised, determined to keep her cynicism uppermost as she opened the flatware drawer.

"If I accept the fact that the shooting was set up as an ambush under the pretense of robbery, like Denman's convinced it was, why would that same individual need to get into my safe?"

"Couldn't he have ambushed you—to incapacitate you—or even kill you—so he could count on your not being there?" Extracting two teaspoons and a sugar spoon, she shut the drawer and turned toward him. "Maybe he broke in because he wanted to steal information or destroy incriminating evidence which he thought you had collected against him."

Berenson furrowed his dark brow. "That statement makes me suspect you believe Denman's theory that I'm on someone's hit list for having double-crossed my partner in a shady deal."

Spoons clattered on the blue saucers. "I didn't say that."

He touched a finger to one of hers, rubbing the tip along its smooth length. "But your eyes say it for your lips. The gray obscures the blue every time your suspicions of me are aroused. Didn't know that, did you?"

His voice carried an element of reproach that made her wish she could deny what she was feeling: "What you're implying is that in the course of some criminal scheme I collected information that someone now wants to kill me for. A scheme, I might add, that Denman has cooked up in his head with the aid of FBI innuendos—and I'm willing to bet money that their investigators, if they are *really* out there, won't be thanking him for tipping me off." His hand convered hers lightly, his eyes searching hers out. "But the truth is, Bianca, I don't have any information—simply because I'm not involved in anything."

Did he expect that his denial would be all the evidence she needed to trust him? She pulled her hand out from under his. "Could you have documents somewhere in your possession that could incriminate somebody without your realizing it?"

"There's nothing in that safe or that office except what directly deals with the daily operation of my major business, the produce distributorship, and various smaller concerns."

"Like what?" She reached for the coffeepot.

"Like commercial real estate transactions, investments in oil leases, joint ventures with developers, data on companies the distributorship has bought."

She tried to inject a casualness in her next question. "Are any of these concerns joint ventures with the Elizondo and Albañez families?"

"Yes."

She had to hand it to him. He certainly seemed to be unabashed by the question and unashamed of the connection. "Why didn't you go into detail about these business dealings with Denman or Barber?"

He leaned forward, his weight on his elbow. "Because it isn't any of their damn business."

She poured coffee into each cup with an admirably steady hand and avoided his eyes. "Wouldn't it have been more helpful to your own cause to be forthcoming about the information, regardless of whose business it is?"

"My dealings are legal, and ethical, as well as unexploitively profitable. What more can you ask of a commercial enterprise?" His voice had a definite edge. Was it a dangerous one? "I have no intention of doing the police's investigation for them. If they suspect that my Mexican friends are involved in underworld activity, let them prove it. As for me, I don't believe it."

Once again his loyal defense was laudable. But was it justified? She handed him a cup and, picking up her own, walked back to the sofa. "All right, let's accept your innocence and the innocence of Elizondo and Albañez. Why were you ambushed and your office burgled?"

Walking around the brass table, he finally shrugged off his leather jacket and put it on a nearby chair. "Because someone in Harvest Enterprises—who is in a position to understand the finances of both the distributorship and its side ventures—could be embezzling funds from the company's coffers."

Her brows arched over her widened eyes. "From that remark, a disinterested party might conclude that you concocted a story which neatly and conveniently cancels out your suspected involvement with the Mexican underworld."

"Or conclude that I'm paranoid."

"That, too, had crossed my mind, but you don't fit the usual mold of the paranoid businessman." Some of the belligerence she had seen flash in his eyes was mollified. "He's usually so deeply insecure in his success that he thinks every employee is stealing from him."

"Should I be content to have your esteem on at least one point, or should I press my luck tonight and try for more?"

The man had a real knack for turning every fork in a conversational road into a personal avenue. She avoided the maneuver and sat down. "I suppose you've got, if not evidence, then at least clues that make you suspect embezzlement?"

He gave her a smile for her evasion and sat down beside her. "In searching for anything and everything to explain the events of last week, I came across a number of irregularities. Irregularities which assume greater significance in the light of a police investigation." He reached into the cookie canister she pushed toward him. Then she took one herself. "First off, ledgers and cash transaction receipts were missing from the office for three days. They weren't returned until the Monday following my release from the hospital."

"Not a usual practice, even for an accountant who might need to work overtime at home?"

"Never. Not in my business." His quick response made her believe him. He ran a tight ship, she imagined. "And when I questioned the accountant about the absence, he couldn't come up with a plausible explanation either. He had already finished the work for the fiscal quarter that those ledgers and cash receipts dealt with."

Interesting but hardly conclusive of embezzlement. Maybe he had a snooper on his staff, a rival's corporate spy. "Anything else?" she asked as she lifted the rim of her coffee cup to her mouth.

"The computer terminal which logs all Harvest transactions shows that someone has been regularly retrieving financial account documents on transactions dating back to the previous two years. I haven't been able to discover to what end those retrievals were put to use." In silence he devoured a few cookies and drank his coffee, then with his eyes fixed on her face, he announced, "This is where you come in."

"Me?" She replaced her cup in its saucer. "Where?"

"The business I was talking about. According to Charles Roper, you have quite a reputation for unearthing fraud."

"I had a few lucky hunches that paid off with conscientious investigation," she dismissed what he called reputation. "Mr. Roper would never have heard of me if that last investigation hadn't been done for an executive who needed his name cleared *before* he ran for political office in the spring primaries. My everyday business as a CPA is not usually so melodramatic."

"Even if I defer to your modesty by accepting what you say, I think you are certainly capable of taking on Harvest Enterprises, Inc., as a client."

She put her cup on the table. The man was serious. His announcement was a heavy order if Harvest were as big a holding company as she suspected. "What *exactly* do you want me to do?"

"I want you to discover if my suspicions of embezzlement are correct. If they are, I want to know how it is managed, to what extent it robs the earnings of each and every concern, including the produce company, and what effect it has on Harvest's present and future financial state."

She reminded herself not to trust what her eyes saw, what her ears heard. Had he already fixed the books in order to cast the eye of suspicion on someone other than himself? Was he just trying to use her, then, to prove his innocence to the police? Was she to be the backup he would later need if police investigations revealed a closer connection between himself and the Mexican underworld?

"You're perfect for the job," he declared with a keen glance at the frown on her face. He put his cup in the saucer and shoved them away from the edge of the coffee table. "I don't especially want anyone to know what I'm up to. Most people will just assume the time we spend together as a result of your auditing the books is time spent in furthering a growing fondness for each other." The hand he extended along the back of the sofa found its way to the nape of her neck. "A suspicion we could make even more credible with just a little effort."

Just looking at that interesting face which had regained a terrific healthy nutmeg color did something to her good sense, and she had to struggle against the breathless quality creeping into her voice. "I'm just a private practice of one individual. I don't have an employee to share the work with."

"I know that." He moved toward her until his thigh was against hers, his arm resting on her shoulder. "That has one distinct advantage, Bianca—no one will know of our arrangement except you and me."

"But it has disadvantages."

"For instance."

"One, I couldn't get started for at least another two days."

"Condition accepted."

She narrowed her eyes, trying to study the play of emotions on his face, which was definitely too close to hers. "Two, without a colleague to share the workload, it would take me, after I collected the data, at least twenty hours of concentrated work just to determine if there really was anything suspicious. Then if I found discrepancies which were worth pursuing, I might need another forty."

"Fine. What's the matter, don't you think I can afford to pay your fee for sixty hours of work?"

That brought a reluctant lift to the corners of her mouth. "I'm not so expensive, Jared, that you can't afford me."

"Then what's the problem?"

She made herself stare directly into the golden explosion of his eyes and say steadily, "If you're really trying to find the criminal before the police decide *you* are the criminal, time should be a fundamental consideration in hiring a investigative CPA."

He stared down on her as though he hadn't heard a word she'd said. Lowering his face to hers he quietly asked, "Do you realize you've never called me by my first name before? Now that I know that this is the way to get you to become more familiar, we'll have to do business together more often."

Business? This was business?—his fingers silently stealing into her hair, his eyes on her breasts, his body slowly, decisively, gliding toward hers? Her mind was getting muddled. Was it really the first time she had called him by name?

Business. That's right. One of them had to remember what it was they were discussing. "It's only fair for me to tell you that you ought to reconsider and engage the services of another CPA, one who is immediately available." *And one not half so susceptible to your charm.*

"No way. Honesty is more important to me than immediate availability. If I want you"—his voice went velvet and low—"and I do, I'll just have to be patient with time, won't I?" He searched her features for her response to the double entendre. "You'll come to me in time, won't you, Bianca?"

His directness took her breath away. She tried to keep alive the suspicions she harbored about his criminal culpability, his convenient silence about his relationships with suspect Mexican families, the suspicions of city, and county, and federal authorities, but he touched his cheek to hers just then and, before she could pull away, his lips brushed against her lips.

"Business completed," he whispered into her mouth.

And his kiss was sweetness tingling on her tongue, delight welling up in her heart, a touch of madness burrowing beneath her skin. Just as she had before in his office and in his hospital room as well, she let the solid argument of good sense dissolve into vapor the moment she felt the heat of his lips. What would happen, she wondered, if he ever drew her into his fire? Would she simply let herself melt into pleasure and ashes without a flickering hope of ever rising again?

With his hands stealing into her hair, he silently persuaded her to lean back into the corner of the sofa while he leaned forward, keeping his injured arm out of harm's way. Gently he probed first her lips, then the inside of her mouth with a rigid tongue. Delicious invasion. He pressed the right side of his body against the softness of her breasts, making them grow hard with sensation while he kissed her, their heads moving from side to side with growing ardor. Tentatively she spread her hands across the expanse of his chest, careful not to hurt him, elated because for the first time it wasn't a bandage she could feel beneath her fingertips. It was lean muscled flesh.

She eased a hand up to his neck, sliding her cool, delicate fingers into the open collar of his shirt. She heard his low moaning laugh and felt a deep sense of satisfaction in having aroused him.

Leaving her lips, he touched her eyelids on his way down the side of her face and her neck while she inched her fingers up his neck to curl them through his thick hair. "You drive me a little mad, Bianca, a little crazy." His voice caught on the ragged edges of irregular breathing. Bending his leg at the knee, he shifted his weight to move his hip more surely against hers. "I want you, Bianca. Badly."

Her hand dug convulsively into his hair, the other massaging the side wall of his chest. How long had it been since she had heard that desire in a man's voice? He flicked his tongue lightly against her earlobe and nuzzled his cheek in the curve of her throat as her body involuntarily began to move beneath him.

"Silk hair," he murmured like a chant, "silk face," and moved his head beneath her chin, searching for the high mound of her breasts with his mouth and a hand that stealthily slid around the column of her throat to the row of buttons on her bodice. "Tell me that you want me, Bianca."

The instant his teeth gently bit her breast through the fabric of her dress, an explosion of sensation went

through her. "Jared!" she cried, her voice a breathless, quivering imitation of itself, and willed herself
to resurrect the ghost of her reasonable self. It had
been too long, too long. She knew the symptoms in
herself to watch for, and she was experiencing all of
them. Her pulse was quick, her breathing shallow,
her breasts rising and falling dramatically, her
thighs hurting with need, her loins eager to swallow
up fire. If she let him unfasten even the first button
of her dress, she was lost. And if she let him into her
body, she was mortally afraid that she would never be
able to get him out of her heart.

"Tell me that you want me, Bianca," he said again,
his voice filled with a need she knew too well herself.

"I can't," she cried and slid her hand out of his hair,
around the strong column of his throat, and covered
his hand at her breast. "I can't, Jared. Don't ask it of
me."

Immediately his hand was still. She wanted to take
that hand and kiss it, in some way make up for allowing him an intimacy, then arbitrarily withdrawing
from it. But she held back from expressing her feelings with such a tender gesture.

Slowly he lifted his face to look down on hers, and
she saw the disturbed passion gleaming in his eyes
and knew that in her own he must have seen desire
dampened by fear, fear heightened by desire. She
didn't realize until that moment how very much she
enjoyed looking at him, wanted him to enjoy looking
at her. He was a feast for her senses but she couldn't
indulge her appetite.

"Too much about you is appealing, Jared Berenson," she whispered intensely. "And too much is
frightening."

For a moment he said nothing, his face and body
precariously balanced above hers, his breathing deep,
his eyes cynically narrowed. "Do I frighten you, Bianca?" he asked her in a hard voice. "Or do you

frighten yourself? Are you frightened by your own desire?"

She shut her eyes as if that would clear the confusion in her head. "I don't know."

"I don't know either. Maybe it's both." When she opened her eyes, the hard lines around his mouth had softened, and she heard the harsh quality in his voice give way to sadness. "Every time I get too close to you, Bianca, I see a shadow fall across your face, across your heart. What are you afraid of? Memory? I don't know. But I'd like to believe that if you could get free of it, you would be mine."

Without waiting for a comment on his analysis, he flattened his hand against the claret velvet and pushed himself into a sitting position. When he got to his feet, he seemed not in the least self-conscious over his unrequited excitement. From his superior height he watched her sit up and smooth out the woolen folds of her dress. For what seemed to her an eternity both of them were silent.

Then she tilted her head back and looked at him directly. "Are you being entirely fair, Jared?"

He picked up his leather jacket, and slipping his good arm into one sleeve, arranged it slowly over his incapacitated shoulder. At first she thought he wasn't going to answer her. "Do you mean in making you doubt yourself so that you'll give more than you're ready to give?" he inquired with one of his ironically arched brows. "Possibly not. Something about you, Bianca, makes me forget the knack of playing fair. However honorable and honest my intentions, they manage to get submerged beneath this incredible compulsion I have to get my hands all over you. I find myself saying and doing the most remarkable things to get what I want."

He shook his head at his own behavior and reached into his pocket before she had time to evaluate his admission. When he extended his open hand to her, she realized he was offering something to her, and with a perplexed look on her face leaned forward to see what it was. Resting in the palm of his hand was the pearl earring he had ripped out of her ear ten nights ago.

"Was it a gift from Richard?" he asked in a distant voice as her slender fingers reached into his hand to take it.

The abrupt question startled her but she didn't avoid his gaze when she answered, "No." She was relieved she could say that truthfully. "It was a gift from Arthur and Marianne when I passed the CPA exam."

Jared turned his head in the direction of the marble mantel. "I don't look anything like Richard."

For a second, no more, the seeming nonsequitur threw her. She swallowed a heartbeat. "No. There isn't even the slightest similarity between the two of you. Not in physical features, not in mannerisms, certainly not in temperament."

He was looking at her when she pulled her eyes away from the photograph. "I'm glad of that."

"So am I." Then she added softly, "Nor were the police ever interested in his activities."

"Ah! But their interest in my activities is misplaced."

"Is it, Jared?"

"Time will prove me right, Bianca, just as this injury is going to heal in time. I'd like to think that without this damn sling I could move so fast and so expertly when I touched you that you wouldn't have the time or the will for second thoughts." He tossed his head back then and laughed, lightening the tone considerably. "In the meantime, I damn these wounds, and I damn your distrust."

Now that he wasn't touching her, now that he seemed relieved of frustrated anger, she felt safe enough to admit, "If it makes you feel any better, I've damned them both thoroughly myself."

"Does that mean that you are sending me home tonight to my cold and solitary bed comforted by the knowledge that your rejection doesn't spring from an absence of desire?"

She held her lower lip between her teeth and raised her brows. "If I were wise, I wouldn't let you leave comforted by anything at all."

"Oh, but that's what is going to save us, isn't it, Bianca? When it comes down to matters of the heart, at the final reckoning you're not going to be wise at all." His thick curling lashes dipped once over his golden eyes. "Thank God." And he bent down to kiss her sweetly on her parted lips. "Sweet dreams."

Chapter Five

FROM her position at the best table in the exclusive restaurant she could see the Riverwalk on the other side of the glass wall. Two stories below her, thousands of tiny white lights twinkling like stars were scattered in the trees that lined the Paséo del Río, and outlining the arched bridges that spanned the river's banks. Because it was the first night of the Fiesta de las Luminarias, countless numbers of paper lanterns stationed along the banks were lit to symbolize the lighting of the Holy Family's journey to Bethlehem. And because it was a Friday night, the banks were jammed with people.

Even in the relative seclusion of the restaurant, Bianca could still hear strains of the Christmas caroling processions. The peace and joy they sang was at great odds with the pressures of the past two weeks and the ambivalences they had set up in her heart. She was sure that she had only added to those pressures when, a half-hour earlier at Jared's offices, she had picked up the documents she needed to undertake the examination he had requested. Now, when she turned and looked up at the face of the dinner partner seated next to her, she saw that his golden eyes were trained on her. She looked away to hide her thoughts since she couldn't quickly disguise them. What sort of peace could Christmas possibly bring this year?

She moved her arm aside for the waiter to serve the first cups of after-dinner coffee and four cordial glasses of liqueur. As soon as he quietly slipped away at Jared's unspoken dismissal, the hazel-eyed Mexican banker, Pedro Elizondo, who sat directly across from her, leaned forward, both elbows anchored on the table.

He spoke earnestly. "I cannot imagine, Jared, what the American authorities could possibly find suspect in any banking transactions I have ever completed in the States or in Mexico, or in any other transaction for that matter. This information takes me completely by surprise." His hazel eyes narrowed beneath the heaviest pair of eyebrows Bianca had ever seen. "Are you *absolutely* sure, my friend, that they *are* interested?"

"Frankly, Pedro, I'm not absolutely sure about anything anymore. But my guess, shared by Bianca"—he inclined his head in her direction—"is that no county sheriff's investigator would verbalize, however clumsily, such suspicions unless he had been given information from the FBI or had stumbled into their investigation himself."

"But we have heard nothing," José Albañez softly interjected, his face the study of a deeply troubled man. "No questions from any police, yours or ours, no investigators at any Elizondo bank or any Albañez hotel—and, what is more," he added with a flourish of perfectly manicured hands, "no unusual procedures at customs when we arrived yesterday."

Bianca surveyed Elizondo, whom she guessed to be near Jared's age, and then Albañez, whom she guessed to be about ten years older. Why had Jared invited her to dine with these two men? To let her see for herself that they were what they seemed—two Mexican gentlemen whose integrity was as intact as their Old World charm? To show her he had nothing to hide by informing them in her presence of the police's interest? From what Jared had said about Denman's clumsy interrogation, she assumed that he hadn't entirely dismissed the possible connection between the attempt on his life and an international underworld ring. Then why did he continue to insist that she study his books for evidence of an embezzlement scheme?

Her eyes fell on Jared again. Without the encumbrance of a splint or a sling, his muscular frame was shown to advantage in a well-tailored navy three-piece suit beneath which he wore a pale blue shirt and a pinstripe, brick-red tie. As Arthur had said, Jared must have been in prime physical condition before he was shot or he could never have recovered so quickly. Undeniably, the man had style. Everything about him, from his honey head of slightly tousled hair down to the tips of his long, firm legs, announced the confidence that comes with success and sexual virility. How difficult was it going to be for her to separate her rational need to find out the truth and her emotional response to his masculine appeal? Which of her contradictory responses should she trust?

"It could be, Señor Albañez," posed Bianca, forcing her thoughts back to the business at hand, "that the FBI had no intention of making itself visible until they completed more of their investigation, if indeed there is one. It could also be that the very clumsy investigator Mr. Denman jumped his own gun by inadvertently tipping Jared off. You see, I just learned earlier today from a client that Mr. Denman's planning to run against the sheriff in the spring primaries, and assisting in a federal conviction could certainly boost his credibility with the voters."

"Es posible, Señorita Bianca, pero yo no puedo . . ." Recognizing the blank look that came over her face at his speedy retort, Señor Albañez immediately abandoned his native language for English again. "All of that is possible, Señorita Bianca, but I find it difficult to understand how information would have gotten into the hands of a sheriff's investigator, and more

difficult to understand how any law enforcement agency could suspect any one of the three of us of wrongdoing. All three of us have unimpeachable reputations. One hears things about other international businessmen, of course." Palms up, he spread out the fingers of each well-manicured hand to indicate the reality of the world marketplace, then wagged one of those fingers. "But not a word about any of us here."

"Never until now," amended Pedro Elizondo. "And what could account for such suspicions, which, from what you two have said during dinner, practically amount to serious allegations?"

She abandoned reticence in favor of directness. "Perhaps it has something to do with that record-breaking freeze last December that virtually destroyed all of the Río Grande Valley crops at a cost of more than a hundred million dollars. Agricultural experts have predicted that there won't even be a grapefruit crop to brag about in Texas for another nine years, if then." She glanced at Jared, who returned the look with concern. She had surprised him by making the connection, but it was too late to back down. "Put lower profit margins together with subsequent increased competition for produce coming from Mexico, and what would the FBI come up with? A motive for Harvest Enterprises to get involved in an illegal scheme to ensure its financial solvency in uncertain times."

She had apparently been too convincing in her recital, for a deathly silence greeted her speculations. Elizondo looked at her with the raised brows of incredulity, but Albañez's face had withdrawn into worried preoccupation. Jared she couldn't see at all unless she turned to her left to look at him, and she kept her head absolutely still. What had gotten into her? Had she been trying so hard to exorcise her suspicions of Jared Berenson's guilt that she had foolishly blurted them out, hoping that they could be contradicted by facts? And to whom had she voiced

her misgivings? The very two men whom the police
suspected were involved in the same scheme! What
supreme idiocy!

"I trust you do not share what you assume to be the
FBI's conclusions?" asked Elizondo as he lowered his
cordial glass slowly to the white damask tablecloth.

"I've assumed nothing," Bianca answered, uncurl-
ing her finger from her cup handle, then added when
his face tightened at her lack of outright support, "I
offer the theory only for consideration."

The banker's facial muscles relaxed but his eyes
watched her intently. "But even if Harvest Enterprises found itself in such difficulties, we know that
the theory is"—he momentarily stalled on his English—*"una incongruencia caprichosa*—how do you
say—ah, farfetched, since it rests on the fundamental
assumption that José and I are underworld figures.
And that assumption is patently absurd."

"In addition," Señor Albañez offered in his gentle
voice, "the FBI must surely know that Jared, unlike
many of his competitors, is fortunate. He does not
have to search for good produce across the border—he
owns forty-nine percent of not one but *two* of the largest and most fertile farms in the Elmante region of
Tamaulipas. It is the area which produces four times
more crops per square area than any other farmland
in Mexico."

"And about his ownership of that land," Elizondo
interjected, correctly anticipating her next question,
"there can be no doubt. As the banker involved in
those property sales, I know that the loan he took out
to buy the property was repaid."

"So you see, Bianca," Jared posed in a silken drawl
that carried a hint of silent laughter, "you're out-
numbered." Unexpectedly his hand closed over hers.
"You may just have to resign yourself to trusting
me."

"But you, *mi amigo,*" Elizondo said, "should not be
so trusting of anyone. These are difficult times for al-

most all produce brokers. You should be on guard against your share of cutthroats who aim at eliminating you as competition."

"And the disloyalty of previously dedicated employees who see their opportunity to destroy you," added Albañez soberly. "Even your drivers might be using company trucks to transport merchandise to sell for their own profit."

"You know as well as I do, José," Jared responded without removing his hand from hers, "that the use of trucks for personal gain is always a possibility in the best of times."

"If a federal investigation is actually under way," Elizondo said, rubbing his hands together, "these are definitely not the best of times."

"And we both appreciate your having told us, Jared, what to guard against for ourselves," added the hotelier.

Had Jared just issued a warning to his friends to clean house before the investigation got as far as their front doors? Bianca continued to wonder throughout the remainder of the evening. She could not resign herself to trusting Jared. Not yet. Some of the pieces in his puzzle made a poor fit. As the two of them made their way along the winding Paséo del Río after leaving the restaurant and the two men, she didn't try to avoid his left arm, which curved around her shoulder, but she didn't encourage any advances either. He didn't need any encouragement. As he talked, his fingers, with a strength that surprised her, found a way to massage her tense muscles through the layers of her black cape and red dress. Disturbing. Disruptive.

"Your arm is really much better, isn't it?" she asked, glancing up at him. The cut on his lip had healed nicely as well.

He gave her a wicked leer complete with a cocked brow. "You'd better watch out. In a few more days when it's back to normal, you're going to have one helluva time eluding me. I'll be too strong for you then, sweetheart."

God help her in that case. She might not be able to help herself.

"You hadn't mentioned anything about Denman's political aspirations to me before," he picked up an earlier topic. "How come? Because you didn't want me to think you were piling up evidence in my favor?"

"Something like that." She smiled in spite of herself, for the man had a decided knack for keeping her on her toes with lightning-quick changes in tone. "Besides, you don't need my support, you've got two friends back there who are as loyal to you as you are to them."

A chill wind suddenly blew along the water and through the wide-leafed fronds of the monsteras, forcing her to shelter herself even closer against Jared's side. She didn't have to look at him to know he was smiling. She could feel his delight in the protective tightening of his arm at her shoulder.

"Why shouldn't they be loyal when I've never failed to keep up my end of any business bargain between us?" He paused, and on a more sober note said, "But make no mistake. I'll always need *your* support." He took up his easy stride again.

Following his lead, she ducked her head in time to avoid the slap of banana leaves against her face and found the distraction a good excuse not to comment on his last remark. "I couldn't help wondering why José Albañez looked so worried."

"Wouldn't you be worried if you were suspected of having committed a crime that doesn't even have a name?"

"But it was more than that."

He dismissed the notion with a shake of his head, the clover-honey hair falling forward onto his wide brow. She suppressed the urge to brush it back into place. "It's only natural that two personal friends as well as joint investors would be concerned about the ambush, the burglary, and the financial state of Harvest Enterprises."

Maybe, but she couldn't shake the feeling that Albañez's face revealed a deeper anxiety. "You didn't tell either one of them anything about the work I'm doing for you?" she said.

"No. If you remember, I said only you and I would know about that." And it was clear from his brusqueness that he had other things on his mind.

Things like coming to an abrupt halt and adroitly turning her toward him while containing her within the warming curve of his arm. They had reached a stretch of closed boutiques whose storefronts were shadowed by canopies the color of the indigo sky overhead. All around them were the laughter of the crowds and the songs of Christmas carolers in the streets and aboard the decorated barges coming down the river, glowing with the golden lights of the *luminarias*. But beneath the canopies of the storefronts the two of them were secluded.

In that seclusion Bianca could hear her heartbeat and Jared's as well. She could smell the scent of his fragrant pipe tobacco mingled with his masculine cologne just as she had the fateful night she found him. She could see the good strong bones of his face dramatically carved with shadows, a face she was never likely to forget.

"Now that my arm is so much better and I've presented you with two excellent, indisputable character witnesses," he drawled as he arranged one arm on her shoulder and the other around her waist, "are you still not going to come home with me tonight?"

His indirect proposition, spoken half in jest, half in dead seriousness, nearly choked her—exactly what he was counting on. Instantly he enfolded her in his arms and, pulling her toward him, kissed her very thoroughly.

For a minute or two he had the advantage of surprise, and she forgot her resolve to know him better before she kissed him more. Instead she felt the sensuous exultation of letting her breasts press against his rock-hard chest. It was frightening—all he had to do was touch her, however briefly, and her entire body rose in response. The moment his tongue touched hers, she forgot fright and remembered pleasure. She slipped her hands inside his open coat, feeling the silk of his vest when she reached behind his back. He rewarded her with a deft thrust of a firm tongue deep into her mouth and let his hand fall a little below her waist.

An eternity later when his lips left hers, she was shaking and concentrating on trying to disguise the reaction. She bit her lower lip to still its trembling.

He stared down at her, shaking his head at his own impetuosity. "I've been dying to do that all evening long! You and those great big almond eyes, just slightly tilted in the corners, are going to be my undoing. Those eyes and your damn seductive long-legged body."

"My eyes, my body—your undoing?" How preposterous, when the golden explosion in his eyes had become an obsession with her, when most of her daydream life was consumed in imagining what his naked body would really feel like lying alongside hers.

"They make me want to do something, anything, to make the blue in your eyes rub out the gray." Beneath the lighthearted banter there was a hoarse fervor in his voice. "Bianca, I want you to believe in me."

She did better with the lighthearted banter. "Anything else?" she inquired, determined to stop quivering inside.

"Of course there is." He tossed his head back in a throaty laugh as if to say her levity wasn't going to do her a bit of good. "Then at any cost, at any price, I want you all to myself for one night."

That hurt. "One night only, Jared?"

He put a caressing hand to her face and his thumb played with her lower lip. "When I've had that, I'll beg for more. I'm counting on your begging, too."

Her hands released their hold on his back, then fell to her sides. "Each time I'm with you I realize how little I really know of a very complex man."

He dropped his thumb to her chin and kept her face lifted to his. "If you work on the assumption that I am what I appear to be, I am a very simple man. A simple and direct man who is sure that he has never wanted a woman the way he wants you."

She wished he wouldn't say things like that. Not when she couldn't control what it did to her. It set her up for passion that wasn't going to be fulfilled, for hunger that wasn't going to be satisfied. Every time he alluded to making love, his words were like expert fingers stroking her intimately. And he knew it. He knew he made her heart race, her body throb; he liked tantalizing her with the fruit she wouldn't let herself taste.

She looked above his shoulder and made herself concentrate on a distant falling star while she lied to him, "Passion could too easily confuse the professional business between us."

He dropped his arm from her waist, his hand from her face. "I don't believe what you're saying any more than you do. But if it's more convenient for you to pretend otherwise tonight, I won't pressure you for the truth."

"The truth, Jared?" She took her eyes off the shooting star and trained them on him. "Where is it?"

His voice was as soft as his eyes were bright. "Hidden inside the love we could make together."

Her gloved fingers securely fastened to the shoulder strap of her leather envelope portfolio, Bianca walked across the parking lot of Harvest Enterprises five days after she had picked up the company's documents which she was presently carrying under her right arm. She looked at the high Gothic structure ahead of her, instantly deciding that it was too dark and dreary an evening to let her gaze wander any higher than the fifth floor. The last thing she wanted to see tonight were the bulging eyes of the hideous gargoyles perched on its stone facade.

A glance at her wristwatch, which read six-twenty eight, made her quicken her steps. Her high heel tee-tered on a small pebble as a sudden noise made her come to an abrupt halt. Apprehensively she peered into the darkness over her left shoulder. In what seemed to be a deserted parking lot, she saw two men working on a Harvest truck. The face of one was ef-fectively hidden beneath a broad-brimmed cowboy hat, but the other's head, with its noticeably receding hairline, was uncovered. She saw the glint of metal flash in the dim moonlight and then a surprisingly quick movement, as if to hide it.

I must be imagining conspiracy everywhere, she concluded and returned her attention to the office building. *On the other hand, maybe . . .* She turned around to take a second, closer look, but there wasn't a human soul in sight between the trucks.

Forcibly dismissing the incident as an absurd prod-uct of her overstimulated imagination, she took up her stride again. Precisely because so many circum-stances surrounding Jared Berenson were weighted with inexplicable mystery, she ought to guard against imagining intrigue in every murky corner, in every innocent face, in every commonplace activity.

As her heels clicked against the rough asphalt, however, she had to admit that the now-you-see-us-now-you-don't quality of this last incident nagged like an inexplicable irritant on the edges of her mind. She *had* seen two men and they *had* disappeared when she had taken a second glance. As she opened the door to the building and exchanged an absentminded greet-ing with Benjamin, she had an uneasy feeling in the pit of her stomach that somewhere in the darkness behind her, intent eyes were watching her every move. That uneasiness remained with her as she rode up in the elevator and then walked up the last two flights of stairs to the executive suite on the top floor.

She decided to tell Jared about the incident at once, but when she walked into his spacious office, he immediately rose from his chair behind the desk and walked enthusiastically over to her, taking the heavy package from beneath her arm and closing the door behind her.

With an engaging smile on his face and a teasing brightness in his eyes, he asked quite casually, "Considering the professional nature of your visit, am I allowed to give or to receive one tender kiss of welcome?"

Well, what in the world was a woman to do with a question like that from a man whose burnished hair was slightly tousled on his wide brow, whose lower lip was outthrust in a counterfeit pout of self-pity, and whose hard-boned face possessed all the right ingredients to break her heart?

She opened her mouth, having successfully pushed that heart out of her throat. "Of course we are on—" but the rest of her professional formality was lost as his mouth took advantage of hers, making a soft smacking sound when he released it.

"Ah, so much better," he declared, laughing while she, mildly disoriented, could only stare wide-eyed at him as he led her to the moroccon leather chair across from his desk. "It would have been impossible for me to concentrate on business without taking care of a little pleasure first." His voice went a notch deeper. His arm lay like a familiar weight across her shoulders. "I've missed you. I don't see you often enough."

She sat down in the chair, gathering a protective poise around her, and he dropped his arm. "I've had your business to tend to, remember?"

He walked in front of her and, crossing his arms at his chest, his long legs at his ankles, leaned his

weight against the corner of his desk. As well he
knew, the stance gave her a wonderful view of his
very male physique dressed in fine fitting dark
brown flannel slacks, a rust corduroy jacket that
sported suede patches at the elbows, and a cream oxford cloth shirt, down the center of which hung a
lightly patterned tie.

"Now that you've completed the first part of my
business," he asked, "what will you do for excuses?"

She tilted her finely coiffed head to the side. "You
do that purposely, don't you? Every time we're together."

"Do what?" he asked innocently.

"Switch back and forth between moods, tones, conversational avenues like a quick-change artist," she
exclaimed with a graceful wave of her hand, "just to
throw me off balance."

He threw back his head and laughed at her indignation, making an expansive gesture with outflung
arms. "Well, of course I do. It works every time. I
never know when throwing you off balance will make
you fall right into my waiting arms, so don't expect
me to abandon my strategy." But the waiting arm he
instantly extended toward her now was back to business. "Let's see what you've discovered."

One minute he was kissing her and the next minute he was addressing her in the passionless voice of
commerce. She eased the portfolio strap off her shoulder. The snap of the lock was loud in the hush that fell
over her. She took out the report and, staring straight
into his bright eyes, delivered it into his open palm.
Apparently he was an old hand at masquerade. She
was the neophyte.

He took the chair behind the long mahogany desk,
framed on either side by dark bookcases and ornately
carved stone that bordered the pointed arched windows behind him. With a slap of heavy paper against
the desk's black leather insert, he deposited her report and the documents she had returned. Bianca

crossed her legs at the knees, one hand resting on the arm of the chair, the other lightly curled on top of the notes she had placed in her lap.

Shining through the unshuttered windows were a few hesitant moonbeams and a suggestion of starlight that glanced off the honey head of hair bent over the report she had begun five days ago. While he studied it she let her eyes wander around the room, which was divided into two areas—at one end, the desk and surrounding bookcases of the company's chief executive officer, at the other, the conversation area with low leather couches and a discreet bar. As her eyes roamed, she picked out details like the stenciled ceilings and Oriental carpets she had remembered on the two previous occasions she had been here; others like a polished wood pipe with its now familiar aroma she had missed.

Her eyes came back to Jared. Didn't they always? With a fountain pen he made notations on the sheets from time to time. Only a few weeks since he had been shot, she thought, and already he appeared to have regained most of the strength in his left arm. Arthur had been right. The wound itself had not been as serious as his loss of blood might have been. Jared looked up from the papers, a puzzled expression on his face.

"As you can see, I followed the usual procedure of an initial audit," she explained smoothly. "I picked eight months at random out of the previous twenty-four to study closely. I looked for the typical red flags, like checks written to petty cash, checks written for nonexistent rent since Harvest Enterprises owns this building from which it conducts all its businesses, checks written to places of business outside the expected and normal, and any checks written to support personal hobbies."

"Or loose women?" He raised a brow and lifted one corner of his mouth.

"Or loose women," she replied with a raised brow and a wry smile of her own.

"Did you also satisfy yourself that I had really made the last payment on those Mexican farms some time back?"

"I can't deny that I checked it out."

He ran a hand through his hair and smiled at her candor. "So you didn't find even one red flag waving in the breeze?"

"Not one. As the comptroller of Harvest Enterprises, Charles Roper has every reason to be proud of his department. Even an Internal Revenue agent would find it hard to fault your accounting."

"And all eight months appeared to be in proper order?"

"Every one of them checked out. The books do not reveal the slightest sign of mismanagement or intent to embezzle." She watched him put the papers down and cap his pen. "However, I should add that the produce distributorship does complete what I consider to be an extremely high number of cash transactions. The only way I can be perfectly satisfied that someone didn't understate the amount of the cash received is to take more time to cross-check the amount against the receipts."

"Just to be sure someone didn't pocket the difference?"

"Precisely." She shrugged her shoulders. "But even then I might find absolutely nothing." For the first time she noticed that Jared's usual confidence was disturbed. Had she underestimated his conviction that an embezzlement scheme had motivated the attempt on his life as well as the burglary?

He leaned back in his chair, planting his elbows on the wide arms. Slowly he passed the black and gold fountain pen back and forth between the fingers of both hands. "If the incidents aren't tied up with an attempt to embezzle from my company or undermine me through financial mismanagement," he asked of no one in particular as his fingers abruptly ceased their exercise, "what's the motive? Could Pedro be right? Could competition outside the company really be at the root of all this?"

Bianca couldn't give him an answer. She wasn't even sure his question was sincere. Uncrossing her legs, she sat on the edge of her chair. "I don't know the answer, Jared, but I do know that since I accepted the job of examining your books . . ."

He leaned forward in his chair immediately at the sound of the knock on the door. "Come in," he said sharply, and she lost the opportunity to inform him that she had noticed the suspiciously frequent appearance of a dark blue car on her block.

Martin Goerner, the man she remembered as the director of trucking operations, walked into the office. In his hand was a sheet of yellow paper and on his face the same cynical smile she remembered he had worn for her at the hospital.

"Ah, Ms. Cavender. Nice to see you again."

She definitely didn't like the man. It was obligatory politeness that made her acknowledge his greeting with a handshake and an equally innocuous "Nice to see you again as well, Mr. Goerner."

"Sorry, Jared, I didn't know you were with Ms. Cavender." He looked from one to the other, seemingly puzzled by the professional distance which separated them from each other. "I wanted to speak with you about something that just came to my attention, but it can wait."

"No reason to wait, Martin. Ms. Cavender would only hear it from me later."

Bianca noticed that the fingers of Goerner's left hand bunched up into a tight fist, though his face remained expressionless. She knew that what he had to say to his boss would be a reluctant disclosure.

"This anonymous message was just delivered to my office." He stepped closer to Jared's desk to hand him the sheet that had apparently been detached from a perforated tablet. "It claims that there's an unspecified number of men working for us who are using our trucks in their normal schedule to pick up produce for themselves to sell on the side."

"But there are no names here, or any particular schedules," said Jared, tossing the sheet on his desk and looking, Bianca thought, more chagrined by an inconvenience than concerned with a serious violation.

"Last week you said that this sort of thing was always a possibility in your business, Jared," said Bianca. "But I don't understand how a driver can hope to get away with it."

She could have sworn that Martin Goerner had to force his entire body into a more relaxed position. "It's really not very hard," he said when he faced her. "All a driver has to do is place an order with farms near the ones we own or trade with in the States or Mexico."

"Exactly," agreed Jared as he came from behind his desk to stand no more than a few feet from her chair. "He loads his scheduled Harvest shipment, then makes room for his own shipment, which he pays for in cash, and then heads back home, making a detour to sell his merchandise for cash to buyers who make it their business not to know what the driver's ethics are."

Martin availed himself of the leather chair to Bianca's right. "I've been wondering," he said, settling himself down, "just what connection, if any, there is, between these anonymous tip-offs and the two drivers who walked off the job three days before you were shot."

Bianca quickly flipped through the files of her memory for anything Jared might have said to the sheriff's investigator or the city police about two suspiciously abrupt resignations, but she couldn't turn up a thing. She watched as Jared pulled back his corduroy jacket to shove his hands into his pockets. He leaned his hip back against the desk's edge and crossed his ankles.

"Are you suggesting that the men who resigned are the same ones who are accused in the note?" Bianca asked.

"Could be," answered Goerner.

"So many avenues to pursue." Jared gave his head a shake. "Part of me wants to find the sucker who ambushed and shot me just out of a deep-seated desire for revenge. Self-preservation, even. And yet another part of me wants to believe that my enemy, having already gotten what he wanted—whatever the hell it was—has retreated permanently, and, therefore, I have all the time in the world to wait for the police to solve the mystery."

Was it his earnestness that reached out to convince her of his innocence, that he really didn't know why he had become someone's victim? Or was it the mesmerizing quality of his golden eyes, the strength of his personality captured in the well-defined line of his jaw, the powerful virility of his male body shown to advantage in the flannel slacks that outlined his long, muscular legs?

She might as well test all her suspicions. "Do you think there's any connection between the dishonest drivers in that note, the two who walked off the job, and the two I saw stealthily working on one of the trucks?"

"What?" came Goerner's brusque syllable, followed by Jared's swift "When?"

"This evening on my way up here."

"Why didn't you tell me this before?" Jared asked as he straightened up from his relaxed position at the desk.

"Why didn't you tell me about the resignations?" she immediately volleyed in return and, receiving no answer, simply said, "I didn't have the opportunity until now."

"That's too bad you were distracted from the issue," Goerner said curtly, looking at her as though, in having handed them a new problem to think about, *she* was now the problem. "We might have been able to get the security guards on it right away."

Jared ran a hand through this thick hair, too preoccupied even to have noticed the tense exchange. "Look, Martin, suppose we talk about this tomorrow morning at eight." His voice was definitely weary. Maybe he wasn't as fully recovered from his wounds as he appeared to be. "We need to discuss a plan by which to verify these messages and find the men they accuse just in case their activity is related to a bigger issue."

"Right. See you tomorrow at eight sharp." Martin got to his feet. With his hand on the door, he said, "Good-bye, Ms. Cavender," and closed the door behind him.

She replaced her notepad inside the zippered compartment of her portfolio, slipping its strap onto her shoulder. When she got to her feet, Jared was immediately by her side.

"Don't go yet, Bianca."

"It is long after seven now, Jared, and I need . . ."

"I don't want you to go." He stepped directly in front of her. She felt the back of the chair press into her legs, the leather strap slip off her shoulder. He put his hand to her hair.

Something in his eyes disturbed her as much as the curtness in Goerner's manner had. "I really need to go, Jared," she protested just as his other hand followed the first.

"I thought we could have dinner together, this time at my place." He rubbed his fingers into the nape of her neck. "I was hoping that I could persuade you not to act your professional age and let down that wonderful silver-blond hair of yours." He took another step closer but she had no more room to step back. "Remember you said I would be the first on your dance card?"

In spite of herself, she smiled at the memory. "Yes, I remember. It's just that . . ." He brought his head down to hers and gently pressed his mouth against her temple. ". . . I didn't hear anyone strike up the band." He lightly kissed her lips and she felt his impossibly curly lashes flutter against her cheek.

"Baby," he crooned, his breath cool on her face, "just let me know the piece you want them to play. If anyone asks, my favorite is 'I Only Have Eyes for You.' "

She found her voice with difficulty. "Mine ought to be 'Enough Is Enough.' "

"Don't give me those 'ought to be's,' Bianca," he commanded in a seductively silken voice. One strong hand slipped down her back. "Especially when you know as well as I do that neither one of us is ever likely to get enough of the other."

When he put a hand to her face, she touched it. How she wished she hadn't done that. He turned his face and kissed the palm of her hand, then turned again until his bright eyes burned into hers.

"You drive me a little mad, Bianca. I don't know what else to call it when I find myself willing to believe that the leather couch over there would serve us quite well if I locked the door." He nuzzled his face against the sensitive curve of her neck and laughed quietly when she trembled in his arms. "I do have enough sanity left, however, to realize we'd be a devil of a lot more comfortable at my place."

"And vulnerable," she whispered.

"Sounds great, huh?"

"Jared," she began hesitantly.

But obviously he already knew her self-control was firmly intact. He held her back a little and looked down. "I didn't think I could seduce my very cautious accountant who's totaled up my character assets and put me in the debit column." He pulled his head up. "But you can't blame a guy for trying."

When she studied the humor in his face, she saw a

great deal of sadness too, and it pushed its way into
her vulnerable heart. If he asked her again to go home
with him, self-control and self-recrimination be
damned, she would. But he said nothing and her weak
moment passed. He let his arms relax his hold on her
and waited for her to make the next move.

"Nothing is simple with you, Jared."

"Yes it is. You mean nothing is simple with you."

She shook her head. "It's complicated by—"

"—an earlier love?" he asked in a cool voice, not
gentle, not harsh.

Her heart muscles contracted for a moment. "By all
of the circumstances surrounding my relationship
with you," she neatly evaded a direct answer.

"And its attendant suspicions. Can't you push all
of that aside and see straight through to what you feel
for me?"

Her failure to answer was answer enough.

His voice was edged with bitterness when he spoke
again. "I should have fixed the books before I gave
them to you, Bianca. If I had given you false evidence
of embezzlement, you might now be viewing me as an
innocent man."

"Perhaps not," she admitted before she realized her
error. "I had expected to find that evidence."

"What did you say?" He furrowed his brow in puz-
zlement, then raised them in comprehension. "My
God! You thought all along I was setting you up to
discover a convenient ambush motive so that I could
use your testimony to evade a criminal indictment."
His hands slipped away from her body. His body
slipped away from her side. She felt her heart crawl
back into the shadows of fear and loneliness that had
only deepened with her deepening feelings for this
very forceful man. "Didn't you?" he demanded.

She raised her head and released her lower lip from
between her teeth. "Yes, I did," she admitted in a
tight voice.

He kept staring at her as though he could hardly

believe her admission. When he finally spoke, the rich timbre of his voice was disturbed. "I don't know how you can bear to be touched by someone you believe would use you so shamefully—unless getting used is what turns you on." A muscle worked madly in his lower jaw. "Someday when this damn investigation is all over, I'm going to try to forget that you thought so little of me."

The hideous irony of it all came crashing in on her as the awful silence hovered over them. Just when she had learned how to laugh again, had been finally able to reconcile Richard to memory, Jared had come into her life and lengthened, not shortened, the last stage of her healing process. She forced back the tears ready to spill down her cheeks. Jared had come at the right time. Why did he have to be the wrong man?

She tore her eyes away from the condemnation glowing like bright coals in his eyes and picked up her portfolio. "If you decide that you'd like for me to check the cash receipts against cash deposits," she managed in a hollow voice, "let me know."

If he was the wrong man, why was her fragile heart breaking quite decisively in two as she walked out his door?

Bianca's eyes snapped open at the unexpected sound that had penetrated the barriers of her sleep. Had the sound originated in her dream? She didn't think so. She caught the satin comforter between her trembling fingers while fragments of that dream floated up to her consciousness. Colliding cars, the mangled body of a man whose hair was Richard's but whose face was Jared's, the wailing sound of an ambulance siren, blood splattered on her frozen face. She crushed the comforter in her fists and heard another unfamiliar sound. This one couldn't have come from the dream. She sat bolt upright in her bed, pushing the long hair back out of her eyes to stare into the pitch black darkness of her room for any sign of move-

ment other than her own, for the slightest suggestion
of another presence.

Nothing. No one.

Heart pounding hard against her rib cage, she
looked at her bedside portable clock. Eleven forty-
five. After leaving Jared's office, she had finally suc-
cumbed to two glasses of wine on an empty stomach
to produce the sleep and solace she craved. Even at
that, she hadn't been in bed longer than an hour at
most, hadn't been asleep longer than half that.

Another sound reached her ears, a high scraping
noise this time, followed by what sounded like a
drawer opening. Fear was like two hands on her
throat, a heavy stone in her chest. What was one supposed to do under these circumstances? Scream to
alert the intruder that the owner was in the house?
She couldn't make a sound, not even a whisper. She
wasn't even sure she could breathe. Get a gun fast?
She didn't own one. Even Arthur had agreed that
burglar bars and an alarm would be enough protection for a single woman. But the alarm switch was
downstairs. Find a blunt instrument and catch the
burglar off-guard before he found her? Her only al-
ternative. Unless, of course, she could find a way to
escape. And how could she do that when every upstairs window was sealed with the bars that should
have sealed out an intruder?

If she didn't imagine consequences but simply took
action, she told herself, she'd be much better off. She
threw off the satin comforter, making herself believe
she was doing the right thing. Frantically she began
to shove her arms into the velour robe that matched
the sapphire gown she was wearing and though her
feet were cold on the wooden plank floor, she dis-
dained slippers for fear of the noise they'd make. As
she walked past the armoire on her way to the door,
she picked up a heavy brass candlestick, leaving its
ivory taper behind.

In her living room she saw nothing but night shadows undisturbed. The gown and robe floating at her feet whispered around the edges of her furniture as she went to the door. Cautiously she put her hand on the crystal knob and ever so carefully turned it. Along the gallery overlooking the foyer she sensed not a sound in the silence, not a movement in the stillness, not a shape in the shadows.

Soundlessly, her bare feet touched each carpeted riser of the staircase with slow deliberation, the fingertips of her right hand gliding along the banister, the other hand clutched tightly the intricately carved weapon as she made her way down into the darkened foyer. Then she heard a sound. She stopped dead, her hair swishing on her shoulders when she brought up her head, her heart thundering in her ears. She was almost positive it was the sound of pages being flipped briskly, one after another. A thief was going through her things behind the closed door of her private office. But looking for what?

Swiftly she descended the last five steps and depressed the button of the silent alarm cleverly hidden beneath the curved wooden banister. It would bring the police to her townhouse within minutes.

Having taken that precaution, she should have stayed where she was, or, at the very least, hidden within shadows or behind the doors of other downstairs rooms. But there was this irresistible urge to see with her own eyes the identity of the intruder. She had to know that it wasn't . . . that it couldn't be . . .

Still as a statue, cold as stone, she waited at the foot of the staircase, listening for the piercing cry of a police siren. The instant she heard it, she floated across the foyer toward the japanned credenza near the office door, her heart still firmly lodged in her throat, its thunder heavy in her ears. Was she stalking the stranger who had deceitfully stalked her heart? Was she stalking the man who had turned her suspicions of him into an indictment of herself? She depressed the button of the audible alarm situated directly behind the credenza just as she heard the police car preparing to brake to a stop at her curb.

Silence.

She depressed the button again. Silence. No raucous clanging alarm. She flipped the light switch above it.

Darkness. Not so much as a flicker of light. And the police siren she had heard coming down her block was now retreating like a lonely wail into the distance. But it must have been enough to alert the stranger behind that door, for she heard a muffled curse and a sharp sound of heels on the wooden floor.

When the door swung open, the shaft of moonlight that fell across the threshold caught her in its spotlight, though she could see nothing but a shape huddling in its own shadow. Startled, she realized her vulnerability and tried to lift the weight in her hand, but it was too late to do anything to save herself, anything at all.

All she took in of the moments that followed were a swishing sound of garments flapping against the air and the scent of fragrant tobacco as a dark figure came barreling toward her. In the next instant, the dark body pushed her out of its path with such violent force that she fell backward, catching the left side of her head on the edge of the credenza. She heard the candlestick she had tried to throw bite into the floor with a thud. Colors burst into flames like a meteoric explosion behind her eyes before she crashed into black and soundless space.

Distinct waves of nausea washed over her as she tried time and again to surface from the high, dizzying tides which were pulling her under. Time passed in seconds? minutes? hours? She didn't know. She didn't care. Her head fell to the side and pain split her skull once again. All of her impressions came through drugged senses as though her entire body were drowning beneath the whitecaps of pulsating pain.

She felt warm breath tingle along her cheeks, rustle against her neck, and then someone placed her arms around a sturdy neck and lifted her from where she lay. She breathed in the mingled scents of pipe tobacco, and cologne, and a body's natural musk. Roused by fear, her mind groped for consciousness, her body struggling for release, but a will greater than hers subdued her halfhearted rebellion and she went limp again in the strong arms that swooped beneath her knees and around her back. A convulsive spasm passed along the length of her figure when she was thrust against an unyielding masculine chest. She was cold. Ice cold.

She struggled to open her lids, heavy as dead weight, a quarter of an inch. She saw darkness cut by a thin, hazy stream of light just bright enough to illuminate the head of a man whose disheveled hair was the color of clover honey and whose eyes, when he turned them to her face cradled at his shoulder, glittered like chips of broken glass. At the sight of the familiar face she cringed and a shadow fell across her heart.

My God! It's Jared! her mind shouted against the walls of her shuddering skull. *It's Jared who attacked me!* How else could he be here now, so soon after she had been struck down? Wasn't that begging too much of coincidence? Wasn't he the very person she'd been afraid to find when she had come down those steps? Yes, yes, of course he was, and yet, and yet . . .

"Why did you . . . do this . . . to me?" she breathed in a plea for understanding, her fingers clutching the collar of his shirt.

The corroboration of her deepest fear was as much a physical blow as the impact that had stunned her. As Jared, still carrying her, slowly walked the length of the foyer, opened her front door and closed it behind him, she could feel her mind closing out the world and its knowledge again. It was better that way . . .

The leather seat was hard beneath her head. A deep voice next to her ear was gentle. ". . . all right, baby. You'll be all right. . . . with you now. I won't leave you." She was drifting in and out of the sound of his voice, the mellifluous sound she tried to hold on to. "I called, Bianca," the deep voice explained. "I called again, but you never answered." Hands moved like ghosts on her arms. Hands grasped her ankles and, putting them side by side on the floorboard, straightened out her legs and rearranged her gown over them. ". . . operator said the lines had been disconnected. So I came right over."

She didn't know what that velvety baritone voice was talking about. For the moment she didn't care. At least she didn't care as long as he resumed the crooning reassurances about her being okay, about caring for her and staying with her. The car door closed. She heard the lock click into place.

The voice must have understood her silent entreaty. "You're safe with me," it said. Someone slipped behind the wheel of the car. "I'm going to take you to the emergency room."

She turned her head toward him. Her eyes opened slightly with fright.

"You're okay, baby," he said as the car's engine came to life. "I'm sure of it. But I just want to hear a qualified doctor tell me the same thing. Okay?"

"Okay," she whispered, and closed her eyes again.

The soft comforter reached to her shoulders when she opened her eyes in the dim light of her own bedroom two hours later. She smiled softly at the dark shadow of the man who sat beside her on the edge of her bed.

"How do you feel now?" he asked.

"Much, much better, thanks to you," she answered.

"Go back to sleep," he gently encouraged her. "You'll feel even better by morning." He must have sensed her reluctance to follow his suggestion but misinterpreted its motive. "I love you, Bianca. I'm staying to watch over you, baby. No one's going to hurt you while I'm here with you."

He leaned forward and his mouth pressed softly against hers. She opened her lips ever so slightly to taste. It was cool, moist. Tentatively she sought the tip of his tongue with hers. Her tongue tingled with his sweetness. Her arms fought their way free of the confining covers and of their own volition wrapped themselves around his strong neck to bring his head down to hers again when he would have retreated.

Breaths mingling, mouth took mouth again, this time with greater pressure, the beginning of demanding need. She opened her mouth to receive his tongue, and when he gave it to her, she coaxed him into tasting every part of her depth, twisting her tongue around his to arouse an exploration that could leave them hungering for greater intimacy. She heard him moan with pleasure and with need as he pressed the weight of his upper body down on hers, and the sound of him filled her with unbearable anticipation. Her hands fell to his back, her fingers rubbing the fabric of his shirt.

Folding back the corner of the comforter and slowly moving to her right to make room for him beside her, she said with a light laugh in her throat, "The clothes have got to go, you know."

"Not now, Bianca," he gently contradicted her. "Not when you're hurting."

She smiled at his reluctance and put determined fingers to his tie and when she had stripped it from his neck, started on the buttons of his shirt. "How often have you told me," she scolded him in a seductive whisper, "that it's when you're hurting that I could be of most assistance?"

"I didn't mean that kind of hurt."

She licked her lips provocatively. "But that's the only kind I mean. It's the only kind I feel right now.

The doctors at the hospital said I was fine. You heard them." It was so dark she could hardly see him. She wished she had thought to light a candle. "Don't you want me?" she asked as if she didn't know the answer, pulling back his shirt and delightedly running her fingers through the wiry curls that covered his chest.

It was a voice unsteadied by frustration that answered her. "Baby, you couldn't know how much." He put his hand in her hair and fingered the long platinum silk spread out on the pillow.

She let her voice go down deep. "I want you, badly."

"Tomorrow will be better for you. Trust me."

Why did he continue to tease her with reluctance? "No. I need you." Her voice was a caress as her hands pushed his coat and shirt off his shoulders. He caught her hands in his as if he wanted to put an end to her advances. "Tonight," she breathed, almost a little angry with him as she gripped his fingers between hers. "Now."

"Bianca, we haven't notified the police yet," he resisted with words, but she felt the eagerness in his body.

"Later," she said, releasing his fingers to work on the buckle of his belt. "We'll call them later, in just a little while. Please."

For a moment he said nothing but she could sense his desire. He yielded to her intensity, soothing her anxiety by stripping down to his slacks. At long last his naked body slid in beside hers on the bed beneath the sheet, and pulled the comforter over both of them. She gave a deep sigh, content in her anticipation.

"I don't want to hurt you, Bianca."

A whisper of a laugh bubbled up in her throat. "You won't, I promise."

"Bianca, about what I said to you at my office—I'm sorry. If I hurt you by implying you enjoyed the shame of being used, forgive me."

"Hush." She put a finger to his lips when he would have said more. "Nothing to forgive. Forgotten."

It was nice the way he slipped his arm beneath her head, rubbed his cheek against hers, but carefully so he wouldn't hurt her tender skin with the late night's whiskered growth.

"Silk face," he said, running a finger along her high cheekbone and into the hollow beneath it. "Silk hair, long, loose, wild, just the way I've longed to see it."

Foolish, she thought. She usually wore it like that and meant to tell him so, but he was kissing her shoulders, and then removing the sapphire straps of lace. He cupped her breast in his hand, tenderly pinched its hardened center between his fingers, and through the filmy gown alternately kissed and bit the engorged center. She undulated against him, persuading him to let her move her leg between his, and with her own hands took her gown down to her waist, exposing her nakedness to her lover. Supporting herself on her elbow, she raised herself and leaned toward him. He put his hungry mouth to her breast again and she responded with all the feverish excitement that had been kindling inside her for weeks, for years.

She fell back among the pillows, his muscular body lying against hers, both eagerly anticipating each other's movements, intimacies, imagining the pleasure lying in wait. Her hands drifted down the length of his back, its sinewy warmth welcoming her while his hands traveled to her waist, stripping the gown over the curve of her hips and down her legs. His head glided down to her navel, then the flat of her abdomen. When the gown was free of her feet, without moving his head, his hand came up behind her leg, along the inner line of her thigh that was wedged between his. Then his hands smoothed the flesh of her hip, crossing forward over the bone, moving inexorably down toward the center of her hurting.

She closed her eyes tight, luxuriating in the minor

explosions of every nerve ending in her body. *Touch me,* she silently pleaded with him as his head came up to hers again. She moved her hands below his waist to his muscled buttocks. A shiver passed from his body to hers.

"Touch me," she begged.

"Over and over again, baby," he vowed.

Between them, his fingers danced along the edges of her feminine center, teasing and cajoling until she was dizzy with spoken and unspoken pleading. Then he pushed aside its walls and caressed her with delicate strokes over and over again until she could hear herself tell him that she wanted him, needed him, her voice quivering with shameless longing. Then his hand glided away to reposition their legs, his moving between hers. Warm pressure flooded through her. When his fingers returned to their tender labor he put his rigid strength between her legs as well.

"Jared!" she gasped against his lips, tossing her head from side to side as his fingers continued to perform their intricate magical pattern, teasing, promising ecstasy if she could wait a little longer. She moistened her lips with her tongue.

"God, how I need you inside me," she told him as she had so many times in her dreams.

"Not yet," he answered, his voice a rich, throaty sound she hardly recognized. "I have so much more to give you, darling."

More? Already she was burning, pierced with the tightness that stretched between pleasure and pain. How she wanted to wait for him, to explode together in a triumph of passion, but he had already stolen away her will, her self-control. It had been so long, too long, since a man had touched her like this. Frantically her hands ran along his legs.

"I'll come," she warned him breathlessly, hating to bring to an end what he wanted to prolong, but she couldn't bear it. "It's been too long."

Still he didn't cease his magic. Her head tossed from

side to side. In desperation she tried to push his hand aside, but he was determined, and stronger. His hand resisted her coercion and his fingers and his male passion continued to hone her to that fine sharp point of pagan pleasure until finally it drove itself back into her, and sensation burst into flaming light. She went wild.

"Richard!" she cried out, her voice sustained by anguish, her body repeatedly convulsed by waves of pleasure. With fingers digging into muscled flesh, she cried out again, a sound both savage and sweet, as she absorbed the fullness of passion and thought she must be dying.

Swiftly he thrust his swollen maleness into her, his passion burning her back into life as the physical boundaries between them began to melt into one blaze of urgency.

He was on top of her now and she welcomed him. He was bigger and heavier than memory; but she gladly, fully, gave herself over to the span of his shoulders, the expanse of his chest, the weight of his legs. How she needed him, needed to give, to receive, to become one with everything that was Love in the present. Raising her knees, she surrendered to him, thrust upon thrust, pulling him deeper and deeper inside herself.

"Bianca," he quietly screamed in agony. "My God!"

Then all was silence except his panting and her own. She felt a convulsion start to ripple through the muscles of his legs and his chest but it was her explosion, too, somewhere deep inside, further than she had ever been. Frantically she clung to him, her fingernails biting deep into the flesh of his back, sobbing with the enormity of ecstasy as he threw his head from side to side like a wild animal. Then the wild cry of agony was wrenched from his throat and he exploded inside her dark womb.

Chapter Six

INSTANTLY a stillness stole into her limbs, a freezing chill into her bones. Her head ached from its earlier injury and her heart ached with the pain of hard, cold fact. Richard was dead. And she hadn't been dreaming. There was a live, warm body poised above her, its passion spent in a feverish riot of her own.

It was Jared's magnificent body, now recoiling from hers by slow degrees. The events of the night that had begun when she had left her bedroom at the first sounds of the intruder rushed into her brain with biting clarity. The veils of confusion which had mercifully protected her from recognizing the enormity of her response to Jared slowly dissipated into thin air. A mild spasm coursed through her as Jared slowly eased himself out of her warmth and lifted himself from between her legs. Putting his weight on his right arm he turned on his side, lowering himself onto the sheet, and then turned again until he lay on his back, one knee raised. In the dark quiet, he lay utterly still against her side, the lengths of their bodies touching at leg, hipbone, arm, shoulder. But no physical contact could bridge the rift in her shuddering heart. She felt utterly bereft and alone.

Was there pain in his eyes over the name she had mindlessly called out? Perhaps it would be better for her not to look, not to know. She closed her eyes against the surrounding darkness that poured into

her soul and turned her head away from him to face
the wall. Perhaps he had no pain, she told herself,
only the disappointment of a criminal who had tried
to use seduction as the means to distract his victim
from his real objective. Or was there lying beside her
the bitter triumph of a man who, after having heard
her call out the name of her dead husband, had thrust
his desire into her to punish her, not to please her. She
shuddered. She didn't know which suspicion was the
more horrible.

She felt him elevate his right arm and supposed he
had repositioned it in a curve above his head. She
heard his deep, heavy breathing and could feel the
rise and fall of his powerful chest muscles as they expanded and contracted against her ribs. She lay perfectly still without trying to move her body from its
intimate proximity to his. She blinked back the moisture collecting in her wide blue-gray eyes, tears that
sprang from a fabric of complex emotions she couldn't
unravel.

With tentative fingers she searched for the edges of
the covers that lay across the lower part of their legs.
She pulled the comforter over her nakedness to es-
tablish some distance between herself and this
stranger named Jared and heartily wished that she
could as easily recover her heart. Yes, she had called
out for Richard. She couldn't deny it. But she had
called out in memory, in confusion. Not in desire. *I
swear, not in desire.* Had she, since the night she had
found Jared slumped over the wheel of his car, so confused the two men in her mind that she was no longer
capable of distinguishing the present from the past,
the living from the dead? She squeezed her eyelids
tight against the tears. *God help me! Don't let that be
true.*

Minutes passed. The chimes of the old grandfather
clock resonating through the foyer were carried
throughout the rest of the house. She had all the time
in the world to imagine what his first words to her

would be. He might say something casually cruel like, *Do you prefer to sleep with dead men?* Or he might choose, instead, the stone cold inquiry, *How does my technique compare to that of a dead man?* She tried to drown out the painful accusations she deserved with other thoughts. What had he said once? Something about wanting their first time together to be memorable for them both? Well, it had been, hadn't it.

His left arm reached across his body to touch hers, his hand passing briefly across her breast as it went upward in search of her face. Finding it, his fingers closed on her chin and coaxed it toward his. When she relaxed the muscles in her neck and turned her head on the pillow, his fingers lightly wiped the moisture from her cheeks. She tried to make out his features in the gloom. Was he being kind so that his cruelty would hurt all the more? She held her breath as he moved his lips to speak, wishing she could drown them out if they were more than she could bear.

"Don't cry, Bianca." The ragged edges of his voice carried the notes of unspeakable sadness, unendurable weariness. But she heard not a hint of cruelty, not a trace of punishment. He leaned forward and kissed her eyelids. His lips were cool against the heat of her flesh. "I didn't think I could trust my self-control once I was inside you," he spoke softly. "I didn't want the first time to be a disappointment for either one of us." He laughed lightly, a self-abusive laugh fully aware of the irony in his words, and in the situation he had tried to orchestrate. "But when it was his name you called out, not mine, it was already too late for me to retreat. I was too far gone to think of your feelings. Maybe I was also a little damn mad that your head was filled up with someone else when I wanted your body to be filled up with me."

She had been so keyed up in expectation of the worst that at first she could hardly absorb what he was saying to her. When she did, she wanted to tell him all that had gone through her head while they had forged their physical bond, but she held back, afraid that if she tried to explain too much, she would cry.

"I didn't expect you to retreat," she made herself begin. "I . . ."

"Did I hurt you?"

She turned on her side and laid a hesitant hand on his chest. "No," she whispered, her voice quivering, "of course you didn't."

"I wouldn't want to hurt you."

Nor would I you. And yet—I have. Or had she? Already she could feel the length of his body tighten as though he were gathering his emotions, like his manhood, back into himself. Where was truth? Where was illusion? How much of Jared was real? How much had her need manufactured? She felt so helpless, so utterly ill-equipped to find the right pieces to the puzzle.

"Remember, Bianca, in the days ahead, that in spite of what was in your mind, your physical pleasure tonight came to you through me." Though he didn't speak roughly to her, his voice had lost that soft, sad quality that had wrenched her heart. Covering her hand with his, he pushed it down his chest to the bed. "I'm going to get dressed now, Bianca," he said matter-of-factly. "Then I'm going to wake your next-door neighbor to call the police. Will you be all right while I'm gone?"

Don't leave me now, Jared, not when we still have so much to say to each other, her eyes beseeched him, but her lips answered, "Yes."

Hours later, after Lieutenant Barber and Investigator Denman had come and gone, she sat on the third to the last step of the staircase, her slim legs covered by gray wool slacks, her royal-blue sweater a striking contrast to the hair spilling over her shoulders like white gold. Having located her prized eighteenth-century candlestick, she had replaced its taper and planted it securely on the step below her. Assisted by a glimmer of moonlight through heavy clouds, the candlelight illuminated the foyer. The flame threw into dramatic relief Jared's facial structure as he stood leaning against the foot of the banister, one loafered foot propped on the bottom step and one hand in his hip pocket.

Avoiding his scrutiny, she rested her head against the stair rail and wrapped her arms around her body. The room seemed suddenly cold. She kept hearing Barber's cynical observation that the entire incident was most likely nothing more than a lover's quarrel and he, for one, wasn't interested in helping lovers work out their differences. A lover's quarrel, for God's sake! Was the man an idiot? Then, there was still Denman's deep-seated conviction that Jared was involved in an illegal scheme and she was acting either as his reluctant accomplice or as his enemies' go-between trying to betray Jared through seduction.

"Tonight ought to teach us something about the wisdom of calling in the police," commented Jared bitterly.

"Especially when you and I are the only ones left at the scene of the crime." She pushed her hair behind her ear with a weary hand. "Since when does calling on the police for help make you a criminal?"

"Since whenever the police start making up facts to fit their preconceived theories, instead of formulating a theory based on the facts." From the corner of her eyes she noticed that he definitely seemed to be favoring his left arm. "I imagine it happens often enough."

She recalled the image of Denman puffing on his malodorous cigar, his broad, hairy hand shoving it in and out of his fleshy mouth as he assisted Barber at an address outside his jurisdiction. "I don't think Denman much cared for this new piece in the puzzle."

"Certainly not. He doesn't know where it fits and he certainly doesn't want to go through the trouble of readjusting his version of what the jigsaw puzzle looks like."

She looked up at him. "Do *you* know where it fits— someone breaking into my office?" He didn't answer. "I've tried to see a connection between what happened tonight and everything that's gone on before, but the logic eludes me. I begin with—" She stopped as he suddenly swung his head in her direction and planted his foot almost violently beside her hip on the step which she was sitting on.

"What do you begin with?" he demanded, a shade belligerently. "The obvious fact that just as soon as you audited my books, you were someone's target?"

"Naturally. Wouldn't you begin there?"

Instead of answering, he stared at her coldly and asked, "How did you jump from that starting place to the assumption that I was the one who broke in and knocked you unconscious when I pushed you out of the way?" His voice was rough with a sarcasm he seemed to be enjoying. "I mean, besides the obviously conclusive evidence that the fragrant pipe tobacco you got a whiff of is used by no human being in this city other than myself!"

"I didn't say that," she protested firmly, but all the while she was really wondering if she had heard in his peculiar phrasing a confession of guilt. Had he slipped up and said more than he could have known? She couldn't think.

"You don't have to say it!" He was equally angry. "Your eyes said it for you."

She put her elbows on her knees, her head throbbing in her hands. She hadn't told the police about the tobacco scent, the fragrance that clung to the jacket he was presently wearing. Wasn't that enough for him? "It doesn't make sense, does it?" she murmured, the heat of her protest having robbed her voice of strength.

"If you mean that it makes absolutely no sense to suspect me of trying to steal the very books I gave you in order to discover an embezzler in my operations, you're damn right! It *doesn't* make sense!"

Her bright silver head came up. She thought that in spite of his explanation that he had driven over to make up after the fight they had had at his office, his arrival on the scene had been suspiciously coincidental. She didn't much believe in coincidence.

"But it might make sense if you were all along trying to . . ." She stopped, seeing that she had gone too far.

"Trying to *what,* for God's sake?" he snapped, bringing his face down to hers in a menacing attitude. "Are we back to accusing me of altering my own books and setting you up as the CPA who discovers embezzlement?"

She couldn't hurl the accusation at him again. Danger and desire, and the danger in desire stood between them, a barrier no words from either of them could pull down. The bed they had shared, its unresolved dynamics that they weren't talking about, was a palpable presence that wouldn't go away.

"I can't think anymore, Jared," she said instead, hating the sound of defeat in her voice and trying to combat it by pulling back her shoulders and emphasizing her words with her hands. "The police and their cynical animosity don't make things any easier for me, Jared, or any clearer. They just muddy up the whole damn thing! I find myself suspecting everyone and everything one moment, and suspecting no one and nothing the next."

As she stared at him, her volume keeping pace with the fervor of her explanation, she suddenly realized that she might never know the motives or the feelings that lived behind the bright eyes of the tall, muscular man poised menacingly over her. Bleak desolation swift as an axe stilled her hands and silenced her voice.

His right hand shot toward her. Involuntarily she flinched and was nearly blinded by the pain that jolted straight down from the top of her head to the back of her throat. She felt her head spin on her neck. The emergency room doctor had been right. When she was pushed against the credenza she had taken a very hard fall.

"At least do me the favor of not cringing when I give you a hand to bring you to your feet," he said sharply.

The bitterness in his voice cut through her physical pain and overwhelmed her with despair, even though she knew she had no right to expect anything else from him. She gave herself a moment or two to recover her equilibrium. Then she took his hand and as he pulled her up, he removed his foot from the riser and stepped back from the staircase. She walked down each of the last steps slowly toward him. Lifting her eyes to his face, she watched as the tight line of his mouth softened unexpectedly into the sensuous fullness that was so appealing. She kept her hand in his when she probably shouldn't have and she stood closer to him than she probably should have, but she didn't retreat by even the space of a heartbeat.

"Bianca, we'll find out who's responsible for hurting you."

But will I be able to endure knowing his identity?

"Before something else happens," he added in the silence that greeted his vow. She might have asked what he thought that something else might be and when he expected it to happen, but almost in the same breath he asked quite gently, "Will you be able to get any sleep?" He dropped her hand and lifted his own to her shoulders where his thumbs rubbed lightly into her flesh.

She shivered at the touch as though all the voiced and unvoiced accusations of the moments before had been a sham, nothing more than an excuse for making up, a prelude to forgiveness. Why was it her fate to have all her suspicions dissolve at the first sign of gentleness in his voice, at the first touch of tenderness in his hands? Had she so little self-control, so little pride?

"If I can't sleep, I can always resort to these pills the doctor ordered." She reached into her jacket pocket and pulled out a clear plastic bottle rattling with blue capsules. "I think they're big enough to drug a horse."

He smiled but he was clearly not going to take his cue from her attempt to lighten the mood. "You know I'll stay if you want me."

Oh, I want you, Jared. That's why you can't stay. She shook her head. "I'll be all right, Jared. I'm a big girl and I need to take care of myself."

He took a step closer to her. She could feel his muscular legs pressing against hers. "I wish you'd share that responsibility with me."

Her heart stopped beating for a moment or two as his hands glided from her shoulders to her neck. A tingling sensation ran along her flesh as his fingers splayed out against the back of her head.

"If you live too long in the shadows of one love, baby," he said earnestly, "you won't be able to recognize a new love for what he is when he comes into your life."

It was his first reference to what had happened between them in her bedroom. She swallowed down the tears that caught in her throat. "The terrible irony, Jared, is that a few months before you came into my life, I thought I was free of those shadows."

"And now?" he prodded her, threading his fingers in her long hair, pulling gently on the white-gold silk.

"And now—you stir up so many emotions, I can't sort them all out."

"Let me help you." And he bent down to kiss her so thoroughly that her body leaped up to hold him. When his lips finally released hers and he stepped back, she was breathless.

"Some help," she confided to him, still holding on

to his upper arms to steady herself. "Don't you know that's the very thing that adds to my confusion?"

"I'm counting on it" was all he gave her for an answer. His hands fell from their embrace. He turned on his heel and walked to the door. "Use the latch chain this time and take your remote alarm to bed with you," he cautioned her in a distant voice before he opened the door and closed it behind him, leaving her to what remained of the dark hours until dawn.

She stared at the emptiness around her and felt a greater emptiness in her heart. It was better this way, she tried to convince herself as she wrapped her arms across her breasts, her hands reaching to her shoulders, trying to replace the warmth he had taken away. Better to keep sending him away. There was no future in love that could be destroyed by distrust, no future in passion that could be aborted by fear. Or worse—what if her passion and fear were so scrambled up in her head that her desire for him was actually a perverted reaction to the danger that surrounded him? Horrible, horrible thought!

And at the end of all those horrible ruminations that left her trembling with self-doubts her flesh still carried the memory of his body burning within her.

"Now that I have had you, Jared," she asked of the empty air around her, "how do I fill up my life without you?"

"Please excuse me, Señorita Bianca," exclaimed José Albañez with a glance in the direction of the slim, fair-haired young man who was his son. "I must speak to Gilberto about a small matter before he leaves to fly back to Mexico."

She creased her brow. "I didn't know there were any commercial flights to Mexico at this hour."

"There aren't," Señor Albañez responded, a well-manicured hand briefly touching her arm. "He flies with a friend in a private plane, but I do not know this friend very well." He shrugged his shoulders as if to say any concerned parent would want to know more. "So I must speak with him."

She smiled at his Old World manner. "Of course you must."

For a moment she was alone, standing between the sputtering fireplace and the old-fashioned, brightly lit Christmas tree that reached at least three-quarters as high as the two-story living room ceiling. Something about the burnished woods and cream walls made her think that the outdoors had been brought inside. Like Jared himself. She looked across the room, seeing her reflection in a mirror into which Jared, from another angle, was also staring. Though the man beside him was trying to engage him in conversation, it was she who apparently had his attention.

Her silver-blond hair was coiled high in a 1940s style, setting off the excellent lines of her face, and her figure was sheathed in dramatic black with glittering black sequined bands at her narrow hips and at the cuffs of the billowing dolman sleeves. Having accepted, against her better judgment, Jared's invitation to the holiday buffet at his home on Cross Mountain outside the city, she had armed herself in a color that announced her resolve to remain aloof. Jared, she couldn't help but notice, looked alarmingly virile in black tie and tux, the formality of his attire pointing out by contrast the earthy vitality no clothes could conceal.

She dropped her eyes, repeating to herself once again that she was here smiling at every Berenson relative and guest for one purpose only—to discover why she had become someone's victim caught in a web that Jared might have spun. She had reckoned, she hoped not falsely, that among his associates and friends she would overhear a clue from a tongue loosened by liberal drinking and the deceptive holiday spirit of trust. But the other self in her that demanded honesty reluctantly admitted that although she was afraid of Jared's criminal culpability, she was in his home because she was still drawn to him ineluctably—like the moth to the flame that will burn it. After all, hadn't she come early at Jared's suggestion and dressed in one of his guest rooms: convenient, they both knew, if she spent the night.

Thus far, her amateurish investigation hadn't unearthed a clue. She felt she was simply skimming the surfaces of conversation, filling her mouth and her ears with social prattle that had no beginning and no end. Earlier in the evening, Charles Roper had approached her with a suggestion that the two of them might want to sit down to talk shop. She took one look at the nearly palpable animosity that glared out of his pale eyes and wondered why in the world he even bothered—except to disguise his distrust, which, considering that she had given him no cause, was a gesture she found deeply annoying. Then, when she accepted the offer, thinking she had at last found the chance to pursue her sleuthing, he immediately tensed, shifting his slight weight from one foot to the other, and told her he would get back to her before the evening's end.

Nor had Martin Goerner looked anywhere close to abandoning the cynical smile he always had in place upon seeing her. "Jared and you seem to be seeing a great deal of each other," he had said in a deceptively pleasant voice when he had cornered her a half-hour before. "For the last few years he's managed to avoid being linked with one woman. Maybe his luck's run out at last."

She looked him dead in the eye. "Why, Mr. Goerner," she very nearly cooed, "I know he believes his luck has just begun." She took a leisurely sip of champagne from her fluted crystal glass, then, without another word to encourage further disagreeable exchanges, had turned on her heel and walked away, determined to find someone pleasant, like José Albañez's son, to talk to.

Presently she watched Jared from a distance, the congenial host who moved easily among his fifty-or-so guests. Though he had been attentive to her most of the evening, he had often retreated into a dim corner as he did now, she noted with a sinking heart, for whispered conversations with Pedro Elizondo, another Mexican financier whose name she couldn't recall, and José Albañez. If she questioned him about the intrigue and the secrecy, no doubt he would say he was trying to discover if any of the men could remember an incident or conversation which would help him reconstruct the criminal scheme around him. And that explanation could be true, she supposed. She was using the screen of a party to do the same thing herself, wasn't she?

Christmas was less than a week away. And where, she wondered, was the special peace which, even in the first years following Richard's death, it had always held for her? It certainly wasn't in the world she lived in now, the one that was tumbling upside down and around without a prayer in heaven of ever coming right again.

"I believe I made a mistake about your man, Berenson. He seems to be a very decent sort of guy."

She turned around at the sound of her brother's unexpected praise. "I didn't think I'd live to hear you admit it." Obviously, the hospital's emergency room staff had been true to their word that not a whisper of her most recent visit would reach her brother through them.

"Did you know he was a college swimming champion?" her brother asked her. He obviously appreciated from his medical standpoint the man's good cardiovascular form. "National event medals and all that, one of his sisters was telling me. Swims fifty miles a week at a private club even now." He nodded his head sagely. "No wonder he recovered so well from that shooting incident."

Interesting. Arthur had now relegated the horror of that night to a mere "incident."

"We've got any number of friends in common, I've discovered."

Hmmm. God knows, he's bound to be respectable then. "Have you?"

"And he's thought of rather highly in the business community. Some San Antonians think he's the most honest entrepreneur the city can boast of. I wonder if he's going to honor his original commitment to developing that downtown property Charles Roper's been talking about."

She laughed lightly to herself. "I can read you better than that, Arthur. What you're really wondering is whether he has *honorable* intentions toward your baby sister."

He gave her one of his most infuriatingly patronizing grins. "It had crossed my mind."

"And Marianne's mind as well?"

"And Marianne's," he acknowledged without the slightest show of embarrassment.

"And at least a hundred times since both of you set foot in his beautiful home, no doubt," she pressed her point.

"Actually, our speculations date from the moment we saw the two of you together tonight," he conceded with a self-congratulatory smile. "Would you expect otherwise from a concerned brother?"

"I'll tell you what I expect," she answered, wagging a finger in his overprotective face. "A little trust. I'm a big girl. You can relax and watch me take care of myself."

"Just you remember he's a big boy. And in addition to having a reputation as an honest entrepreneur, if he hasn't actually asked you to marry him . . ."

She put up an open palm between them. "Don't tell me. I think I've got this speech down pat. I certainly heard it often enough throughout high school and col-

lege. If he's not interested in marriage, he's bound to
be a philandering playboy, right?"

Arthur assumed the look of reproach he had per-
fected. "Bianca, you need to take relationships more
seriously."

She shook her finely coiffed head. "No, Arthur.
You're dead wrong there. That is the *last* thing I need
to do." But when she saw the hurt he tried to hide behind his bluff exterior, she relented just as she always
did. He really was a good brother, but honestly, she
wished Mother Nature had thought to bless him with
a wild daughter or two to make his anxiety worth his
while. Smiling, she put her arm through his and
waltzed him back to the bright face and bobbing curls
of Marianne, who was thrilled to have him returned
to her adoring care.

Before he could protest her rather neat dismissal,
she had wandered out of his sight and down the wide
corridor, away from the main entertainment area and
toward a study in the north wing of the house she had
passed earlier. From the open doorway she could see
that the room, lit solely by the small lamp on the central desk, was unoccupied. Immediately she saw it as
the temporary respite she needed from the bright
chatter of the party.

The deep pile of the area carpet covering the slim
planks of the oak floor hushed the click of her heels
when she advanced into the room. She smiled in the
realization that Jared, whose muscular physique
would probably look more at home on a playing field
than in a library, was apparently a prolific reader. On
bookcases built into three of the walls stood a rather
substantial number of volumes behind the beveled
glass doors. In fact, from the condition of rows of
leather-bound manuscripts, she wondered if some of
those cases contained a rare book collection. It was to
those shelves on her left that she headed. But the instant her fingertips figured out the intricate brass
lock on the bookcase door she froze.

Snatches of heated conversation from voices she could easily identify drifted into the study from the hallway. The two guests obviously assumed that in this deserted part of the house no one could overhear them, for her position to the left of the open door and behind it effectively blocked her from their view.

"All that you've said could be true." The voice of Roper was firmer than Bianca had ever remembered hearing it. "But I still say that working as the comptroller for a produce broker like Jared, who has many diversified interests, can be a very risky business if the books have been adjusted behind the comptroller's back."

One by one her fingers released their hold on the brass lock, but otherwise she remained perfectly still.

"Adjusted?" repeated Goerner's voice as though the idea stretched his credulity. "Adjusted—as in falsified?"

"Correct."

"Falsified by a certified accountant like—"

"—like Bianca Cavender. And I don't know what you're so surprised about. You've seemed as suspicious about their meeting on Old Boerne Stage Road as Jared said the police were."

Goerner didn't deny or affirm the statement. "Just what do you think Jared would gain by having her adjust the books—that is, if you're assuming Jared has put her up to it."

"Of course he has." Roper immediately dispensed with his colleague's reluctance to accept the fact while Bianca cautiously turned on her heels to face the sounds of their conversation. "It's quite simple, Martin. He wants to have the books *meet* the needs of Harvest Enterprises, not *reflect* the holding company's actual transactions."

There was a moment of complete silence before the voice of Goerner burst out in anger, "What in the hell are you talking about?" followed by a muted crash. Bianca could only suppose that he must have slammed his glass down on the flower table in the hall. "What is 'meet,' not 'reflect,' the needs of the company supposed to mean, for Chrissake?"

"I think Jared knows what I mean."

"Well, I don't, and it's me you're talking to, not Jared!"

For a second or two Bianca thought she wasn't going to hear another word, but Roper's voice finally filtered through to the study, repeating his conviction. "Sometimes a company *needs* to show a greater volume of business than it actually transacts."

"Really?" inquired Goerner, his words underscored with heavy sarcasm. "Why is that, Charles? Because it wants to pay *more* income tax than its fair share, no doubt?"

Another muted crash followed the first, and in the ensuing noise Bianca took a chance on taking two steps to her right. Through the crack between the door and its frame she could just make out the two figures.

"Because with proof of a greater volume the company is in a better position to impress investors or lenders for a business venture. In cases like that, two sets of books are usually kept. But it's a dangerous double deal to play when you are trying to attract big-time investors. I don't think that's what's happening here."

Goerner didn't hide his impatience. "Then what *is* it you suspect?"

"I suspect that Harvest's books are being adjusted to reveal greater income than the company actually earns because it's a good way to conceal Jared's income from a source other than those I know about. An illegal source."

"What!" Goerner was clearly outraged.

"Even though I haven't got a shred of evidence, I've wondered if Jared wasn't shot by a partner in that illegal source of income. One who thinks he got double-crossed." He readjusted his rimless glasses on the bridge of his nose.

"If you recall"—Goerner enunciated each syllable as he leaned forward menacingly—"the police report maintained that Jared was shot by the same sociopath who had shot five other men in this area."

"I don't believe that story for a minute," Charles asserted with a wave of his hand. "That's only what they want the public to think until they come up with the right answers. And I won't be in the least surprised if the right answer includes a complex scheme involving at least four men at the company, three of whom are drivers. And possibly Elizondo," he added as an afterthought.

"Drivers? Why drivers?" Goerner was aghast. "And how would Pedro Elizondo fit into whatever the hell you think is going on?"

"Because the operation I'm thinking of needs a contact across the border."

"Jesus H. Christ! Do you have any idea how mad this sounds?"

"It isn't so mad. And although I'm not a gambling man—unlike *others* in the company," he said pointedly, "I'm willing to bet that when the police uncover the operation, you're not going to be in any better shape than I am if someone's looking for a scapegoat. No one else stands between the two of us and the head honcho."

"Roper, you've always been a bit nervous about your position since old Berenson left Jared as CEO of Harvest," he spat out the words as he turned on his heel to leave, "but this is paranoia of the first degree and you better get it out of your head!"

Roper threw out a hand to stop him. "Lots of things can cross that border with produce, Martin."

Goerner swiveled around again, but not before Bianca glimpsed the taut expression on his face. "Like what?" he asked, his voice wooden.

"Like dope," Roper answered, "like guns, like jewels. There's big money in all three. And I certainly don't intend to go to jail for any of them."

"Where in the hell did you get this garbage?" Martin waved a hand in front of Charles's face. "Out of the clear blue?"

"I have my sources."

"What sources?" demanded Goerner.

"Drivers who come to me with their suspicions."

"And you've built up this elaborate story upon the word of . . ."

But Martin's skepticism was lost in the barrage of hearty good cheer from a voice that sliced straight through Bianca's beating heart. "Why hello, Mr. Goerner, Mr. Roper! Why in the world are the two of you hiding out here at the end of the hall?" trilled that familiar east Texas twang. "Have you seen Bianca? I've been looking for her everywhere."

Before they could answer, Marianne pushed the door to the study back against the wall and with one of Jared's numerous first cousins in tow, exclaimed, "Why, Bianca! Leave it to you to sneak away from the fun! Honestly! Arthur said we'd . . ."

The rest of her sister-in-law's admonition was lost on its intended audience. In a reflex that was anything but rational, Bianca scanned the study for a place to hide even as she knew it was hopeless. Alerted to her presence, the two men quickly dropped their earnest discussion to stare at Marianne as she sailed into the room. Bianca gave up any attempt to make an escape. Trapped like an animal hunted down for the kill, Bianca just stood there, rooted to the spot. The venomous looks that froze the two men's facial muscles told her she'd been caught eavesdropping. She knew they wouldn't forget it.

Bianca walked the length of the gallery, from which vantage point high on Cross Mountain she could see the distant city lights below competing against the sky's star-glitter above. In between the city and the mountain top stretched miles and miles of shadowy oak and cedar, wild persimmon and purple sage.

Under the clear crystal stars she could see how the multilevel house was built into the natural terrain. On one level above her to the left, a swimming pool that began below the terrace off the master bedroom jutted out into the edge of the cliff. On the lower level where she was standing was the gallery that spanned two small humps in the rocky cliff. Exploring didn't interest her here, for the long steps leading down to yet another level looked treacherously steep at this hour of the night. If she missed a step, she could easily plunge into the rock garden below, or worse, fall down the steep face of the cliff with little to break her fall except sharp rocks and scrub brush.

At two in the morning, the final good-byes had been said, the last friends and relatives escorted to their automobiles. Jared was somewhere inside talking to his housekeeper, and as soon as he joined her Bianca would ask him to take her home.

Even though for the last three hours she had tried to make sense out of the disclosures she had heard from the study, she was still unable to put the pieces of the jigsaw puzzle into any recognizable picture. Had Charles Roper openly accused Jared of smuggling dope or guns across the border, using Pedro Elizondo as his Mexican connection? Had Martin Goerner been angry because he thought the comptroller was guilty of character defamation and company disloyalty? Or had Goerner been angry at Jared because he too stood to lose a great deal if the boss was guilty of a major felony?

She shook her head and kept her fingers busy with the clasp of her bracelet. None of the information seemed to fit the engaging personality of tonight's host, the unaffected, open-faced charm that attracted even hard-core cynics like her brother. Unless, of course, a serious personality disorder made it possible for him to be both charming and cunning in the same smile, both beguiling and scheming in the same breath.

A cold gust of wind rushed across her face, and dry dead leaves rustled in its wake. She shivered and steadied herself with her hand against the rough cypress post at the top of the steps. She supposed the gust had been but the first blast of the predicted cold front that would plunge moderate temperatures down into the twenties. Common sense demanded that she go back inside. But inside she would have to face Jared with a mask in place to disguise her fears and suspicions. She was too tired for disguise and he was too clever not to see through it. Again she shivered as another gust of wind rushed past her with greater force than before.

The decision was taken out of her hands. First she heard a whistling in the air behind her, followed by a deep thud. Then she felt a vibration of nerves originating in the center back of her hand and another more violent vibration that traveled from her shoulder to the back of her neck, snapping it forward. Sharp pain spiraled madly up and down her spine and her knees nearly gave way under her.

In a flash of understanding she realized that a hard object which must have been thrown at considerable speed had struck the post, grazed her hand as well as her shoulder, and nearly toppled her over into what would have been a headlong flight some fifty feet down onto a bed of jagged rock and scrub brush.

Her brain was momentarily stunned into paralysis. Then before shock could give way to fear, she sucked in the crisp night air and angrily whirled around to confront her assailant, nearly losing her precarious balance on the step with her precipitate movement. Within seconds, slow, deliberate footfalls on the gallery deck resounded in the dark quiet like muffled cannon shots going off, one after another. Stealthy footfalls of someone she couldn't see, someone who didn't want to be seen, though she herself was clearly visible in the light of the moon and the outdoor lamps that illuminated the steps.

Her own vulnerability sunk into her like a heavy stone. In an instant she knew she had to run for cover. Whirling around again, she searched the dark landscape for refuge. She sighted the sanctuary of thick shrubbery and a stand of high trees to the east of the pool where no light could find her. It would mean a mad descent down these steps, then a frantic ascent up those that led to the pool, but she saw no other choice. Once concealed behind one of the mammoth boulders beyond the dense vegetation, she could decide what her next course of action should be.

With her heart hammering madly in her chest, she flew down the steps, barely touching the wooden posts with her high-heeled shoes, mindless of the ripping sound at the bottom of her long straight skirt and the burn on her hand from holding the rail too tight. Following hard after her came the sound of footfalls sharper and faster across the deck she had just abandoned. She must have been disoriented, for she thought that the steps both receded and advanced. Were footsteps coming from opposite directions? Was she being stalked by two assailants? She stumbled on the edge of the rock garden but quickly picked up speed again.

"Bianca! Stop!" There was a frantic note in the deep rich voice that called out to her.

She wouldn't listen. She mustn't. *Keep running,* she told herself. *Keep running for cover behind those boulders.*

"Bianca! The cliff drops off abruptly at the end of the pool deck! Stop!"

It was Jared's voice, charming and cunning, beguiling and scheming. She wouldn't believe him. It was a ruse to throw her off her stride, halt her momentum, ensnare her in his trap. She stumbled again and felt the lacy cedar leaf slap her hard against the face, the thorny branch of pyracantha cut into the flesh of her leg. She pitched forward onto the steps leading to the pool, but desperation made it possible for her to push herself into an upright position again and force her legs up the steep incline. And all the while she could hear the footsteps coming closer, coming closer.

"Bianca! There's nothing but an arroyo behind the boulders. Don't be a fool!"

Fool? Who was he kidding? That's exactly what she was to have gotten involved with him in the first place! She should never have fallen for the glint of gold in his eyes, the generous smile, the endearing way his tousled hair fell onto his forehead. She should never have cared so much if he lived or died that fateful night in November. She should have known he was the wrong man though he had come at the right time. She should have kept her heart locked in the shadow of memory—it would have been safer.

She stepped onto the wide flagstone pool deck. Her heart pounding like timpanic thunder in her ears, she ran hard into the night, desperately searching for cover even as she heard the footsteps close in on her. Immediately behind her she felt the rush of breath exhaled, breath that wrapped its warmth around her neck.

She didn't even stop when she felt the heavy hand clamp down hard on her right shoulder, then slash forward in a diagonal stroke over her breast and down to her waist. It wasn't until the other arm of her assailant came from behind and wrapped itself around her, gripping her below her breasts, that her body was finally forced into stillness against the rock-hard chest.

For a moment she stopped breathing as they tottered precariously against each other. She shut her eyes, then opened them, able to see beyond the vegetation and the boulders. A deep chasm of jagged rock yawned for hundreds of feet below. Her body began to tremble. Without warning, he abruptly whirled her around to face him.

But he must have been overconfident of his victory, or he had seriously underestimated her determination, because he relaxed his hold. In a split second, she twisted sharply to the right to extricate herself and headed in the direction of the house. If the housekeeper was still there, it might be a sanctuary yet.

His surprise at her escape gave her enough of an advantage that she was able to run the length of the pool deck and head up the terraced steps leading to the north wing of the house. With luck, one of the two doors opening onto the terrace would yield to her touch.

That hope was smashed the moment her foot touched the second to the last riser. She stumbled and the body that was only one step below her slammed into her, his strong arms grabbing around her waist to steady them both. She was caught. This time for good. She knew it in her bones and abruptly ceased her frantic attempt to escape. Seconds passed while he pressed himself so close to her she couldn't be sure whose heart was hammering inside her chest.

Keeping his hands on her, he turned her around. She backed up one riser, then another, he advanced two, then one more. On the terrace he stood in front of her. Her eyes shut down, then opened again, this time wide with fear. She saw his face against the backdrop of crystal stars. It was a face both charming and cunning, beguiling and scheming. Hadn't she known it would be? Her breath came in short, uneven gasps. Deeply afraid, she put out a hand, its fingers splayed as if to ward off evil.

"Stay away from me," she hissed, her voice hoarse and quivering.

The eyes that looked down on her were bright slits, the shadows of their curling lashes like sharp needles on his skin. The planes of his face, frighteningly sharp, tightened with anger, a muscle spasm working madly in the lower right jaw. His arms gripped her like a vise.

"Never!" came the quiet shout, its vehemence ringing in her ears. "And I'll never let you go!"

Was it a threat or a lover's vow? Suddenly she was uncertain all over again, her emotions thrown into turmoil. His arms—were they refuge or prison? The warm blanket of security or the cold shroud of death?

He took one hand off her body and shot it around behind her. She heard the metallic click of the door lock when the handle was turned and a low thud when the glass swung wide and hit the rubber shield on the baseboard. She backed up into the room as he advanced.

"Why in the hell are you trying to run away from me?" His voice was hard and intransigent.

She tried to mouth the right words, but nothing came out. With a quick tongue she wet her lips and kept backing up into the room, the deep carpet swallowing the sound of her heels. Finally, "Someone tried to attack me on the gallery."

He slammed the door shut behind him. The sound reverberated in her skull. "What! When?"

Was the fierceness in his eyes spontaneous outrage at the attack, automatic disbelief, or anger at her escape? "Just now. Someone threw something, a rock maybe—I can't be sure what it was, but it very nearly knocked me down those steps. I could have been . . ."

"But you and I are the only people here, Bianca. Even my housekeeper has gone, and the security guard I've hired won't arrive for another half-hour. Are you sure?"

"God, yes!" What had she ever done or said to cause his mistrust? "Of course I'm sure! I don't fabricate danger! When I turned around to find out who had done it, I heard the footsteps of someone on the deck stalking me." His face was practically touching hers. "So . . . I . . . I made a run for it."

"But I was the one coming after you."

A hush descended on the room. "I know." Her blue-gray eyes felt enormous in her face. Suddenly she was very tired; her voice resonated with the hollow quality of resignation. "I loved you and you wanted to hurt me. I made love to you, and you hunted me down out there like an animal. I . . ."

"Stop it, Bianca!" He shook her hard until she was sure the throbbing in her head would never cease. "Stop it!"

One of his hands moved down her back and the other moved up behind her neck. Did those stealthy fingers want to strangle her or caress her? They were alone in his house. He had said as much. He could do anything he wanted with her and no one would ever know.

"You don't really believe that," he told her harshly, his eyes boring into hers. "You couldn't."

Your own men who know you don't trust you, Jared. How can I? She was dizzy, disoriented. She grabbed the lapels of his coat to steady herself. "I don't know what I believe. Sometimes I don't even know what I feel."

"Why in God's name would I want to hurt you? What possible motive could I have?"

She shook her head, the tears collecting in her eyes obvious in her broken voice. "I don't know, Jared. I . . . don't know anything anymore . . ."

"But you know that I love you. You know that you're safe with me always."

The longer she looked into his eyes, the deeper she felt the heat of his body pass through the black crepe silk into her flesh. Reality started to recede. Her compulsion to uncover reality ebbed. Resistance to everything he stirred in her began to crumble. Slowly he inclined his head toward hers. How could she not respond when the steel bands of his arms relaxed only to pull her closer against his hard legs, his narrow hips, his broad chest? Was she falling into empty space instead of eager arms? She couldn't know.

"Don't ever run away from me, baby," he said, his voice husky with deep hurt, his head seeking the warmth in the sensitive curve of her neck. She could feel his tears wet on her cheeks. "I can't stand it. It makes me wild."

If he was wild, she was weak. Why not just surrender to her weakness for him and let his arms enfold her? "Jared." Her voice, both frightened and wistful, caught in her throat. "I want to believe you."

He lifted his head and searched her face. "Let me make it easy for you."

His mouth touched hers with a cool pressing softness. Gliding his tongue back and forth along the dark outline of her mouth, he suddenly bit her lower lip, sucked on it gently, then eased his tongue past her teeth.

She took the delectable wine of his kiss inside her honeyed darkness. She was lost. She knew it now. She released his lapels and flattened her hands on his chest, feeling, through the pleated shirt, his heart beating madly against her palms.

With a hint of savage impatience, he pulled the pins from her hair with one hand and with the other unfastened the first in the long row of small buttons at her back, all the while continuing to kiss her with ever increasing demand for her uninhibited response.

Then his lips released her and his face came up. Slowly he edged her forward until her knees met the foot of the bed. Through the glass panels that lined the wall, long, wide spools of milky moonlight rolled out into the room's darkness. Caught in the cold light, they stood together. Beyond his shoulder, she glimpsed the glistening sheet of water in the pool below and the sheer dramatic drop of the cliff behind it. A chilling sight.

"I never stop wanting you, Bianca," he said with husky breath as he stared with intensity into her blue-gray eyes. His cool hands touched the smooth skin of her back as he deftly managed the next four tiny buttons. "I can't think of anything else when I'm not with you. And when I'm with you, I'm drunk on desire."

He pressed his soft lips into the hollow of her throat and finished off the last tiny button below her waist-line. She shivered again, recognizing the pressure of anticipated pleasure rising inside her and quietly offered him her wrists. Unfastening the sequined cuffs as deftly as he had managed the back, he pulled the silk crepe from her shoulders and coaxed the cloth over her narrow hips. The dress fell to her feet as his hands slipped behind her again. She stepped out of her dress and out of her heels. Instantly she heard the snap of her black brassiere give way to his purposeful fingers.

Her breaths came now in shallow, uneven little gasps as she watched him take one, two, three steps back. Fascinated by his unselfconscious grace, she watched the arc of the black dinner jacket as he tossed it onto the chair. Black tie, white shirt, wide cummerbund followed. Arms crossed at his sides, he pulled off his undershirt, shaking his head of hair when the shirt came free. Then his trousers. In the cold light she had a marvelous view of Jared Berenson, naked to the waist. As always, she was struck by the fact that he was a very big man, but his stomach was perfectly flat, his flesh finely toned over long, powerful legs and the broad span of his chest. She caught a glimpse of the scar on his left side, relieved because it appeared to have healed well.

"Your body is incredibly beautiful, Bianca," he breathed as his hand reached for her face. "Small waist." He crossed back to her, stroking her cheek. "Long, slim legs." He rubbed his thumb across her lower lip. "Full breasts."

She opened her mouth to bite his thumb gently. He laughed deliciously and put an arm around her waist while she slipped her hand into the mat of wiry golden hair heavy at the top of his chest and tapering down below his navel. She let her hands roam along the

sides of his torso, sliding down into his briefs while a
smile played on her lips. Slowly she put her cheek flat
against his chest and her cool fingers glanced caress-
ingly along his tight skin. She felt him shudder
against her and heard him groan.

She could hear his deep breathing and the hammering of his heart in her ear. She buried her head in
his embrace, wrapped her arms around his neck, and
waited still as a stone for him to touch her.

Both of his hands went down her back at once and
over the curve of her hips, pulling her inexorably toward him. "You're like luxurious velvet," he whispered above her head as his hand dipped into the
black lace of her panties. "I want that velvet to fold
over me."

A long shuddering sigh escaped her parted lips and
her body began to move with a rhythm to match the
beat of his fingers, which alternately touched her
with long sliding strokes and shorter, softer glances.

"Jared!" she cried as he persisted in fondling her
with delicate, determined strokes.

His breath fanned the tendrils of hair damply curling at her temple. "Give yourself up to this. To me."
The hand at her back pulled the black lace down her
thighs.

She began to waver on her legs. She thought she
would faint. She wanted to touch him, to give him
pleasure, but how could she when he persisted in
driving her body mad with sensation until she no
longer knew what to do with her own limbs.

Following his silent directions, she fell back onto
the bed, taking him with her, and felt time fall away.
All that was left in her spinning world was this man
with burnished hair and golden eyes, this man with
strength enough for two. She held on to him for dear
life while he stripped off his own briefs, and then in a
frenzy of desire, she moved her hand down his chest
and over his hipbone, madly searching to touch him,

to communicate her feverish excitement, to generate the same excitement in him.

She touched him. The agonizing groan that hit the night almost satisfied her longing to return his pleasure. Side by side they lay, mouth searching for mouth, tongue probing warmth, warmth sheltering strength. He moved his leg between hers, lifting the knee until it met her wet warmth. Leisurely she rubbed against his leg, delighting in the tingling sensation of his hair against her skin, then surprised him by rolling on top of him.

His mouth curved in a broad smile and his laugh was low and deep as he undulated like a strong wave beneath her. His hands glided up her legs, thumbs probing the flesh of her inner thigh, and as she leaned forward, caught her full breasts. Gently he rubbed the tender centers between his thumb and index fingers. Little explosions went off in her body, scattering into every crevice of her flesh as she continued to fall forward, balancing herself on hands flattened on either side of his head. First his tongue circled the rose aureole with maddening deliberation, then his mouth clamped down on the erect center and sucked long and hard as one hand slipped down behind her back to her hips and the other searched out that familiar pathway between her legs to the center of all erotic sensation.

Poised above him, she felt helpless as her breathing turned swiftly into panting and the sounds welling up from her throat turned into drawn-out notes of yearning. His expert fingers fondled and teased in intricate patterns, determined to drive her a little mad before he let her have him.

Suddenly she felt every sensation intensify in her nerve endings and gather into one throbbing force controlled by his fingertips, a force whose electrifying power she couldn't contain, not for one more instant, not for one more moment.

"Now, Jared!" she cried in anguish, lowering her hips onto his, sliding her legs alongside his. "Now!"

Swiftly both of his hands moved to cup her hips and, holding her in this way, he buried himself inside her. She bit down on her lip, trying to hold back the ultimate pleasure until he was ready, but her body was too full and too desperate with sensation. Flight and capture, fear and longing, reticence and desire—all the ambivalence of the night exploded inside her with terrifying power, sending her senses spiraling into ecstatic madness.

Jared's hands moved in a frantic rhythm over the flesh of her legs, her back, her hips while his body writhed beneath her. Suddenly his fingers ceased their frenzy and the tormented cry "Bianca!" rushed past her ear as she felt the thrust of his energy reach the deepest part of her sexual mystery. Another dark spasm convulsed her body and, turning her head beside his on the pillow, she delved into his ear with a moist tongue, taunting and probing with ardor.

"My God!" he cried out, and thrust his need into her again and yet again until she was sure that in this crucible of sexual awareness and release she would surely die.

Then his hands went gentle and his caress went smooth and she felt her mind transcend the body, floating effortlessly into deep and deepening contentment. Slowly he withdrew himself from her shelter. Rolling both of them to the right, he coaxed her over until her back was against his chest, his knees lifted into hers, the curve of their bodies perfectly fitted to each other's contours.

He lifted the white-gold hair from the back of her neck and spread it out on the pillow they shared. He kissed her softly below the ear. "We're going to keep each other safe and warm . . . always," were the last words she heard him whisper before she drifted into sleep.

Chapter Seven

LIKE a weightless sheath of lavender gauze, early morning light came through the long, wide panels of glass on the east wall of the bedroom. She could see the world of surrounding cliffs, their greenery white-tipped with frost. The world inside whose colors were cinnamon, and saffron, and salmon was warm, deliciously warm and peaceful. Even the oak logs in the hearth were alight with the dancing, warming flames of a fire someone had thoughtfully made.

Appreciatively she snuggled beneath the comforter. A soft smile played on her lips, a deep contentment settled in her soul. Vaguely she was aware of the shower sounds coming from somewhere off to her left. Yawning, she stretched the tips of her toes down to the edge of the mattress, then brought her knees back up again, and wondered what would happen if she spent the entire day in bed, luxuriating in the cool feel of fresh linen against her skin, without once touching a ledger, checking a receipt, tabulating an entry. She closed her eyes and quietly laughed at the thought of such wanton self-indulgence.

When she opened them again, she saw strong legs covered with wiry honey-gold hair planted beside the bed. As she slowly raised her gaze, she saw the rest of a naked, magnificent male body leaning against the bedpost, the cinnamon velour bath towel around his neck drawing attention to an unforgettable face. In his bright eyes she saw her own longing, which the mere sight of him had awakened. It was then that the reality of the previous night crashed in on her, the reality of having shared herself with a man who might have seduced the fool in her that needed him.

As the soft smile disappeared from her lips she reminded herself that there was another reality to contend with as well. There was the reality of their having loved together, the reality of his tenderness, the reality of her feverish surrender. The shadows on her heart had lifted briefly last night, and in that brief light she had given herself up to the pleasure of him. She couldn't, she wouldn't, tarnish the memory with regret.

"At some point you're going to have to get those beautiful lazy bones out of bed," declared Jared with enough sparkle in his eyes to light a fire. "I've had my shower and I'm running your bath water now." At the surprise in her eyes he laughed lightly, bent down, and put a kiss on her mouth, then straightened up again. "Your skin feels like it's been pampered with all those perfumed oils that go with bathing."

She stalled, hesitant to throw back the covers in the morning light. "I left my things in another bedroom."

He shook his head and a few droplets of water spattered her upturned face. "No excuses," he informed her with a hand at the covers. He threw them back with one swift flick of the wrist. "I brought your case over."

He left her no choice but to swing her legs over the side of the bed and get up. With effort she kept her hands from instinctively covering herself and assumed a sexual poise the equal of his. He stood back, the better to appreciate her slender, willowy shape with softening eyes, and she couldn't help noticing the beginnings of change the view evoked in his manly frame.

He stepped forward, filling his hand with her breast, and she put her hands on his forearms to steady herself. Giving her a gentle squeeze, he said gruffly, "I'll fix the coffee while you bathe. We can drink it before the fire when you're finished."

"I won't be long," she said, taking the first step toward the sounds of bubbling water.

"I'll be here," he promised in a low growl and kissed her shoulder when she brushed by him.

Twenty minutes later, refreshed by her bath, Bianca stood at the doorway to the bedroom. She noticed that drapes were now pulled across the glass-paneled wall. On the hearth she saw a coffee tray, and on a wide blanket in front of it was Jared, his back to her, a short saffron robe covering his chest and the upper part of his well-formed legs, which were stretched out in front of him. His skin really was the most attractive shade of golden nutmeg. He sat there utterly still, his hands palms down on either side of his hips, supporting his weight. She wondered what was preoccupying his mind as he stared into the logs sputtering on the grate. Wrapped in the voluminous towel she had found folded on a chair by the tub, she walked toward him, her feet hushed in the sculptured carpet.

"You forgot to bring me my clothes when you brought my case," she admonished him, a shade hesitantly, when she reached his side.

Taken unaware out of his reverie, Jared swung his head around. She thought that unwarranted alarm flashed in his eyes, but before she could be certain, it was replaced by a devilish gleam. "Did I?" he inquired, covering the span of her instep with the warm palm of his hand. "Well then, I'm afraid you'll just have to wear what you've got on until I choose to remedy my omission." His hand sneaked beneath the hem of the towel to smooth the flesh of her calf. "As you can see, I'm as vulnerable as you are."

"Now why do you suppose that doesn't ease my troubled mind?" she asked as she stepped behind his back to reach his right side, feeling his hand trail down her leg as she went.

"You've got me there, baby." He bit his lower lip on a husky laugh. "I can't imagine."

As she knelt down beside him he pushed himself forward to pour the coffee. He put one lump of sugar in hers and a long stream of cream.

"Didn't think you'd be ready for a full breakfast just yet," he said, putting the saucer into her open hands.

"No, not yet," she said and wished her voice were a little stronger. "I have to be awake at least an hour before I can face food."

"Besides," he said softly, lifting his cup to his mouth, "making love on a full tummy's no fun. It's so much better when the hunger of one appetite increases the hunger of the other."

The coffee splashed against her upper lip. She quickly glanced at him above her clattering cup, but his face was perfectly serious.

She cleared her throat and shrugged one naked shoulder. "I thought that the first item on our day's agenda might be doing something mundane—like getting to work before noon."

He made a tsking sound with tongue against teeth. "What priorities, Bianca! After last night, you should be ashamed."

She knelt there in silence, anxiety's little fist seizing her throat. Perhaps she should be ashamed, but not in the way he meant. She remembered last night's ending all too well, and she remembered more. Charles Roper's accusations about Jared's being a contrabandist came back to sit inside her chest like a block of ice, where it chilled the heart that Jared warmed. She felt cold in spite of the hot coffee. Very cold.

Jared swiveled on his hips until he faced her, his back now supported by one of the big chairs that flanked the fireplace. He put his empty cup back in its saucer on the tray. When he raised his knee and rested his arm on top of it, the saffron velour fell open.

Beneath the robe he was naked. She raked a hand through the hair waving on her shoulders. She wet her dry lips with a hesitant tongue and looked up.

The eyes that caught hers were laughing at her. "Finish your coffee, Bianca." His voice was strong, confident like his body. She marveled at the poise. "Then come over here and sit beside me."

Just because she had probably made a serious error in judgment last night didn't mean she should compound her dilemma with yet another this morning. And if she didn't want to make another mistake, she mustn't let her gaze fall from his face to the triangle of hair at the open collar of his robe and from there down to his legs again. But she did. If she valued safety, security, certainty, she had to stay exactly where she was. But she didn't.

She drank a little more from her cup before replacing it in its saucer. Leaning to her side, she deposited it on the tray beside Jared's. Gliding toward him was easy on the smooth blanket. Her thigh rested against the outer line of his.

"Do you want me, Jared?" she asked, a reckless query when she knew she felt both desire and fear next to him. The flame of desire could melt her reserve. It had before. It could again.

He put a hand to her naked shoulder. "Like I've never wanted anything or anyone in my life," he answered steadily. "It shocks me sometimes how much I want you. I think you're remarkable, wonderful, and I need that wonder."

She kept her hands in her lap. "Do you mean as a sexual partner?"

"That too, of course. But I meant as a womanly person. Inside your womanliness, all the smooth pieces of you fit." He leaned forward and nuzzled his face in the warm line of her throat. "I want to be one of those smooth pieces inside your life that fits."

Her heart set up a hammering that was bound to

become insistent. "Is there any reason you think you can't be?"

"Not a one." He kissed her neck. His hand caressed her shoulder, her back. "Can you?"

About five or six, actually, beginning with Denman's implied accusations and ending with Roper's distrust.

If his hand pushed any harder on the towel wrap at her back, it would fall to her waist. What then of Denman's, and Roper's, and her own suspicions? They weren't going to dissolve into vapor as she dissolved into ecstasy. If they were true, she would lose this man who expertly exacted pleasure from her and then gave it back to her threefold. The sensible self in her realized that each act of love she shared with Jared Berenson increased the devastation she would feel at losing him. But her instincts were asking, if she couldn't have him forever, shouldn't she glory in having him now?

A long, rattling ring of the telephone pierced the silence of her dilemma. Jared's hand went still on her back. His brow furrowed with chagrin at the interruption. Another shrill ring followed. And another.

"I suppose I'm going to have to answer that," Jared sighed heavily.

"You probably should," she quickly agreed, resting her cheek for a brief second on his hand as it glided onto her shoulder.

He kissed her shoulder, then her lips, and reluctantly got to his feet to pick up the persistent bedside phone on its sixth ring.

"Berenson here," he spoke into the receiver. As he listened to his caller she noticed the way the muscles of his forearms and his legs tensed. "Benjamin," he asked in a voice considerably tighter than before, "which two drivers?"

Two drivers? The same two who had resigned immediately before Jared was shot? Or two of those accused in the anonymous note of sidelining with

Harvest trucks? Suddenly all the reality that she had forced out of her mind in order to steal a few hours of lovemaking pushed its unwelcome way back into the forefront of her brain.

"What in the hell would make him draw a conclusion like that?" Jared demanded as though he wasn't ready to cancel out the conclusion himself. "If he slipped up in that way, he's a damn poor agent, or an agent who doesn't care anymore if his cover's been blown."

She shook her head, unable to make sense of his responses without Benjamin's half of the conversation.

"I'm the only one with a key to that elevator and I know it was on my key chain last night," Jared answered, clamping the receiver between his ear and his shoulder while he tied the sash of his robe more securely.

The conversation and Jared's peculiar tension shoved out the implicit trust she had almost surrendered the moment before. With each of Jared's heated and curt replies returned the memory of last night's disclosures, of which she had said nothing to Jared, and her memory of last night's assault on the gallery, the terror of which she had tried to forget in the security of his arms. But there was to be no forgetting, was there?

"No," Jared insisted for the second time. "Hold off contacting the police for at least two hours. I don't want them near the premises until I've had a chance to have a look at things for myself."

Why, Jared? Because you've got to conceal evidence of a crime you're afraid they'll discover? A crime you committed?

He replaced the receiver and then took the few long strides back to her. He bent at the knees in front of her, balancing his weight on the balls of his feet.

"That was Benjamin," he said.

"Yes, I heard you call him by name."

"He wanted me to know about a conversation he overheard."

I've got one to tell you about myself.

"Two Harvest truck drivers, Martínez and Schmidt, pulled in this morning from their route across the border into Mexico. While they watched the produce being unloaded, Benjamin heard Martínez say he was positive that one of the two drivers recently hired is an undercover federal agent."

For a moment she studied her hands lying in her lap, the painted fingernails bright against the velour towel. Then she looked up. "Why would Martínez leap to that assumption, unless, of course, he's paranoid, or has had reason to suspect criminal activity to begin with?"

Those impossibly curly lashes dipped, and when they rose, Jared gave her a blindingly direct stare. She hadn't been as subtle as she had tried to be.

"Not so unusual or paranoid, Bianca, when you consider that every employee has heard the details of the shooting and the burglaries. Some may have even heard and repeated Denman's theory of my involvement in international crime. Why wouldn't any one of them begin to see police in every corner, even if he had no reason to suspect I was engaged in foul play?"

Her heart was heavy in her chest but she didn't look away when she answered, "You could be right, of course."

He put out a hand, his fingers kneading the flesh of her bare shoulder. "Tell me," he asked earnestly, "do you think that in time I'll ever get accustomed to the fact that the beautiful woman who makes love to me one moment can in the next accuse me of unnamed crimes with the same delectable eyes and lips?"

She stared at him as long as she could, but in the end she dropped her gaze and tried not to mourn the loss of that soul-filling passion that had been promised just moments before the telephone had rung. "Is that all that Benjamin called you about?"

He pulled his hand away from her shoulder and got to his feet. "No," he said in a hard voice. "He also reported that the door opening onto the corridor that leads to the executive suite elevator was unlocked when he checked it this morning. I'm the only person who has a key. And I haven't unlocked that door in close to a month. He thinks I need to come down to check out the situation."

Before Denman and Barber get there. I know.

"If you want to wait for me here, I should be back in about three hours or I can drop you off at your place on my way down to the office—if you want to go home."

She leaned back her head to look him in the face and said quietly, "I'm going with you."

"There's no need," he declined her offer abruptly. "Whoever got in by that door no doubt got what he was after and without leaving a trace—except, of course, the careless failure to lock up."

She would not let his tone deter her from her resolve. "Nevertheless, I'm going with you. I'll just change into the jeans and pullover I wore out here yesterday."

"I'm touched by your concern"—he inclined his head as he leveled his sarcasm at her—"if that is what is prompting your interest."

"Concern for you and a determination to find out who has been after me."

Jared's eyes were half-shuttered. His lips were as close to a thin line as their sensuous fullness allowed. His arms crossed in front of his chest announced the distance growing between them. "You don't lie very well, Bianca," he accused her in a low voice. "You want to come because you don't trust me to tell the police the same version that you would tell about what happened to you on the gallery last night."

She fought the constriction in her throat well enough. "Well, of course, you couldn't tell them what I had experienced. After all—"

"Spare me an explanation of the individuality in human experience," he said, summarily dismissing her evasion with an impatient gesture of his hand. "You want to be there so you can check me out and catch me in the middle of a lie. Isn't that it, Bianca? To see if I'm going down to my office to conceal criminal evidence before Denman and Barber can find it?"

He had her. It was all those things. Concern, distrust, determination to find out the real identity of her attacker, even if it were he. "My motivation, when it comes to you, is never simple, Jared."

He planted his feet apart and impaled her with a dark glare. "Not exactly the soothing denial I had hoped for."

"Nor the one I wish I could give."

A hush fell between them and she fought the urge to lay her weary head in her hands.

"In time—I tell myself, in time, Bianca, you'll both love me and trust me. But this mess could be so much easier for us if you could only stop struggling with yourself and give me both your love and trust *now.*"

For that, she didn't have an answer.

"Can you imagine, Mr. Jared, undercover agents here!" exploded Benjamin as soon as Bianca and Jared stepped into the foyer where he had been pacing the floor, anticipating their arrival. He fixed Bianca with a look of outrage. "Like *we* had done something needing investigation! When all along something's being done to *him,* to Mr. Jared! You'd think those policemen and sheriffs could see that, now wouldn't you?" He shook his head and his fist at the imbecility of the absent culprits, the keys on his belt loop jingling with his gesture. "Seems to me that the police have made a mighty mess of things and the situation is just getting worse. Shootings, burglaries here and at your place, too, Ms. Cavender, and now another break-in." He made a growling sound in his throat.

"It's too bad, Benjamin," Bianca posed quietly,

"that the police won't take your loyalty to Mr. Jared as proof positive of his innocence." *And too bad that I can't take it either.*

Behind Benjamin stood Jared, taut lines around his mouth, a deep crease between his brows. She wished she could better read his reaction to the supposition that he and his company were under FBI investigation.

"You're right there, Ms. Cavender." The older man nodded his head. "I sure could give them a piece of my mind. The very idea that Mr. Jared is a criminal is preposterous. Anyone who works for him could tell you that."

Not everyone, Benjamin. Not Charles Roper. "What about Martínez and Schmidt?" she asked. "Could you make a guess of how they reacted to the presence of an FBI agent?"

"I don't have to make a guess. I went up to them and asked them!"

"You did?"

"God bless America, you bet I did!"

"And what did they say?"

"They thought Mr. Jared had given information that made the police think certain drivers were involved in something criminal."

"They must have been pissed off as hell!" exclaimed Jared.

"Well, to tell the truth, they were pretty offended," Benjamin admitted lamely, as though he felt he owed the boss an apology. "And then they thought if someone had given evidence against you, and it was *you,* not them, being investigated, the police were far wide of the bull's-eye they were hoping to hit." He added with raised brows and lowered chin in Bianca's direction, "Martínez and Schmidt had better leap to the boss's defense, after all he's done for their families."

"Ms. Cavender and I are going to take a look at the door you say was left unlocked, Benjamin," Jared interrupted what might have become an explanation of that last remark. Putting a hand on Bianca's elbow, he added, "We'll take a look around at a few other things as well."

"Right. I'll stay on this floor until you tell me it's time to call the cops." Benjamin uttered the last word as if it were a distasteful syllable.

The long corridor branched off to the right of the foyer she had walked with Jared before. On the evening they had discovered a burglar in his office, they had taken the stairs at the end of the corridor. She now realized that there was a door at the end of the hall, no more than three feet from the foot of the stairs, that she hadn't noticed that night, or on subsequent visits.

She watched as Jared pulled out a handkerchief from his coat pocket to cover the doorknob. "Benjamin said he had his gloves on when he first opened it this morning. I thought I'd take the precaution even though I don't really think anyone would leave fingerprints behind to be discovered."

Opening the door wide, he waited for her to precede him, but she was suddenly wary and deeply conscious of how alone they were. Irrational, wasn't it, to spend the night with a man and then to fear him on the following day? Jared was right, she was struggling with her own unresolved contradictions, unsettled ambivalence. Even now, she felt a powerful tension between two equally strong compulsions. Half of her wanted to get the hell out of the building before she discovered something terrible, and the other half wanted to be around when Jared or the police discovered whatever terrible evidence the building concealed.

With its burgundy carpet and the rich woods of occasional tables, the hall looked like the plush reception room on the top floor. "Is this the only elevator leading to the executive suite?"

"Yes," he replied, slowly looking around for any signs of disturbance. "It goes from the basement directly to the executive offices on the fifteenth floor. Obviously, it's far more convenient than having to use the stairs after leaving the public elevator, but I closed it off after I was shot."

She took the first steps into the hall. "Why?"

"Since I had already complained to any number of people about the elevator's creaky ride and faulty switches, I thought someone could seize upon it as a good way to commit a crime and have it look like an accident. You know, elevator containing intended victim plunges from fifteenth floor to basement, and he dies—tragic accident. So I closed it off, saying it was temporarily out of commission."

She could see one light glowing at the end of the hall. Below it was the elevator, a beautiful early-twentieth-century contraption of cast bronze doors, its intricately patterned lacework featuring flowers and foliage. "It's a shame not to use it," she said, her voice sounding a hollow note as it bounced off the sides of the corridor.

"Pedro Elizondo has found a Mexican craftsman who will be here next month to work on it."

She shivered and shoved her hands deeper into the pockets of her tweed jacket; the corridor was as inadequately heated as it was lit.

"Cold?"

As cold as your voice. As cold as my heart. "Quite." Good thing she had thought to take the jacket out to Cross Mountain with her yesterday. The jeans and sweater and boots would never have been sufficient protection against the arctic chill that prevailed in this eerie wing of the building.

"Sorry, I had Benjamin shut off the vents when I decided to lock the entrance. The elevator ought to be even worse."

"Great." Her booted feet abruptly halted a few feet from the elevator door at the muttered sounds behind her. She turned around to look at Jared. "What did

you say?" Did she imagine menace in the play of
shadow and light across his face?

"Jumpy, aren't you?"

She shook her head in a tight pattern. "Just cold."

He put a hand on her shoulder. She was acutely
aware of its warm weight pressing into her. "All I said
is that I can't make any sense of it. Why would someone go to the trouble of making a key for this door unless it was to use the elevator? And why use the
elevator unless it was—"

"—to move easily from floor to floor without being
seen?"

He shook his head. "It creaks something dreadful.
When it's in operation, there's not a man in this part
of the building who wouldn't hear it."

"Then because it's a convenient way to—"

"—to hurt someone?"

She shrugged her shoulders. His fingers inched
their way toward the back collar of her coat. "Or to
move something heavy."

"Like what?" he inquired in a tight voice while his
hand slipped alongside her throat. "A dead body?"

She shivered again. She was sure her lips were
turning blue. "Thanks for the image, Jared." *Just
what my faltering heart needed.* "I was thinking of a
safe, or boxed documents, like account books, actually."

"I wonder" was all he said as he rubbed his thumb
into the base of her neck, his fingers into the waving
fall of her hair, then dropped his hand altogether,
leaving her a trifle breathless. He turned on his heel
and his long jean-clad legs covered the distance between themselves and the elevator. "Let's have a look
inside, shall we?" he asked as the pressure of his fingertips on a wall switch caused the door to slide open.
A gust of colder air hit the corridor and her chest.

Against her better judgment she took the steps toward him, silent apprehension gnawing away at her
nerves.

"After you," he said with a expansive sweep of his arm.

She stepped into the ancient contraption, the light click of her heels followed by Jared's behind her. She looked up at the ceiling and down at the floor. What could they hope to find? They didn't even know what they were looking for. At the first grating sound she whirled around. Jared had pulled the brass doors of their cage shut.

"We might as well take the ride our intruder took, see what he saw," he offered.

"Why not?" she managed to return with nonchalance, though her voice was nearly strangled by her closing throat.

She was inundated by an overwhelming sense of isolation, though at one level she recognized her response was irrational. All she could think about was that they were separated from the rest of the world, she and Jared, locked in the dark paneled cabin. She felt blood rush to her head and quickly glanced at Jared's face. Though it continued to tell her nothing, she couldn't dismiss the feeling that danger was closer than ever before, closing in on them now. She felt horribly trapped by forces she couldn't name, by her own lack of understanding. Desperately she wanted out of that cage.

"Why the apprehension, Bianca?" he asked, his finger poised to press the button marked fifteen. "The ride will be a little jerky, but nothing to make the blood run cold." He pressed the button. Nothing happened. "That is, if we can get it started."

"Perhaps we ought to abandon this investigation to the police," she tendered as he pressed a second time to no avail.

Jared's face was hidden from her as he studied the panel of buttons, but she heard his voice clearly enough. "You know, Bianca, I hate it when you act as if you really believed I was going to hurt you."

Her stomach muscles tightened painfully. He

swung his face around, but for the life of her she couldn't read the dark expression that twisted one corner of his mouth and raised a brow.

Turning away from her mute admission, he pressed number fifteen a third time. The cage laboriously creaked on its hinges and began a halting ascent as Bianca literally shivered at the possibility of reaching the fifteenth floor landing only to come crashing down to the first at a mortally high speed.

A peculiar sound reached her ears above the creaking and grating of ancient bronze and steel. She jumped and looked up to the ceiling of glossy wood. She heard the noise again, an erratic thumping sound, low and deep as though something precariously balanced were rocking to and fro above them. She shut out the image of a dead body that immediately sprang to her stimulated imagination. When she opened her eyes again, both their attentions were riveted to the trapdoor directly overhead.

Unexpectedly the elevator lurched to the right, she hit the rail behind her, and the trapdoor fell open with such force it slammed up against the ceiling in an arc. Bam! Bam! Instantly she went rigid with fright at the inevitable, intuitively apprehending the worst. Abruptly a man's arm dropped through the opening, and while she watched it dangle back and forth, like a pendulum announcing the hour of doom, she screamed.

She could hear the cry curdling in her throat, rancid with fright, and still she could not stop screaming. It was a terrifying sound yanked up out of her guts and forcibly ripped out of her throat. She felt the brass rail bite into her spine with sharp pain as she slammed into the paneled wall, and still she could not stop screaming.

Jared's fingers bit through the fabric of her coat. "Stop it!" he commanded her brutally and just as brutally shook her without mercy. "Stop it!" he yelled again, his face looming above her transformed into unfamiliar fierceness.

Abruptly his fingers ceased their merciless digging into the flesh of her arms. Wrapping one arm around her in a rough embrace, he pulled down the back of her head against his chest with a harshness and swiftness that knocked the breath out of her.

"Stop it, Bianca!"

But it was a quiet shout now, and as suddenly as she had begun to scream, she was mute, silent except for the mad gallop of her heartbeat against the rhythm thundering in his chest. As suddenly as she had gone rigid with fright, she now went limp, her breath coming in short, uneven gasps muffled by his coat.

Gradually sensory awareness returned. The palms of her hands were punctured from the way her nails had bitten into the flesh. Her leg muscles ached from having been locked in place. Her face burned from the contact against his wool jacket. She supposed that it would have felt worse had he slapped her to bring her to her senses.

"It's Charles Roper, isn't it?" she whispered, her voice a quivering testimonial to the fright that was still on a slow boil inside her.

But she didn't need Jared's answer. She knew it was Charles Roper. Hadn't he accused Jared of smuggling contraband across the Texas-Mexico border? Wasn't this the way Jared had avenged the accusation? *Then why did he take the chance on my discovering the body?* she asked herself, and then answered, *Because I'm his next victim.*

Had Roper been the one who broke into Jared's office the week following the shooting in order to discover the boss's schedule for the transportation of illegal goods? Had Roper gone on to inform the city police and the federal officials? Was it Jared who had tried to harm her on the gallery because she had overheard Roper's accusation? Was it Jared, not Roper, who had broken into her office that night to . . . *To do what, for pity's sake?* She couldn't think straight anymore. Nothing made sense.

"Are you mad?" Jared demanded as he roughly pushed her away, his hands, anchored on her shoulders, shoving her against the paneling.

She studied the rage and disbelief that contorted his features and realized that she had spoken aloud all the questions that had silently plagued her heart.

"I don't know." Each syllable was a tortured gasp of breath. *Dear God, how I love you and I don't even know who you are.* Desperately she searched for some light of innocence behind the rage that flashed in his eyes.

"So I staged my own shooting, Bianca?" he asked sarcastically without expecting an answer. "What could I be so involved in that I need to drag you into it and then knock you off for being involved?" A hand slid up the back of her neck, fingers digging in her scalp. "Did I carve out a place for you in my heart only to rip you out of my life? God!" he exclaimed, his voice a deadly whisper now. "You can really be a witch, sometimes."

Chill, brittle silence crackled between them while he wrapped the long curling strands of her platinum hair around his fingers. Taking her utterly by surprise, he brought his head down swiftly, but when his lips touched hers, they touched her with incredible, heartbreaking gentleness, and when his lashes fluttered against her cheek, she thought a drop of moisture touched her cheeks as well. But she couldn't be sure, and when he raised his head to glare at her, she could see no telltale sign of sadness in his bright eyes.

"Pull yourself together," he said brusquely. "The police will no doubt expect sensible answers."

Chapter Eight

UNFORTUNATELY, Bianca didn't have any sensible answers to give the police. How could she when she couldn't see any pattern in the events that had taken over her life, or any way out of the feelings that had taken over her heart. And all of this confusion in the face of death made her utterly miserable, utterly weighted down with grief for all that had been, all that would never be.

Fortunately, Jared, watching from the door of his office as a police team lifted Charles Roper's body from the elevator dome to a stretcher without disturbing the chalk marks that outlined it, had had answers enough for two.

"Ms. Cavender," Denman asked, taking his cigar out of his fleshy lips as he walked from the doorway to where she sat on the leather chair facing Jared's desk, "is there anything you'd like to add to Mr. Berenson's description of the events between his receiving Benjamin's phone call and finding Roper's body?"

Bianca shook her head, the movement adding to her blinding headache. "No. I can't think of any detail he left out."

"Astute powers of observation, your Mr. Berenson," said Denman with a malevolent smile. "Almost as if he expected to be quizzed on the crime when he got here."

Honestly, the man was as obtuse as he was unpleasant. What in the hell did he think had been going on in their lives recently that they had time to think of much else? "Considering the events of the past few weeks," Bianca said tightly, "and Benjamin's phone call this morning, I don't think there's anything odd about it."

Denman grunted at her defensive explanation and looked at the subject of his remarks. "Too bad his antenna wasn't tuned up last night when you thought you were being attacked on his gallery. We might have been able to find evidence of an attempted crime had we been called right away." He shoved his cigar back into his mouth.

She wasn't convinced he could have found a thing but neither was she absolutely certain about Jared's motivation in not alerting the police, so she asked a question of her own. "What connection can you make between the conversation I overheard between Charles Roper and Martin Goerner last night and Roper's death this morning?"

"Charles must have gotten into the building to find proof of the suspicions he discussed last night with Martin." It was Jared who had spoken, having come up behind Denman while the investigator thoughtfully chewed his cigar. "Evidence which, if I were guilty of crime, I wouldn't want anyone to see. Right, investigator?"

Denman glared at him from the small dark beads that passed for eyes below his brows. "I reckon that's a distinct possibility."

"But as of this moment, you can't be sure that Charles's death was anything but an accident, and, should you decide otherwise, as I overheard Ms. Cavender point out to you, I've got an alibi for my whereabouts last night."

Of course you do! Why hadn't it occurred to her before? Jared had had someone take care of Roper at the exact time she was providing him with an alibi! She heard whirring sounds in her ears, felt a queasiness in the pit of her stomach. How could she look into his face, remember what had passed in love between them last night, and doubt his sincerity? Maybe she didn't have to doubt it. Maybe he was the kind of man who could genuinely desire her and in the same breath have no scruples about using her.

Denman wasn't impressed. "Convenient, I'd say."

Jared wasn't intimidated. "And true."

"We're about finished here," Lieutenant Barber called out as he advanced into the room. "My immediate report will show that Charles Roper, having mistakenly walked into the empty space where he had expected the elevator cabin to be, appears to have died in the fall." He looked first at Bianca and then a bit longer at Jared. "But if the medical examiner's report shows that a blow to the back of the head caused that purple bruise we found on the body, then homicide is going to go looking for a murderer."

Bianca involuntarily put a hand to the back of her own neck and tried to restrain a shiver. Jared, she noticed, looked nonplussed by the animosity Denman and Barber almost palpably exuded.

In fact, he immediately responded, "The sooner the better, Lieutenant Barber. When homicide apprehends the criminal, we will all sleep safely in our beds."

Barber thrust a crumpled white sheet of paper at Jared. "We found this note clutched in the victim's hand. Does the name Villanueva mean anything to you? Does Harvest Enterprises employ anyone by the name?"

As Jared snapped the edges between his fingers to straighten out the paper he creased his brow in concentration and then slowly shook his head. He handed the note to Bianca and then looked up at Barber again. "Right offhand I can't say that we do, but I'd have to check the personnel records to give you a definite answer."

"Make that as soon as possible," Denman growled.

"Not an instant's delay, investigator," Jared smoothly assured him with a mocking smile while Bianca fervently wished he wouldn't make things any more difficult by baiting the humorless man who held their futures in his hand.

"And you, Ms. Cavender?" inquired the police lieutenant, hiding his skepticism none too well, "can we also count on your cooperation?"

She looked up from the note on which someone had scrawled the Spanish surname. "Naturally," she said, too miserable to be offended or frightened by his suggestion that cooperation was the last thing he expected from her.

"Good. I'll expect to hear from you, Mr. Berenson, tomorrow, by which time we will have also spoken to Martin Goerner." Taking the note from Bianca's fingers and putting it in his pocket, he moved his loose-limbed frame toward the door, followed by Denman. "By the way," he said, turning toward the two of them, "we've located the two drivers who gave notice three days before you were shot, Mr. Berenson."

Bianca was sure Barber enjoyed the theatrics of his parting shot as he ever so casually informed them, "The most we can glean from their stories thus far is that they wanted to quit because they suspected that they were going to be forced to get involved in transporting contraband."

Jared's face, when she quickly glanced to check it, didn't reveal a trace of what he was really thinking, but she was sure hers had nearly frozen with horror.

"I wonder," Jared spoke with his usual steady confidence, "who planted such an idea in their heads."

"I've wondered the same thing myself," Barber returned. "And I also wonder if it's not time for you to start looking for a very good lawyer."

Having driven her home in uncomfortable silence, Jared brought the Porsche to an abrupt halt in her drive. Before she could say a word, he was out of the car swift as an arrow, coming around to the passenger's side to open her door.

"I want to talk to you, Bianca," he said brusquely, his voice brooking no argument as he looked down at her surprised face.

She swallowed hard. Dear God, but she didn't want to deal with the determination that squared his jaw and ignited his eyes. "Perhaps this isn't the best time to talk, Jared. We've both done a lot of that—and a lot of listening—this morning," she resisted him as she swiveled her legs out the open door. "Maybe the best thing we can do is take a little time away from each other to sort things out."

Extending his hand, he pulled her out of the bucket seat and slammed the car door shut behind her. "There's a helluva lot more left to say," he returned. Leaving her to accept his resolve as best she could, he went to the trunk of the car to get her things. "I'm not particularly fond of the conclusions you come to when you sort things without me," he said harshly when he returned to her side. He took a firm grasp of her elbow and began to guide her up the brick walk to her front porch steps.

"It's already so late in the day, Jared," she insisted, even though she began to see she might not have a chance against his obstinate will. "Couldn't it wait, at least until tomorrow?"

"No."

They stood at her door and glared at each other. She almost hated him for the powerful personality that came pouring out of every part of him, for the conviction, the undeniable virility, that emanated from his body. And loved him for it. That was the grief of it. She loved him—too.

"What's so important that it can't wait?" she demanded, angry with him for his ability to weaken her resolve, and angrier with herself for letting him.

"You and me, that's what."

"I don't believe that the two of us together are much

of a priority just now," said the fool in her that couldn't accept defeat as she reached into her purse for her keys.

"Liar." He took the keys out of her hands and opened her door. He ushered her across the threshold and followed immediately behind her. "I'll take coffee, black and hot, thank you."

Twenty minutes later he was pacing the floor of her living room and she was still trying to accustom herself to the events of the last twenty-four hours which, like a high tide, had trapped her in its vicious undertow. From the sofa she watched him. Holding his coffee cup in one hand, the other stuffed in his back hip pocket, he stopped to study the photographs on the mantel—one of a fair-haired young man, and the other of a laughing bride and groom. Bianca suddenly realized that those precious moments of the past had fully been superseded by the present. How could it be otherwise when the emotional currents Jared had swept her into left no room for any others?

She looked down on the brass table top at the paper where Jared had written a chronological sequence of events since that fateful morning-night of late November. On the second sheet he had tried to discover a pattern by writing down the details that all the incidents held in common. Thus far, the only pattern she could see was the pattern which Denman and Barber believed in. And Charles Roper.

"Let's concede the possibility," Jared said as he pulled his attention away from the pictures, "that Charles Roper was correct in a few of his assumptions, assumptions held by the police as well."

"Like the fact that Harvest Enterprises is acting as a front for a scheme to transport illegal goods into, or out of, Mexico?"

"Right. And let's assume that the American contact in Mexico is connected with organized crime over there. Then, federal and city authorities, aware of the operation—"

"—possibly from information Charles Roper supplied—"

"—could have planted an undercover agent to work as one of our drivers, as Martínez suspects, in order to verify that info and catch the criminals red-handed."

She took a sip from her cup. "It seems to fit the scenario."

"But it doesn't necessarily follow that I'm the mastermind behind the operation." He made do without her agreement. "I could have been shot with a twenty-two-caliber 'Saturday Night Special', not by a smuggling competitor to warn me off desirable territory"—he stood behind the sofa she faced—"nor by a partner in crime who Denman thinks I double-crossed, but, instead, by the smuggler himself. Maybe he needed me out of the way for four or five days so he could use Harvest trucks to transport the biggest shipment of smuggled goods he'd ever received."

"But why did the criminal break into your office four days after you were shot, when it would have been safer to break in when you were incapacitated in the hospital?"

Jared creased his brow. "Suppose it wasn't the criminal mastermind who broke into my office. Suppose it was Charles trying to find evidence of the smuggling operation. The shooting just reinforced suspicions that had been planted long before."

"And who broke into my office?"

"Charles must have done that as well because he wanted to discover if I was using you to fix the books."

She had thought the very same thing herself. But it bothered her that Jared was so quick to offer this explanation. "Where would Charles Roper get the idea that the books were being falsely adjusted if they weren't? Who fed him that kind of information? A comptroller just doesn't come up with that out of the blue."

"I can only assume that the sources he told Martin he had were the truckers who walked off the job. They had probably confided their suspicions to him, based on some pretty good evidence, or terrific instincts—if the shooting, the burglaries, the attempt on your life last night, and Charles's death this morning are anything to go by. The truckers's actions followed by my being shot must have been fuel for Charles's fears."

"So Charles leaped to the conclusion that you were behind whatever scheme was brewing."

"Or assumed it had to be someone with enough influence in the corporation to run an operation involving both trucks and drivers. Why not start at the top with the holding company's chief executive officer?"

"And check out the books to see how the chief could be managing it?"

"Of course. Even you believed I had adjusted them and then ordered your audit to cover myself." It was a statement delivered without a trace of emotion. He ran a hand through the hair that had fallen on his forehead. "If Charles could have seen that Harvest Enterprises books had been adjusted, then he would have known for sure that the profiteering smuggler had to be me. Anybody else would need to conceal his haul by laundering his *own* accounts, not *mine.*"

At least he was right about that. "I don't understand why Charles was obsessed with becoming a scapegoat for a smuggling scheme."

Jared emptied his cup. "Me neither, except that Charles has been extremely nervous ever since my father handed over the day-to-day operation of the company to me following his heart attack five years ago." Jared suddenly looked very tired. "Maybe he got it into his head that because of our differences I wanted to replace him, even though I've never considered such a plan. A good corporation thrives on differences at the top."

"What exactly did you and Charles differ about?"

"About what he calls my 'aggressive willingness' to acquire smaller concerns even when a high risk is involved, aggression almost always supported by people like Martin Goerner, but not always by the conservative members of the board. Perhaps Charles believed my batting average on those high-risk moves couldn't be as high as my reports to the board showed it to be."

She remembered Roper's comment to Goerner that, unlike others in the company, he was not a gambling man. "Could Charles have thought you were covering those business gambles with an outside source of income?"

"Possibly. But I'm not. I never gamble what Harvest can't recover."

I wonder. If Charles was right about the gambling losses and the smuggling ring to cover them, then the person who killed him is you, Jared. And that makes you the person who tried to hurt me last night on the gallery.

Thinking wasn't taking her anywhere she wanted to go. She wished she could pull in her arms and legs and roll herself into a tight, protective shell. She didn't want to know any more. She was tired and heartbroken. When she opened her eyes, Jared was standing immediately beside her, on his face a look of tired defeat that wrung her heart. Deep sorrow at her distrust and her suspicions burned in the brightness of his eyes. She could have wept.

"I don't think you really believe that I am guilty of any of this." His rich voice was heavy with sadness. "If that were so, you could never have been so completely mine when we made love to each other last night."

He touched the truth but she wanted to avoid being touched in that way. "Jared," she whispered above the constriction in her throat, "right now all my emotions are so tightly interwoven with each other, how can I be sure—how can you be sure?—that my desire for you isn't stimulated by fear, or loneliness, by the peculiar circumstances of our first meeting which made me link you with—"

"—your dead husband?" He finished her lengthy rationalization for her in a passionless voice. "Let me take out the dagger, Bianca. The heart is already bleeding."

She stared up at the naked emotion she saw in his eyes, heard in his voice, and blinked back the moisture collecting inside the lids of her eyes. She swallowed down the first words that came to her, a petition for his forgiveness. She beat down the desire to use a gentle hand and a tender kiss to smooth away the lines of sorrow on the face she loved.

"But it could be true, Jared," she insisted, though she knew it wasn't. Something in her, tight and hard, just wouldn't let it go.

"You made love to *me,* Bianca. It was *my* body that gave you pleasure. It was to *my* body you offered pleasure. I hope to God you're not lying to yourself about this the way you are trying to lie to me."

She looked down on her hands that were not doing such a good job of balancing the cup and saucer in her lap. She couldn't give up the struggle to sustain her distrust even when, *especially* when everything about him beckoned her to jettison all her reservations and accept the truth as he gave it to her.

He sat down beside her and, taking the blue cup from her unsteady hands, placed it beside his on the brass table. She could feel his hand settle along the back of her neck. "I love you, Bianca. I love you completely with all my heart. I loved you from the moment I opened my eyes and saw you beside my hospital bed. I loved you even when I falsely suspected that *you* might have tried to set *me* up for the gunman. Can't you at least grant me that in return? Can't you at least admit right now that you love me, even though you're scared to death that I'm guilty of crime, even murder?"

She knew herself to be a fool, but as she turned into
the curve of his arm she couldn't lie to him. "I love
you as deeply as I can without trust."

He put his face against hers. He must have felt the
tears fall on her cheek. "Then I'll have to be satisfied
with that, won't I?" She felt the flutter of his eye-
lashes against her skin. He gently pushed her away
from him and, picking up his jacket off the sofa, made
his way to the door. As he was about to close it behind
him he turned around. "One last thing. Rake your
mind for any allusion you might have heard last night
to someone named Villanueva. That name could hold
a more important clue than we realize."

It was three o'clock in the morning and she was still
unable to sleep. Having abandoned her bed in frustration, Bianca paced back and forth across her living
room floor, the hem of her sapphire robe swishing
against her ankles, the fall of silver-blond hair swishing on her shoulders and against the finely drawn
lines of her face.

Time and again she searched the scribbled notes of
outlined evidence Jared had left behind on the coffee
table for a new interpretation that would exonerate
him. And each time that she failed to find it, she returned to pacing the floor or looking dejectedly out the
window on the cold night.

What would she do, she wondered, if the final evidence did in fact condemn Jared Berenson? Could she
bear a second loss? Pressing her forehead against the
cold pane, she felt the weight of her misery like a
stone in her chest and a pressure building in her head.
Her mental wrestling gave her no peace. She had to
stop herself from trying to work it out, resign herself
to accepting the evidence they had—whoever it con-
demned. And yet, if only she could find proof of his innocence, or evidence that would . . .

Pealing sounds spiraling up the staircase startled
her. From the insistent rhythm of the notes, she as-

sumed that someone had probably been pressing her doorbell for some time while she had been caught up in her mental convolutions. She quickly glanced at the mantel clock. Who in God's name would be at her doorstep at three-fifteen A.M.?

The police! Dear God, something must have happened to Jared! She knew it. An unreasonable fear worked its way around her heart but she made her legs take her to the door, her feet flying down the staircase to the deadbolt lock and the safety chain. As soon as the metal chain jingled in her hesitant hands, the chimes stopped ringing and a voice yelled:

"It's all right, Bianca. It's me. Open up."

Quickly disengaging the chain and slipping the deadbolt back into place, she pulled the door into the foyer. Jared Berenson, his hair mildly disheveled, his bright, intelligent eyes rimmed with darker circles than she ever remembered having seen there before, stood on the doorstep. She saw the determined set of his jaw and the firm line of his sensuous mouth. The very sight of him dressed in casual cords and a bulky cable-knit sweater beneath a leather jacket, much as he had been on the night she had first seen him, pulled at her heart.

"You're safe!" she exclaimed, not able to disguise the relief that rushed over her. She was more successful in forcing down the impulse to beg his forgiveness for her mind's infidelity over the last few hours since she had seen him.

"For now," he said, apparently puzzled by her reaction, then understanding widened his eyes. "Did I frighten you?" he asked with concern.

"Yes," she admitted, a laugh of self-mockery lurking in her breathy voice. "Wouldn't you be frightened by a three-fifteen ring of your doorbell? I thought the police were here to tell me something dreadful had happened to you."

"I'm sorry," he said quietly, and stepped across her

threshold, taking his welcome for granted even now in spite of the distrust that had marked their last good-bye. "I didn't think of that. I just assumed you wouldn't be able to sleep any more than I could, so I never thought about the time."

She held the collar of her robe up against her throat, warding off the rush of chilling wind that had pushed its way into the foyer, and shut the door behind him. Still a bit dizzy with the vestiges of subsiding anxiety, she leaned against the door and looked directly up at him. "It's all right. You're safe." *That's all that matters.* "I tried to sleep," she acknowledged, "but I couldn't."

With a knowing smile for all the emotions she held in check, he opened his arms. "Come here, Bianca," he ordered in a voice smooth as velvet.

And she walked right into the voice and the arms and let them enfold her with warmth. He bent his head down to hers and kissed the gleaming halo of her hair. Putting his thumb and index finger below her chin, he lifted her face for a soft, tender kiss on her lips.

"I'm sorry I frightened you," he whispered, then released her face and held her body close against his. For a moment she let herself hold him as well.

It was a moment of silent understanding she would always treasure. What difference did it make if he had done something illegal when she would continue to love him in spite of it? At this moment she knew in her heart of hearts that whatever her lover had done, he could not have deliberately killed Charles Roper nor would he ever deliberately hurt her.

"I've worked hard on the name Villanueva in the last twelve hours since I left you," he said softly as he combed her hair away from her face with his gentle fingers.

She pulled her face away from his chest. "And you've come up with something?"

He stepped a few inches back but he left both arms

wrapped around her waist. "I think that Charles must have written the name on the sheet of paper he died clutching in his hand. But I don't think it's the surname of any employee, or anyone else, for that matter." She waited with raised brows, not knowing where his thoughts were taking him. "I don't think it's one word. It's two. I think it's the name of a small village in the northeastern Mexican state of Tamaulipas."

"A village?" She flattened her palm against his chest and took one step back. "What makes you think that?"

He shook his head. "It's just a hunch. When I couldn't find any employee by that name, and my calls to Pedro and José didn't unearth any business associate, I took out a detailed map of Mexico, and looking over the Harvest truck route, I discovered the village name. The route a smuggler would have to follow from there to the Texas border is not very different from the regularly scheduled route for our drivers."

Releasing her, he reached into his jacket. He unfolded a map and walked over to the credenza. She followed him and, when he laid the map out on the japanned surface, bent down to peer at the area the size of a half-dollar which he had circled in green. His finger pointed to print which read "Villa Nueva."

"As you can see, Villa Nueva is located approximately forty kilometers to the west of one of the two farms in the Elmante region which Harvest owns and from which it imports most of its Mexican produce."

"Do you think the illegal goods are exchanged there?" she hazarded a guess.

He nodded his head. "If Charles was correct in assuming that illegal goods were being smuggled."

"The very presence of an FBI undercover agent at

the company, which neither Barber nor Denman denies, seems to bear out that possibility."

He folded the map and put it back in his pocket. "Because of that possibility I'm going to leave for Mexico tonight in order to check out the situation."

She blinked her eyes, then opened them wide. "But you can't do that, Jared."

"On the contrary, Bianca. I have to."

"If you've figured this out, so will the police." Putting a hand on his arm, she tried to convince him. "Let the people trained in apprehending criminals take care of it."

He gave her a sad smile. "Wrong, sweetheart. Dead wrong. At the rate the authorities are proceeding with this case, I could turn out to be the scapegoat Charles was sure he was going to be."

She was furious with him for taking his safety so lightly. "And looked what happened to Charles for trying to unearth the problem by himself!"

For a moment or two his obstinacy battled her concern in quiet warfare. The image of that dead body, she mused, must have flashed across his mind as clearly as it did her own.

"Harvest trucks are scheduled to pick up produce tomorrow night, Bianca. If they are actually being used to transport contraband, then I have to get to Mexico before the next exchange takes place." Jared decreased his volume and his vehemence. "I want this entire matter settled *before,* not after I'm indicted and convicted in federal district court for crimes I did not commit."

What could she say against that kind of logic when in fact the investigative talent of Denman and Barber had never impressed her? She dropped her hand from his arm, forcing herself to accept a decision she could say nothing to change. "When are you leaving?"

"Now."

For better or worse, she could not let him go alone. "Then I'm going with you."

"No, you're not."

She could never be sure of anything unless she stayed with him during investigations, during interrogations. "In a situation like mine," she quietly announced, thinking of the constant conflict waged between her mind and her heart, "the only solution is to know everything, Jared, or to know nothing. It's already too late for me to go deaf and dumb."

It was his turn to put a restraining hand on her arm. "Bianca, you intimated yourself that this could be dangerous. You haven't got any business coming with me. I came here tonight only because I wanted you to know where I'd be."

"If it's dangerous, you'll find trouble," she responded, covering his hand with one of hers. "And when you find trouble, you'll need someone to go for help. I'll be there to do that." Before he could say another word, she slipped out of his grasp and made her way to the foot of the stairs. "Call Barber's office, or Denman's, or both, and tell them where we're going while I get my things together."

When she reached the landing, she heard him sternly call out, "Bianca—"

"When you're finished with the police and the sheriff, please call Arthur's exchange and leave a message with his answering service," she let her voice sail down the stairway. "I want him to know where I've gone, but I *don't* want to hear any arguments about it before we leave."

"Bianca!"

She refused to give him the response his voice demanded. "Don't worry. I'll pack a light suitcase. It won't take me any time at all."

Once inside the upstairs apartment, she waited with tightened breath for his angry reply. She sighed only when she heard his grudging concession, "By all means make it light! I'm intending to stay no more than one night at one of José's posadas near Villa Nueva."

An hour later, armed with a revolver that was far more powerful than a twenty-two-caliber 'Saturday Night Special' and a camera the size she had always associated with espionage, Jared drove that metallic red Porsche 928S onto the Interstate that would take the two of them two hundred seventy miles to the Brownsville-Matamoras border.

For better or worse, she kept repeating to herself like a marriage vow as they raced into the cold starry night. But what was the rest of that vow? she asked herself. *Until death do us part,* her memory spoke up, and she shivered in the cold.

By three o'clock on the following afternoon, they had driven one hundred fifty miles into the interior of Mexico to arrive in a picturesque town that had been built during the Spanish colonial period. Jared slowly circled the cobbled pavement of the town's central plaza, then turned right onto the last street that shot out from the circle like a spoke from the wheel. Waiting for them at the end of the street was a magnificent sprawling hacienda of white stucco and red-tiled roof. Lush gardens surrounded the estate, with trailing bougainvillea, colorful begonias, and brilliant crotons that had never seen a deadly cold winter.

"Posada de San Joaquín," said Jared, gradually pressing the brake as they approached the high wrought-iron gates. "One of José's many European-style hotels."

"*Posada* means 'inn,' doesn't it?" commented Bianca as a uniformed servant opened the gates. "He should have used *castilla* for 'castle.'"

Jared nodded at the gatekeeper and sailed on through. "Perhaps, but you'll find that in spite of the elegance, its charm is intimate." He looked over at her. "And contagious."

"The charm or the intimacy?" she asked.

He thrust out his arm and with his fingers lightly touched the back of her neck. "Both."

Jared's assessment of her reaction turned out to be accurate. With their luggage in the hands of a porter who immediately recognized Señor Berenson, they walked across the highly polished terra-cotta tiles of the lobby. Intimate conversation areas were built around gurgling fountains, and the gardens could be seen through glass doors with arches reaching at least fifteen feet high and six feet wide. A cleansing light washed everything, from the tin lanterns hanging on the stone walls to the dark wood of two-hundred-year-old Savonarola chairs and armoires.

"Jared! Señorita Cavender!" exclaimed the surprised voice of the slim, fair-haired young man behind the reception desk as he turned to face the entrance. *"Qué una sorpresa maravillosa!"* At the blank look on Bianca's face, Gilberto Albañez inclined his head in a mute apology and moved easily into English. "Was my father expecting you?" he inquired with what Bianca thought was a little flame of apprehension in his dark eyes.

"Not unless he's psychic," Jared answered, extending his hand to shake Gilberto's as he approached the desk. "But I knew he was coming here after he left San Antonio."

"That is true, though he is out for the rest of the afternoon. But now that he has promoted me to hotel concierge"—he made a flourish with his hand to indicate his amusement with his own importance—"I am at your service instead. You desire, I suppose, a room."

Jared raised his brows and corrected his assumption. "Two rooms."

The young man flushed to the roots of his hair as he made a slight bow of his head. "Certainly," he said, recovering quickly.

Bianca was sure that the young man's tension was

greater than his faux pas warranted, but she didn't ponder it long; she was too impressed by Jared's concern for observing the proprieties for her sake.

"A suite for Señorita Cavender," ordered Jared. "A room for myself if no other suite is available."

"If that can be arranged, Gilberto," Bianca interceded with a softer voice.

"Fortunately, though it is Friday, we have just received a last-minute cancellation. We have two rooms and one suite available in the east wing," he assured her as he reached to his right for the registry book. "For how many nights do you expect to be here?"

Jared creased his brows in thought and then said, "I think we should be ready to leave tomorrow in the latter part of the afternoon."

The young Albañez's head came up. "So soon?"

"There's business to conduct, Gilberto. We'll come back another time for a holiday."

"Ah, business," José Albañez's son released the syllables slowly and shrugged his narrow shoulders as if to say he did not understand such a fast-paced life. "Just like my father. Here one day, in the States another." He looked at Bianca with a playful pout on his mouth as though he expected her sympathy for his point of view. She rewarded him with a generous smile, mostly because she sensed that he was somewhat in awe of his father's friend. "If you care to dine with us this evening, dinner will be served between seven-thirty and eleven." When Jared looked concerned, Gilberto immediately offered, "If you would like an earlier meal, I can arrange it."

"We haven't eaten a thing since ten this morning," Jared explained, but Bianca knew it was not for that reason that he was requesting Gilberto to inconvenience the chef. "Would five-thirty be possible, though it is unquestionably early?"

"For the dear friend of my father, nothing is impossible." Gilberto bowed his fair head. "Dinner for two at five-thirty in the dining room."

Three hours later, after having refreshed themselves in rooms that turned out to be adjacent, and having oriented themselves to the geography of the town and surrounding area, Bianca and Jared sat back in their chairs in a garden courtyard serenaded by an early group of mariachis at Gilberto's insistence while waiters served them one delectable course after another. Dressed in the turquoise silk Jared had given her, she wore her hair at his request loose and full at her shoulders, while he wore a very proper navy suit. Together they listened to one Spanish love song after another.

At last the caramel flan arrived with coffee just as a few more of the posada's guests began to wander into the courtyard dining room. Pulling his eyes away from her face, Jared extracted a sheet of paper from his pocket while she stirred the sugar cube and cream in her cup to make the deep brew palatable.

"You've worked out a map?" she asked him, leaning forward.

"Yes." He pushed his pipe to the side. "I think that this should be the most direct route to Villa Nueva, though it means traveling on dirt roads all the way." He shrugged his broad shoulders. "I should have thought of that before we left San Antonio and rented a Jeep rather than put the Porsche through that kind of punishment. Too late now."

"How long do you suppose it will take us to get there?"

"An hour at most I should think."

"What do we do when we get there?"

"Check out the location, snap a few pictures, speak with any *paisanos* we come across, and piece together the information to determine if Villa Nueva is actually the rendezvous. Then I think we'd do best to report what we discover to the proper authorities and hope they arrive in time to see any criminal activity firsthand."

"Who are the proper authorities here?"

"José Albañez. He sits as the area judge. When he returns within another half hour or so, I thought that as a precaution I would explain before we left exactly where we're going and why."

"Would that be wise," she asked, hesitant because she knew the depth of his friendship, "considering the connection the police have intimated between the family and the Mexican underworld?"

A stern look froze his features at the slanderous suggestion and a premonition of disaster and danger suddenly chilled her to the bone. "It would be the height of idiocy, Bianca, to search out a smuggling ring without letting anyone know where we are."

She reached across the table and laid her hand across his while she looked steadily into his eyes. "Perhaps our search for the truth has been hasty, Jared. Maybe we need more time to—"

He shook his head once. "If anything, we could be too late. Charles Roper is dead. Who's next? Me? You?"

"But have we really thought this through? What if we arrive too early and find them right in the middle of smuggling goods themselves? What then?"

"*If* that happens, we'll make sure we're out of the way. Besides, there's nothing to make us think that any merchandise will be disposed of until late tonight or in the early hours of the morning after the Harvest trucks have picked up produce at the farm."

She bit her lower lip, trying to find the words to express the peculiar feeling that had come over her. "I can't help feeling that we're walking into something we're not equipped to handle."

"Bianca, neither the FBI nor the San Antonio police force nor the Bexar County Sheriff's Department is going to come across the border to prove my innocence, especially when they could make me out to be the criminal just by staying put. For all I know, Charles could have been feeding them information against me all along." She stared at him. "No. The time is right. I have to act on my own or be willing to become a victim. And that, my sweetheart, I will never do." He looked at his watch. "When you're finished with that cup, it'll be time to change into jeans for the road if you're still determined to come with me. You know, of course, that I would prefer it if you stayed here."

"Not a chance," she adamantly informed him, and reached for her cup.

Moments later, as he pulled her chair back from the table, she was suddenly conscious of the intent scrutiny of a man on the other side of the room. He definitely looked out of place in the sophisticated surroundings, but somehow vaguely familiar.

"Jared," she asked, turning around to look up at him, "do you recognize that man over there in the far left corner?"

"There are four men in the far left corner, Bianca."

"The one wearing a denim suit," she whispered as she turned her gaze to the corner again, but the rest of the description never made it past her lips. "Well, he was just there a second ago." Her eyes quickly scanned the room. "Where in the devil could he have gotten off to so fast?" She was doubly suspicious. To pull off so fast a vanishing act, a man had to be guilty of something.

"Did you enjoy your dinner?" asked Gilberto, immediately coming up beside Jared.

Without answering, Bianca immediately jumped in. "Gilberto, did you see one of your hotel guests this evening wearing a blue denim suit cut in a western style?" Gilberto showed her a long blank face. "He had salt and pepper hair, about six feet—maybe taller, swarthy complexion."

"He doesn't sound like anybody I've seen this evening, Señorita Cavender. Is it important?"

"It might be. If the description later rings a bell with you, will you tell Jared or me?"

"Of course."

As she looked into his pleasant face, why, she asked herself, did a secretive glaze seem to fall across the big dark eyes?

Chapter Nine

THE occasional call of a nocturnal bird, the rustle of leaf in the tropical vegetation, the shuffling of pungent earth beneath their feet were the only sounds Bianca and Jared could hear in the early evening light streaming down on the isolated patch of forest outside Villa Nueva.

Had it not been for the helpful *paisanos* they had questioned in the tiny village itself, they might never have found this hidden rendezvous at all. And it was the rendezvous—of that they were as sure as they could be without actually having seen a contraband transaction. Too many of the *paisanos* remembered having seen over the last year a number of trucks bearing the Harvest logo. When asked if they knew of a building that could be used as a warehouse in the area, one elderly woman recalled having heard that repair work had been done on a nearby derelict brick structure, which she called a *choza*, more than a year ago.

At the sudden movement beside her Bianca tensed, but it was only Jared, who put his hand on her shoulder and spoke quietly. "If we're correct, Harvest trucks will pick up produce tonight at the farm forty kilometers to the west and a few of them should make a detour to transact their illegal business here. If we work things right," he said, cocking his head to the side, "we should be able to study the area before the trucks arrive and from a distance perhaps identify who and what is involved."

"What are you expecting?" she whispered in spite of the fact that they were alone. "Drugs? Guns? People?"

"All of the above"—he smiled cynically—"and anything else besides. I wonder what Charles must have concluded."

"I don't think he knew, either, or he would have told Martin Goerner when I heard them talking outside your library."

"Possibly. In any case, if we're lucky, we'll find out tonight for ourselves."

She looked down on what he held in his hand. "Photographs of any transaction would no doubt interest the authorities—city, county, and federal."

"I'm counting on it," he acknowledged. Turning his head toward the small brick structure ahead, he suggested, "Let's make our way to the *choza*. Maybe we'll be in luck and find all of the information we need in one place."

She followed Jared's lead, her feet practically nipping his heels to avoid getting separated from him in this virtual maze of trailing vines, towering trees, and foilage gone wild. She was afraid of what they would find, or worse, what might find them.

"Señor Georner," a heavily accented voice called out to them from the silence, though they could see no human figure.

Bianca froze, her limbs held in suspended motion. Jared did the same. She could actually feel the tightening of his muscles, probably because her own were coiling into knots just as her heart was jumping into her throat. Who was it that had found them? She brought her raised foot silently down to the earth and inched up beside Jared. She had time to take a quick glance at the shock which had vividly marked his face before he concealed it. How would Martin Goerner be

known, and be expected in Villa Nueva, unless, of
course, it was he who . . .

"You are here much earlier than we expected." The
heavily accented English that was coming closer bordered on remonstrance, which it tried to disguise with
condescending goodwill. "There is no need, no need.
Your worry these past weeks has been for nothing. All
is under control. My personal assurance I give you."

The human figure came into view. Bianca noticed
the rifle the man carried in the crook of his arm at the
same time Jared spoke up. "The name is Parker.
Goerner sent me ahead."

The man's hand grasped the receiver of his rifle.
The voice abandoned the disguise of civility. *"Por qué
razón?"*

"Just in case there were any last-minute changes
in the volume of the shipment," Jared answered casually enough while Bianca held her breath, waiting
for the man who was approaching them to reply, hoping that Jared's vague answer had satisfied him.

The man she assumed was a guard stopped no more
than three feet in front of them and took in her presence with a scowling visage. *"Por qué tu trajiste esta
mujer contigo?"* the man demanded in a voice growing steadily uglier.

"I never leave home without her," Jared answered,
and Bianca was grateful that the guard didn't suspect the light sarcasm, just as she was grateful that
Jared continued to answer him in English or she
would never have understood what was going on or
what attitude she was expected to adopt.

The guard grunted but his return to English suggested that he conceded the possibility, albeit grudg-
ingly. "You will be able to inspect the shipment at the
shop," he offered with a toss of his head over his
shoulder in the direction of the *choza*, "but I do not
believe we will need more than the usual two trucks.
Now I must return to the gate."

"We'll wait for Goerner at the shop," Jared replied,

and the guard grunted and trooped off, presumably in the direction of the gate he mentioned.

As frightened as she was by their brazen entrance into a world of contrabandists, her heart was considerably lightened by the evidence which pointed to Goerner's guilt and Jared's innocence. It made sense, didn't it? Charles Roper had sealed his own death warrant when at Jared's party he had confided his suspicions to Goerner, the very man whose guilt would eventually be proved by the evidence Roper had collected. It was Martin Goerner who had been waiting for Roper to appear at the produce distributorship yesterday morning. It was Martin Goerner who had killed him.

"Come on, Bianca. We haven't got much time to lose."

She understood. Obviously Jared didn't want to talk about the ramifications of the guard's having mistaken him for his director of trucking operations. She respected his reluctance and kept her own counsel as she began to move with him toward the shop. She bumped up against the revolver he carried in a holster beneath his arm, hidden by his denim jacket. The revolver was hard reality. Whatever they had gotten themselves into, she knew, it was too late to get out of it now. They had no choice but to forge ahead and to find the evidence to vindicate Jared Berenson.

She put a quick hand to his arm. "Listen," she whispered, then froze as she concentrated on the peculiar low hum that reached her ears in the dim light of sunset.

Jared cocked his head to one side, looking just as perplexed. "It sounds as though it must be coming from the *choza* which, from what the guard said, must contain the shipment."

"What kind of shipment is accompanied by a choir of droning bees?" she wondered aloud.

He shook his head. "I can't imagine. But we better have a look." As they both took a step toward the clearing, Jared cautioned, "But let's be careful. Even though the area doesn't look all that well-protected, I don't want to come across another guard and have to come up with another convincing act."

She remembered the first one's eagerness to grasp his rifle's receiver. "Right."

They made their way out of the lush vegetation and stealthily advanced toward the tile-roofed brick structure occupying the center of a clearing probably not more than seventy feet in diameter. She felt a tug at her sleeve and turned in the direction in which Jared pointed. Off to the northeast, a narrow path hacked out of the surrounding vegetation was visibly marked by wide tire tracks.

"The gate must be at the end of that path," Jared said, whipping out his tiny camera and its equally tiny zoom lens again to shoot six frames of the area.

"Good thing we parked the car directly opposite from the gate," she offered in an attempt to convince herself of their safety. "When we leave, we're not likely to bump into anyone."

"Hopefully not."

She wished he could have been more reassuring to alleviate her uneasiness. Side by side, they walked the last few feet to the double doors of the dilapidated building. They looked at the shiny locks above each doorknob and then at each other. Jared lifted his eyebrows as if to say *Here goes nothing* and curved his hand around the right knob.

Intruders must not have been expected, for the handle gave way and the door, though it creaked laboriously on its rusty hinges, opened easily enough. Covering her completely with his broad frame, Jared was the first to cross the threshold.

When she followed one step behind him, she was unprepared for the interior. Ivory enameled cabinets with gleaming steel hardware built into ivory walls, embossed tin ceilings, and shining tile floors were all absolutely spotless. Here was evidence of the repair work the elderly woman in the village had heard about. In the center of the room she could see huge pieces of machinery and two figures.

Two faces, remarkable for their startling similarity and the long mustaches that drooped below their chins, looked up from their work, and two pairs of undaunted black agate eyes stared back at them.

What in the world was the shorter of the two men cleaning? she tried to figure out as she stepped a little more to the left of Jared and got a better view of the machinery. Presses? Plates? What was the taller one packing in neatly stacked bundles inside long, slim wooden boxes? Paper pesos?

The shorter man wiped his hands on a cloth hooked on his belt and querulously grunted in unaccented English, "What in the hell is she doing here? I thought Elijah and I made it clear she's already made trouble between two men. You after being a third? We don't want her around."

"Wrong blond," Jared said curtly as Bianca, fascinated by yet another instance of his ability to ad-lib, took another step toward the light that glowed in the kerosene lamp. Her instincts told her to keep silent in this male-dominated enterprise. "You've got her confused with the woman we used in San Antonio."

The shorter man didn't look convinced and didn't look any less angry, but he turned his attention back to Jared with a sound that could have passed for concession.

The taller one, who must have been Elijah, shut a white box with a loud bang and demanded, "And just who in the hell are you?"

"I'm Parker," answered Jared with faultless poise in the face of their abrupt malevolence. "Goerner sent me ahead to make sure the shipment's in order."

"You're all alike, you clean-hands, lily-white-collar types!" spat the man at the press with disgust. "Always scared of your own shadows. Why you're brought into an operation like this I can't figure out.

Goerner's driven us nuts for the last six weeks with his constant checking up on us and our security. And I suppose he's coming out again later tonight." His black eyes filled with fury. "Tell him to back off! We don't need to see him or his messengers. We learned our craft from the best silversmiths this country's got, and we take care of our end of the deal a *damn* sight better than he takes care of his!"

"At least Caleb and I don't go off half-cocked, shooting people at stop signs to no good purpose," Elijah added with disgust, "and getting that blond woman who hangs around Albañez to help him at that!"

"We sure as hell don't!" exclaimed Caleb. "And we don't go around writing anonymous notes about truckers sidelining with produce to throw the boss off the scent, for Chrissake! You wanna talk about who needs checking up on?" He shoved a fist toward the two of them. "Goerner's the stupid fool who needs to be checked up on and knocked out of the organization altogether!"

Elijah crossed his arms against his chest and pulled his mustache into his mouth with his lower lip. Releasing it, he informed them, "And you can tell Goerner we said so. We got nothing to hide from him and we ain't scared."

Jared put up both hands on either side of his shoulders to indicate that he wasn't responsible for inciting their anger. "I'm just here following instructions," he said gruffly. "Goerner's message to you is that the trucks will arrive one hour earlier than expected. You can be sure I'll deliver your message to him."

"See that you do," growled Caleb. "And shut the door behind you and your woman."

Without another word, Jared turned on his boot heel, and taking her cue from him, Bianca followed close behind. Neither one of them said a word until the *choza* was far behind them and the thick vegetation through which they had come was a few feet ahead.

"Good heavens, Jared!" she finally exclaimed when she felt it was safe to breathe again. "That was paper currency—the contraband is *U.S.* paper currency!"

"You bet it was! Counterfeit style!"

Her mind was teeming with all that they had learned and her lips, forced into such a long silence in that *choza,* were eager to put it into words. "Mexico is the ideal location because it has the craftsmen who could teach Caleb and Elijah to produce it," she said as they traipsed back through the tropical forest.

"Not to mention the added advantage of being outside the jurisdiction of U.S. authorities, yet close enough to facilitate transportation."

"How do you suppose the drivers do it, Jared? Once they leave the Harvest lot, do they outfit their trucks with a compartment big enough to hold those wooden boxes Elijah packed with the counterfeit bills?"

"Probably. That procedure, I think, would call for the currency to be picked up *before* the produce is loaded up, not after. And that, my darling, means that you and I have to get the hell out of here and fast because those two trucks could roll in at any time."

"Jared, that night I was sure I saw two men working on a Harvest truck," she began hesitantly, not sure exactly why she suddenly had such a clear picture of that incident in her head, "do you suppose that the men might have been rolling back odometers to subtract the extra mileage they put on during these special assignments?"

"Possibly, or they could have been removing the compartment behind which they concealed the currency. In either case, they slipped up. Both of those procedures should have been completed long before they drove into the Harvest lot."

"Maybe the failure to do so explains Martin's having been so upset about the incident when I mentioned it in front of him. And maybe he was so furious with Charles's accusations against you the other night at your place because all Charles had to do was make a little adjustment in his perspective and his evidence would have led him to Martin." For a moment Jared was very quiet as they worked their way back to the car they had hidden from the road and her heart went out to him. "I'm sorry, Jared, that it's someone you know and care about."

He didn't respond immediately and when he did it was with a heavy voice. "It was bound to be, wasn't it?" he asked. "But frankly, I'm even more worried by Elijah's reference to a woman connected with Albañez because that means that Denman was right when he said that the FBI assumed the family was connected with the Mexican underworld."

"Jared!" she suddenly breathed as a new idea hit her brain with explosive possibilities and she stopped walking. They had been so caught up with their emotional response to the Albañez reference that they had failed to realize what that reference meant for their physical safety. "They know we're here!"

He put his arm around her shoulder. "Sure they do, baby, but they don't know who we are or what we're after."

She shook her head and looked up into his eyes. "No, I don't mean Elijah and Caleb. I mean the people who are behind this whole scheme. The man I saw at the hotel tonight looked familiar because he's one of the men I saw working on the truck that night." She could tell by his piercing look that he realized the ramifications.

"Martin's contact on this side of the border is someone at the hotel who the driver was there to see," Jared arrived at her conclusion. "So you're saying I made a big mistake by telling José Albañez of our whereabouts."

"Don't be so hard on yourself," she said gently. "The minute that driver saw the two of us in the hotel restaurant he knew why we were there and where we would be going. He would have taken the news immediately to his contact at the hotel." She neatly avoided accusing José of occupying that position; she supposed Jared had already come to the same conclusion.

At the same moment, they whipped their heads around at the loud tire roll of heavy trucks on the dirt road to the northeast of the shop.

Knowing that they'd left a trail behind them a mile long, they had no choice except to run for cover and hope to get to the Porsche and drive away before Martin showed up. One of those truck drivers might believe that a man and woman had preceded them to check up on the shipment, but Martin and the other trucker would know better. From their vantage point behind the gargantuan leaves of tropical plants and overgrown shrubs, Bianca and Jared could see two trucks displaying the distinctive cornucopia logo brake before the shop.

"I was more on target than I realized," Jared quipped, "when I told those master printers back there that the pickup was going to be earlier than usual."

"Amazing how many things you said were right on target—like assuming the blond they didn't want around was the woman who set you up to be shot."

He gave a dismissive shrug of his shoulders. "I was simply playing off their remarks and our own perceptions."

When they looked again at the shop, Elijah and Caleb, recognizable even from a distance by their great, drooping mustaches, threw open the doors. One of them, she wasn't sure which, stood on the step and waved imperiously for the drivers to enter.

Jared clicked the shutter of his camera repeatedly. He advanced the film, locked the shutter, and said, "It's time to split."

"Should we wait just one minute more?" She put her hand on his arm. "Maybe others will show."

Jared hesitated, caught between caution and a desire to capture on film all the players in the intrigue. His decision was made for him when they heard the hum of a car engine approach the *choza* from the road the trucks had followed. A tall man, dressed like Jared in jeans and denim jacket, alighted from a dark car and slammed the door shut behind him.

"It's Martin, isn't it?" she asked.

"Yes," he replied just as another man alighted from the passenger's side of the same car.

"Jared," she whispered hesitantly when she saw the long blond hair of a woman who followed the second man.

But he answered her question before she asked it. "I'm not positive from this distance, but yes, I think it's Gilberto who's come with him—and the woman who waylaid me four weeks ago."

She said nothing more as they silently watched the truck drivers step out of the shop with slim wooden crates in their arms. Coming from the rear of the building, the rifle-equipped guard who had accosted them earlier joined the group.

From the distance she and Jared picked up only the dull roar of words as the conversation progressed into a shouting match between Goerner, who kept pointing in the direction of the trucks, and the mustachioed printers, who took turns shaking their fists into any face that dared to get too close to theirs.

It wasn't long before Goerner swiftly turned around and peered into the surrounding shadows, undoubtedly searching for the mysterious Parker and his blond woman. What was he pulling from inside his jacket? A gun? With lightning speed Jared advanced the film and depressed the shutter time and again until he had at least six shots of his subject.

"God, I hope there was enough light!" exclaimed Jared.

"Me, too!" she breathed, not wanting to think that any of this had been in vain.

Knowing that they had probably delayed their departure longer than they should have, without a word he grabbed her arm to make their getaway and together they pushed their way through the dense tropical vegetation to get back to the Porsche. She knew that he must be thinking that they had to get out onto the highway and head for the border without returning to the hotel for their things.

Jared picked up his head and looked back at her. She heard it too, the sound of tires rolling on the dirt road. Relief flooded through her. Having picked up their shipment, the trucks were heading out to pick up produce. By God, incredulous as it seemed, they had escaped danger so easily. If her sense of direction was accurate, Jared's car wasn't much farther away than five minutes of uninterrupted walking.

But even five minutes was too long.

A single tall figure suddenly shot out of the darkness into the narrow path directly ahead of them, bringing them to a dead stop. Bianca's eyes went wide and her chest ached with the deep choking breath she inhaled. It was unmistakably Martin Goerner—his cynical smile in place, a murderous glint in his otherwise dead eyes, and a gun in his steady right hand. He must have known a shortcut between the shop and the road.

At that moment Bianca wasn't aware of much more than the sensation of her heart galloping in her throat like a wild steed on the run and the painful pressure of something biting into the palm of her left hand.

"Make a run for the car!" Jared quietly screamed down on her head as he continued to face Goerner, who was slowly stalking them as he would stalk his prey. "I'll head north and west."

She just stared up at Jared, unable to comprehend what exactly he was asking of her. Then in a flash she realized he saw that their only hope lay in splitting up. He was pressing the car keys into her hands and letting her escape while he drew all of Goerner's attention onto himself. But she couldn't let him do that.

"I won't leave you," she whispered intently.

She could see the hard intransigence that marked his face in profile. "Your loyalty's not doing either one of us any good right now. Get back to the car and get help!" he ordered through clenched teeth.

She felt physically pulled apart by two opposing instincts, but there wasn't time for deliberation or argument. Nor did she really have a choice about which inclination to follow. She had to do as he said and try to believe that with the revolver he carried he had a chance against his enemy. She squeezed Jared's hand once, then, grasping the keys, turned on her heel and dashed off to the south in order to circle behind Goerner before heading west toward the car. In the same split second, Jared made his move. She heard the pounding of feet thunder after him.

Then all she heard was the thunder of her own heart exploding in her ears and someone slashing through the dense foilage in hot pursuit behind her. She had to reach the car, for Jared's sake and her own, she told herself as her breath came in deep and agonized sounds and her muscles ached from the strenuous demands on her body. She flailed at the leaves and jumped over fallen stumps, forcing her way through what began to look like an ever darkening impenetrable wall of vegetation. The tip of her boot hit something hard and immovable. When she stumbled on it, the other foot hooked underneath a thick, trailing vine. Flinging out her arms and splaying out her hands, she tried to arrest her fall; but the attempt to save herself was futile. The heels of her hands took most of the impact as she hit the pungent earth with a thud.

Her body was momentarily stunned, vibrating from the collision. Before she could be aware of much more than the faint taste of blood and damp earth in her mouth, she began to scramble to her feet, pushing her hair out of her eyes, ripping her cardigan away from the thorny bushes that snagged it. With her knees bent, her weight balanced on the balls of her feet and the tips of her fingers, she was poised to spring up and forward into the dying light. Instantly a large body slammed into her from behind and she hit the dirt again, her arms imprisoned beneath her. She had just enough time to let out one long bloodcurdling scream before her pursuer's arm slid over her head and his hand clamped down hard on her mouth.

Her eyes, frozen open with fright, saw the metallic gleam of a revolver waving in front of her face and she struggled to free her hands from beneath the combined weight of their bodies in order to wrest it from him. Though she felt as if her muscles were ripping apart with the effort, nothing she did made any difference. She tried to rock her body back and forth to throw him off, but he didn't budge. Then, miraculously, she could feel the weight of his body roll to the left. Before she knew what was happening, he was wrenched off her back and she was able to make one, two complete rolls to her right, then scramble to her feet.

Jared, his denim jacket stretched across his broad back, had his hands on Goerner's shoulders as he shoved the man to the ground. Goerner hooked his foot behind Jared's ankle, and Jared fell on top of him.

"The gun, Jared!" she screamed, afraid that he might be too confident because he carried one.

Jared made a lunge for Goerner's right hand. Staggering backward with shut eyes, she heard the deafening blast of a shot. Her heart's fear frantically pounded at the walls of her chest and climbed into her throat. She forced her eyelids open and made herself look at the two men wrestling on the damp earth. Neither one of them had ceased moving. She made herself take a better look at Jared's face. It wasn't wearing the stunned pain of a man who had been hit with a bullet, but rather the stark fury of a man intending to take vengeance at any cost. She had never seen that look before and it made her cringe.

Her brain, still thundering with the echo of that blast, only gradually registered the virulent outbursts between the two men.

"Were you trying to kill her, Martin?" shouted Jared as his hands grappled for Goerner's gun while trying to hold on to his own.

"Like I should have killed her on the gallery if you hadn't come along!" Martin hissed as he pushed his fist toward Jared's jaw.

Jared stopped the fist with his own revolver, but the defensive action cost him the weapon. It flew out of his hand, the sound of its fall silenced by the dense growth into which it must have landed. Bianca heard a triumphant growling sound come out of Goerner's throat as the two men tore into each other, one determined to wrest the gun from his adversary, the other determined to use it. She could only watch with increasing horror, trying to find a way to help Jared, but forced to accept her own helplessness.

Jared grabbed Goerner's gun with two hands. As he rolled to his left side up against a felled tree, he smashed Goerner's hand to the earth repeatedly until the man's grip exploded into an open hand and the gun skittered inches away. Then Jared's hands went for his face and his throat. While the two enraged bodies grappled with each other, Bianca made a dash for the pistol. Just as she straightened to her full height and brought the gun up to aim it, a voice behind her shouted something in Spanish and another gunshot sounded in the small arena where two bodies tore at each other like wild beasts.

Everything happened so fast Bianca wasn't sure what she saw, nor why none of the three men had realized she was carrying a pistol. The guard who had met them before they had gotten to the shop came to Goerner's rescue, pulling the men apart with curses muttered half in Spanish and half in English. Goerner got to his feet, leveling a vicious oath of his own at Jared.

"I should've killed you that Saturday night in November," Goerner gasped through clenched teeth as he wiped his mouth with the back of his hand.

Jared's chest expanded and contracted rapidly. "Why did you even try to get me at all?"

"I needed you out of the way, that's why," he answered with a nasty twist on his syllables as he tried to snatch oxygen out of the damp air. "That week I had extra stuff on the trucks as a favor to some people who had done a few favors for me."

"Stuff like dope, and guns—and people?" Jared taunted him with contempt.

Goerner had backup. He could afford to smile as he replied through labored breath, "To name a few."

"For a bright man, Martin, you've done a number of stupid things," spat Jared. Goerner tensed. The guard held the receiver of his rifle in a tight grip, though he seemed interested in what Jared had to say. "Elijah and Caleb told me to tell you so. First, you do such a lousy job of concealing your operation that Charles learns of it. And then, when you could simply have done away with Charles, you bungle things up by coming after me and Bianca. Not very tidy! What will the rest of your partners think of your sloppy work?"

Incensed, Goerner was angered into defending himself, as Jared undoubtedly intended. "The drivers who abruptly resigned were planning to come to you. That ambush effectively dissuaded them. Charles's death would probably have scared off Martínez and Schmidt from talking to you about their suspicions too. But then, I don't have to worry about that anymore, do I, Jared?"

"It seems to me that just killing Charles will give you plenty to worry about."

"I didn't kill him."

"Oh, no?" Jared's skepticism was palpable. "You

didn't lure him back to the office to wring out all the hard evidence he'd collected, making a key to my executive elevator so you could arrange a little accident there?"

"Believe it or not, my fastidious conscience wouldn't allow it."

Jared made a growling sound deep in his throat that might have passed for a laugh.

"I might have hoped it would turn out that way," Goerner shouted. "But he was the one who opened that elevator door, screaming all kinds of threats at me if I fought his attempt to go to the police with evidence against you."

"Couldn't hack that, could you? You had to prevent the FBI from discovering the whereabouts of your little print shop, didn't you?"

"Damn right I did! I hadn't set things up to frame you for what I was doing, even though it looked for a while like you were going to take the fall without my help. I needed more time to ensure that would happen if Charles was going to the FBI. When I tried to reach for what he had written on the sheet of paper in his hand, like a fool he pulled away from me. He tripped and fell back into the empty space, catching his head on the brass door handle." For a moment something like an awareness of the enormity of what was happening around him crossed his sullen face, then passed. "Now that I've got you, I'm not going to let my conscience prevent me from disposing of you and your accountant tonight."

"Rotten luck, wasn't it, Martin?" Bianca asked when the guard pointed his rifle at her as an implicit directive to move closer to Jared.

Goerner swiveled his head to the right. "What was?"

As she walked toward Jared she did her best to keep her right side, against which she held the gun, concealed from Goerner's and the guard's view. "You're the one who never liked Charles's conservative position much," she observed casually. "In fact, you probably couldn't abide Charles Roper because he never gambled in commercial deals, and you've probably always hated Jared because he knew when to stop." She saw the truth of her comment immediately reflected in his face riddled with insecurity, hate, and fear.

Jared took his cue from her. "So you're the one who fed Charles's insecurities about his position as comptroller at Harvest, made him think he could be easily replaced," he stated more than asked. Goerner's silence corroborated the supposition.

"What rotten luck then, Martin. I really expected more of you." She continued to press the point as she tried to press against Jared's thigh so that he could feel the revolver between them.

"How do you figure it?" Goerner didn't like the confusion she was making him feel or her casual confidence in the face of being told he intended to dispose of her and the man she loved.

"Your trick backfired on you, of course," she answered, sliding ever closer to Jared, who continued her baiting.

"If you hadn't made Charles feel so threatened in his position," Jared explained as she felt his hand touch hers, "he might never have searched for an answer to the riddle that perplexed him. Without that search, your criminal involvement may have gone undetected."

"Do not move so close to each other!" growled the guard as he scrutinized the distance between them.

Bianca and Jared went still as stone.

"I plan to go scot-free anyway, Jared," Goerner informed him with a demonic lift to his brows, "in spite of men like you and Charles who can *afford* to remain uncorrupted. After those idiots, Denman and Barber, plus a few feds, questioned me last night, I decided to make arrangements to fly from here to Paraguay. I don't even need to kill you or her to go free. I'm going to kill you just to protect the others on both sides of the border."

"Now turn around and walk straight ahead," the guard ordered. "Man first with Señor Goerner at his side. Woman six feet behind with me."

They did as they were told because they had no other choice. As they began the escort, Bianca turned her head to her left at the sound of shouting voices and running feet. Leading five armed *federales,* José Albañez burst into the small clearing. More backup for Goerner, Bianca believed with sinking heart. And yet when she turned around to seek silent communication with Jared's eyes, she saw the glint of steel in the moonlight as Martin Goerner stealthily raised his right hand to bring it crashing down on an unsuspecting Jared, standing no more than a foot from his side.

Why would Goerner feel it necessary to strike Jared down now when he was surrounded with his own men? She didn't know the answer but without a second's hesitation, she knew what she had to do. She lifted the revolver, her eyes on her target. In the same instant that Jared looked her way and deftly leaped away from Goerner, she pulled the trigger while she fervently prayed she was aiming high enough to hit Goerner's hand, which clutched a dagger, not his heart.

Deafening silence. Frozen instant in time. Then the mad shouting of wild men shattered the quiet and the arrested activity of human bodies in the arena took up again. The guard fled east while Goerner fled in the direction from which they had come, his wounded right arm bleeding freely against his shirt, pursued not only by Jared but by Albañez and those *federales* who hadn't gone after the guard.

Stunned by what she had done to another human being, Bianca stood frozen to the ground. Totally confused by the melee around her, she didn't know who were Jared's friends and who were his enemies. And there wasn't any time to distinguish one from the other.

When she finally caught up with Jared, he and Albañez and the *federales* had caught up with Goerner. But someone else was in the picture, too. Gilberto Albañez.

The younger Albañez had blood in his eye and a black pistol clutched in his hand aimed directly at Jared, who was standing no more than six yards away from him. Transfixed by the deadly intent of the Mexican stood a woman with yellow hair, her hands clasped at her breast, her profiled face tight with anxiety.

The wound which made Goerner a weak physical adversary didn't keep him from exerting psychological pressure on Gilberto. "Kill him, for God's sake, and let's get the hell out of here!" Goerner hissed, holding his bleeding hand to his shirt.

A cry forcibly ripped out of an agonized soul, *"Gilberto! No, mi hijo!"* shot out onto the air like a quivering arrow.

Father had called to son. The woman whirled around, guilt and fright and anger distorting what might have been an angelic face. Gilberto's hand wavered, but his body, positioned between his two criminal partners, still tensed for the kill. Everyone froze in horror, afraid to move on Gilberto for fear of what their action might trigger in him.

Jared must have made some lightning-quick associations for he called out, "Listen to your father, Gilberto. It's already too late to protect yourself and the kingpins who run this operation. All of us are witnesses here, not just me. You could never kill all of us before one of us got you."

Gilberto's face mirrored his trembling uncertainty as did his voice. "The three of us, Yolanda, Martin, and I, are going to leave on that plane. Do not try to stop us."

"We'll stop you, Gilberto," Jared told him with unwavering determination. "And Yolanda might be the first one hurt. Are you willing to take that chance?"

"Do not touch her!" Gilberto cried out angrily. She's innocent!"

"Not if she allowed Martin to use her as an accessory in a conspiracy to commit murder," countered Jared immediately.

Gilberto's face whipped to the left, glaring at Martin, whose eyes and voice, in spite of the physical pain, conveyed a mesmerizing intensity. "We're in this together, Gilberto. Don't act like a coward now."

"Martin's been using you as a pawn," Jared swiftly called out. "Don't be as big a fool as he has been!"

The young man seemed to grasp the trigger with greater determination. Everyone seemed to be holding their breath. Jared, Bianca could tell, was prepared to spring to the side when necessary.

"Mi hijo," called out José, *"listen to your father and your father's friend."*

For a moment she thought Gilberto had not heard his father's second plea, but then the son's hold on the trigger suddenly slackened. His shoulders fell, his spine relaxed. He let the hand that held the weapon fall to his side. The gun dropped like dead weight to his feet on the damp earth. His eyes, staring at the collected witnesses, were mirrors of subsiding anger and abiding shame.

"Papá" he beseeched José in a broken whisper, *"perdóname."*

Her heart rent by the defeated son's petition for his father's forgiveness, Bianca felt tears obscure her vision. As José Albañez slowly approached his son with open arms, she touched her fingertips to Jared's sleeve. It was over. The long vigil of fear and suspicion that had begun in late November was finished. Glancing silently into each other's eyes, together they turned away in respect for the private anguish that still remained.

* * *

Bianca stood on the balcony overlooking the lush gardens where, at three in the morning, bright moonbeams picked out a host of colorful blooms and brilliant foliage lining the winding cobblestone paths.

In spite of the unrelieved tension which had begun at Jared's home atop Cross Mountain and ended on the damp earth of Villa Nueva, she felt more relaxed than she had felt since she'd first come across a stranger's body slumped over the wheel of his car.

"By now," said that same man, no longer a stranger, who presently stood behind her, his hand resting familiarly on her shoulder, "Harvest trucks carrying the counterfeit currency are probably being detained at the border where federal agents have been patiently waiting."

"Did you ever suspect that Goerner gambled so heavily?" she asked, still trying to make sense of it all.

"From time to time I had wondered, but when Charles actually mentioned it to me once, I wrote it off as a reflection of his own fear to gamble anything at all. I certainly never suspected that Martin lost so heavily in the casinos he frequented."

"I suppose the explanation he gave the authorities was true," she wondered aloud. "He owed so much to so many that the only way he could pay back his losses was to become part of the counterfeit operation on the U.S. side."

"Perhaps," Jared conceded. "It was easy to rationalize as a harmless way to repay his debts—until he shot me with the help of Yolanda. That's what enraged Gilberto, when he discovered her involvement." The hand that ran along her arm was gentle but his voice was gruff when he added, "It's a lot harder to understand how he rationalized exploiting Gilberto and luring a kid his age into working with the Mexican underworld."

"Yes, a lot harder." She vividly recalled the elder Albañez's heartbreaking sorrow when he realized his son's involvement. "Does José know enough highly placed people to be able to help Gilberto?"

He dropped his gaze to her and put both hands on her shoulders. "Yes, don't worry. He definitely knows people who know how to work within Mexico's legal system. Even Martin admits that Gilberto knew nothing in advance about the incident on Old Boerne Stage Road, or about his attack of you on the gallery. He was just a bored rich kid, like his pilot friend, who went looking in the wrong place for excitement and found a little too much."

"And the Elizondo family?" she asked, not sure why no one had mentioned anything about Pedro tonight. "Do you think that Denman just got his facts confused about which families the FBI was investigating?"

Jared shook his head. "Not exactly. From what José told me about half an hour ago when he returned to the hotel, the *federales* said that the FBI were convinced that a contact was operating out of this resort hotel. Initially they theorized that José must be one of the kingpins, possibly assisted by Pedro. Apparently the FBI ruled out Pedro's possible connection some time ago but no one bothered to tell Denman."

She smiled ruefully at the pitiful efforts of people who tried to make a name for themselves in the world. "Denman won't be happy that you've solved his crime for him."

"That *we've* solved his crime," Jared firmly corrected her, pulling her close as he wrapped one arm around her and lifted the other to ruffle up her hair. The filmy purple peignoir she wore floated deliciously around her bare legs. "And now, are all of your questions laid to rest? I'd much rather just think about us right now."

"It seems so peaceful now, Jared," she said as she rubbed her cheek on his playful hand.

"I'd like it to be this way forever," he murmured as he lifted her hair to kiss the exposed line of her throat

and her arms floated effortlessly up to his neck, her
fingers curling through the thick tousled honey hair.
"I don't want to wait for spring, Bianca," he said, his
breath a cool breeze on her skin. "Valentine's Day
sounds good enough to me."

"Good enough for what?" she asked, retreating a
step or two from his embrace, her hands falling down
to the chocolate-brown robe that covered his muscled
forearms.

"For our wedding, of course," he answered as
though he were surprised she needed to ask. "What
else? Nuptial vows exchanged in a small church in
front of immediate family and closest friends would
suit me just fine. And if that's what you want, too,
that's the way we'll do it." He lowered his head, the
tousled honey hair falling onto his wide brow. "But I
do have this mother you met once at the hospital who
inquires about you daily, and whose only son I happen to be. And if you could tolerate a guest list num-
bering no more than fifty additional people at a small
celebration afterward, I know she would be thrilled."

She stared at him with growing disbelief. "Aren't
you even going to ask me, Jared?"

"About the date?" Immediately his face was all
penitence. "I'm sorry, baby. If we walk down the aisle
on the fourteenth of February, it will be a weekday
event and that at least should cut down on the number who'll be able to come—if nothing else will."

"No, Jared—I meant aren't you even going to *ask*
me if I want to marry you?"

He threw back his head and laughed heartily. Then
he assumed a very stern visage to inquire, "Do you
mean to tell me that you can make love to me the
saucy way you do, with the sweetest intimacy and the
most insatiable appetite, without wanting to marry
me?" Behind the stern voice were eyes glittering with
golden lights. "You ought to be ashamed, Bianca Lamont Cavender! Have I seriously misjudged you?
How could she hope to sustain her indignation and

resistance in the face of his mock incredulity and out-rage? "No" came out on a melodic laugh of her own.

His voice suddenly abandoned the spirited play and he pulled her into his arms again. "I knew you played for keeps," he whispered as he captured her head beneath his chin. "It's all I could count on to keep me going when the distrust and fear leaped into your eyes each time we kissed. It's what made the heartache endurable."

Her fingers dug into the velour that covered his back. How she loved this man, loved him with a depth that sometimes hurt. "And you, Jared?" she asked, turning her head up to look into his eyes. "Do you play for keeps?"

"You know I do, sweetheart. If you hadn't suspected it, you would never have answered so perfectly what my body was begging for from yours, speaking of which . . ." He let his voice trail off as he gave a meaningful glance at the bed turned down for the night and relaxed his embrace to propel her in that direction.

But she wasn't finished with what she needed to say. "Jared," she detained him, her voice tentative, "does it bother you at all that I was married before?" She waited breathlessly for his answer. "I have to know."

He creased his dark brows as though he were surprised at the question. "No, of course not. Why should it?" He shook his head and eased his hands on both of her shoulders. "It's a big part of what has made you the sensitive, giving person you are." He spoke so earnestly, his lips carefully enunciating each syllable, his brilliant eyes not letting hers leave his face for an instant. "I love, and am in love with, the person you are now, Bianca. If your first marriage were erased, the woman I love would also be erased. I was never upset because you'd been married before, baby, only that I thought, at one time, it prevented you from accepting me as your lover."

Because she had to be absolutely sure of the sincerity she heard in that rich, low voice, she persisted. "And it doesn't bother you that the memory of that first love is something I still treasure?"

He shook his head slightly and kissed her brow. "No, as long as you have enough room in your heart for the memories *we* will make together, enough room for the loving and the living that *we* will share."

"I do, Jared," she declared in truth, her heart overflowing with love, and trust, and desire. "I do now."

He smiled, a gentle curve of his sensuous lips. "It's rather exciting to think that you're a woman who has the capacity to love with such depth and with such loyalty. It's exciting for me to know that I will be loved in that way."

She put a delicate hand to his handsome face. He covered it with his, and pulling it away from his face, kissed each fingertip, and then the center of the open palm. "You know, I almost feel a bond with Richard," he said as he looked up from her hand. "He loved you when I couldn't be there. I'm grateful to him for having kept you safe and loved until I could find you. I don't think that I could ever resent anyone who truly loved you."

"Oh, Jared," she whispered above the tears in her throat, the tears in her eyes, "God, you're wonderful. I love you."

"Keep telling me that, baby," he answered in a husky voice as he clasped her to himself. For a moment or two neither one of them said a word. He just held her tightly against his solid warmth that was her great comfort, smoothing his hand slowly over the glorious silver-blond hair. Pulling away a little, he softly laughed. "Do you realize that you saved my life twice, Bianca? Once on Old Boerne Stage Road, and once nine hours ago?"

She looked at him, catching her lower lip between her white teeth, then slowly releasing it when she admitted, "You saved mine as well, only you didn't know it."

"Oh, I think I do," he answered wisely as he rocked her in his arms. "Maybe that's another reason I'm not jealous of your past—because I'm your present and you are mine. Are you going to share that life with me by letting me become your husband and by committing yourself to become my wife?"

The woman she was now, the woman whose heart had been set free from the shadow of the past and the shadow of fear, joyfully whispered, "Yes. Forever."

THE VELVET GLOVE

**An exciting series of contemporary novels
of love with a dangerous stranger.**

#13 STRANGERS IN EDEN Peggy Mercer   89664-8/$2.25 US
/$2.95 Can

Lelaine Majors poses as a private investigator to discover who's framing her father, but
the trail leads her to an international smuggling operation and love with a dangerous
stranger.

#14 THE UNEVEN SCORE Carla Neggers   89665-6/$2.25 US
/$2.95 Can

A friend's call for help draws musician Whitney McCallie into a mysterious plot of
deception with the magnetic Chairman of the Board of the Central Florida Symphony
Orchestra who may be hiding more than his heart.

#15 TAINTED GOLD Lynn Michaels   89666-4/$2.25 US
/$2.95 Can

Quillen McCain has struggled to hold onto the twelve wooded acres in Colorado that
have been in her family since the days of her gold-mining grandfather. It's love at first
sight when she meets Tucker Ferris, but then she begins to fear that the handsome
stranger might do anything to trick her out of her land.

#16 A TOUCH OF SCANDAL Leslie Davis   89667-2/$2.25 US
/$2.95 Can

Piper McLean is a widow of eleven months when she meets Michael Shepard who
teaches her how to love again. But when she receives terrifying threats which hint at
the mysterious circumstances surrounding her husband's death, Piper begins to fear
that the man she now loves may be after her life.

#17 AN UNCERTAIN CHIME Lizabeth Loghry   89669-9/$2.25 US
/$2.75 Can

Bethany Templeton receives an unusual bequest and meets an unlikely lover all in the
same afternoon. But when danger stalks her, she begins to think that Jonathan Jordan,
the man who has won her heart, may be after her life.

#18 MASKED REFLECTIONS Dee Stuart   89668-0/$2.25 US
/$2.75 Can

When New York City businesswoman Kelly Conover arrives in Blue Angel, Colorado, she
learns her sister Kim is missing. It's only when Brad York, Kelly's too-persistent lover,
follows her to Blue Angel that they discover the secret of the missing twin—and the
perfect balance for their love.

Catherine Lanigan
writing as

Joan Wilder

Romancing The STONE

87262-5/$2.95
Based on the Screenplay Written by
Diane Thomas

LOVING THE FANTASY

Lost in the steaming Colombian jungle with brutal killers closing in, she felt like the heroine of one of her romance novels. Except that romance was the last thing on her mind...especially with Jack Colton, the bold American adventurer on whom her life now depended.

But there are certain times, certain places, and nights that may be the last, when a man and a woman can only be meant for each other. And suddenly she knew that he was the right man for her.